BOULEVARD OF BROKEN CREAMS

Sarah Fox

Paperback ISBN: 9781068970719

E-book ISBN: 9781068970702

Cover illustration by Francesca D'Ottavi.

First edition: October 2024

Also by Sarah Fox

The True Confections Mysteries

Six Sweets Under
Baking Spirits Bright

The Magical Menagerie Mysteries

Murder Most Owl
Dead Men Wag No Tails

The Literary Pub Mysteries

Wine and Punishment
An Ale of Two Cities
The Malt in Our Stars
Claret and Present Danger
Through the Liquor Glass

The Pancake House Mysteries

The Crêpes of Wrath
For Whom the Bread Rolls
Of Spice and Men
Yeast of Eden
Crêpe Expectations

Chapter One

"Is this place for real?"

Cooper Graystone, Hollywood heartthrob and my former co-star, stood in the middle of my family's chocolate shop with a huge smile on his face.

The empty tray I held in my hands gave a loud clatter when I dropped it on top of the display case full of chocolate truffles and bonbons. I tore around the sales counter and tackle hugged Cooper.

"Oof!" he said as I nearly knocked him off balance.

Luckily, he was strong and agile enough not to lose his footing. Otherwise, we both would have toppled over onto the nearby display of chocolate gondolas.

"I'm so excited you're here!" I exclaimed, finally releasing Cooper.

"It's good to see you again, Becca," he said as he removed his dark sunglasses. Happiness lit up his blue eyes, almost making them sparkle. "And this town is freaking amazing. I know you've shown me pictures in the past, but being here is like walking through a fairytale."

"Right?" I said. "Larch Haven will steal your heart before you leave. That's pretty much guaranteed."

"Hey, I've only been here for an hour and I already want to come back."

"An hour?" I feigned indignation. "You mean, you didn't come to see me as soon as you arrived?"

He hooked his sunglasses on the collar of his blue T-shirt. "I meant to come over here as soon as I checked into the hotel, but I got waylaid in the lobby on my way out."

"Let me guess," I said. "A pack of rabid fans?"

He grinned. "Not quite rabid, but definitely enthusiastic."

It didn't surprise me that a group of fans had already found him. Cooper had risen to fame on the show *Twilight Hills*, which aired for four seasons. The drama had featured an ensemble cast, which included me, but it was no secret that Cooper had been the most popular among the show's fans.

He'd since gone on to star in another drama series, which was currently on hiatus, and he was here in Larch Haven to play the leading man in the made-for-TV romance movie *Love on the Canal*. I was also dipping my toe back into my old acting life, playing one of the supporting characters.

"The hat and glasses probably won't do you much good," I said. "Everyone in Larch Haven knows you're in the movie and if they don't all know that you've now arrived, they will in approximately...."

I looked to my cousin, Angela, where she stood behind the sales counter, listening in with a bright smile on her face.

"I'd give it another seven or eight minutes, max," she chimed in.

I took Cooper's arm and tugged him across the store. "Cooper, this is my cousin Angela. She looks after the business side of True Confections. Angie, meet Cooper Graystone."

Angie hurried out from behind the counter, her cheeks pink and her dark brown curls bouncing. She offered her hand to Cooper, but he shook his head and opened his arms.

"Becca's like family to me," he said as he hugged her, "so you and I are practically cousins."

Angie's cheeks were even pinker as she gave Cooper a squeeze and stepped back, beaming up at him.

"Two kids, right?" Cooper said to her. "Bella and Luca?"

Surprise showed on Angie's face. "How do you know that?"

"Becca's told me all about her family."

"And I've told them all about you," I said to him.

Angie's eyes strayed toward the shop's front window and the smile slipped off her face.

"Gossip Granny alert, Becca!" she said in an urgent whisper.

My eyes widened and I grabbed Cooper's arm, practically dragging him into the back of the shop.

"Hey, what's going on?" he asked with alarm as he stumbled along with me.

I shoved him into the office and followed him into the room just as the bell above the front door gave a cheery jingle.

"Didn't I ever tell you about the Gossip Grannies?" I whispered once we were safely out of view of the two ladies who had entered the shop.

"No." Cooper tried to lean past me to peek out the office door.

I pushed him back. "You don't want to go out there. Trust me."

"I've dealt with elderly fans before," Cooper tried to reassure me. "Okay, so that eighty-year-old with the hot pink boa tried to give me a lap dance while I was eating dinner at a restaurant, but most of them are super sweet."

"Sweet is not a word I'd use to describe the Gossip Grannies," I said, keeping my voice to a whisper. "They're much closer to the boa-lady category."

Cooper pushed the office door closed. "Enough said."

I'd never actually known Delphi Snodgrass and Luella Plank—the real names of the two Gossip Grannies—to give anyone a lap dance (thank goodness), but their penchant for making up wild rumors and spreading them around town put them at the very top of my avoid-whenever-possible list. Hiding Cooper from the Grannies wouldn't stop them from coming up with tabloid-worthy stories about my friend while he was in town, but at least he wouldn't have to endure the crazy and possibly inappropriate questions they would no doubt pepper him with if he ended up in their clutches.

Cooper pulled his phone from the pocket of his jeans and checked the time. "Just one problem. I'm supposed to meet Phil for lunch in ten minutes."

Phil Chalupnik of Ever After Films was the producer for *Love on the Canal*. He came to Larch Haven on vacation last summer and found the town so charming that he wanted to set one of his movies here. I was thrilled when I heard he was actually making that happen, and even more excited when I landed a supporting role.

"All right," I said, placing my hand on the doorknob. "Hat and glasses back on."

Cooper complied and I quietly eased the office door open. I peeked out into the hall, toward the front of the shop. Delphi and Luella stood by the display of chocolate gondolas, their backs to us.

I pushed the door open wider, placed a finger to my lips, and then gestured to Cooper to follow me. I rushed him down the hallway to the back door and we managed to slip out into the narrow, cobblestone alley at the back of the building without either of the Gossip Grannies spotting us.

"Thank goodness we have a back door," I said as I shut it behind us.

Cooper removed his hat long enough to run a hand through his blond hair. "I feel like I dodged a bullet."

"You definitely did."

Cooper's phone chimed and he pulled it out of the back pocket of his jeans. He checked it and rolled his eyes.

"Something wrong?" I asked.

"Nah." He tucked his phone away again. "Just my personal assistant wondering where I am. Sometimes she acts more like a babysitter than an assistant."

"She?" I echoed with surprise. "What happened to Wes?"

Wesley was the personal assistant who had worked for Cooper back when I lived in California. He was extremely efficient yet easy-going and fun to have around.

"Wes had to have surgery. Nothing life-threatening," Cooper rushed to add when he saw my look of concern. "But he's taking a month off to recover. Geneva is standing in for him. She gets things done, but...."

"She takes her job a little too seriously?" I guessed when he left his sentence unfinished.

"That's a good way of putting it."

A door opened farther down the alley and we both turned in that direction. One of the local shop owners dragged a wooden pallet out the door and leaned it against the exterior wall of the building. He disappeared back inside his shop without noticing us.

"Please tell me you'll join me for dinner tonight at the Larch Haven Hotel," Cooper said once we were alone again. "Bring Angela, and Dizzy too."

Dizzy was my life-long best friend.

"We'd all love that," I said. "I'll check with Dizzy and Angie to make sure they're both free."

"Perfect." He pulled me into a hug and gave me a good squeeze. "I'm really happy we're working together again, Becca."

I hugged him back. "Me too, Coop."

He pulled away and gave me a grin. "Later, gator."

I smiled at the parting words he'd used so often when we worked on *Twilight Hills* together.

"After a while, crocodile," I returned.

Still grinning, he tipped his hat at me and set off down the alley.

· · · •• · • • · ·

ALTHOUGH COOPER MADE IT out of True Confections without the
Gossip Grannies noticing him, I wasn't so lucky when I reentered
the building. I'd hoped to slip unnoticed into the kitchen so I could
get straight back to work, but Luella spotted me while I was still
in the hallway.

"Rebecca!" she called out. "We were hoping to see you."

I forced a smile and cast a longing glance at the kitchen door as
I passed it on my way to the front of the shop.

"Afternoon, Luella," I greeted. I nodded at her friend. "Delphi."

"Is Cooper Graystone in town yet?" Delphi asked, her eyes
gleaming behind her large glasses. As usual, her gray hair fell past
her shoulders in frizzy waves.

"Oh...." I silently scrambled around in my brain for a way to
answer truthfully while protecting Cooper. "He's scheduled to
arrive today."

Delphi shook her head and tsk-tsked. "He should really give up
the hard partying."

Luella, the shorter and rounder of the pair, nodded eagerly. "A
stint in rehab would do him good." She'd recently taken to wearing
her short, gray hair in spikes, and today they were tipped with blue.
Not a single one moved, even with her enthusiastic nodding.

"Cooper isn't a hard partier and he doesn't have any addiction
issues," I said, feeling protective of my friend.

"Why else would he look so rough?" Delphi shoved her phone
at me. "It's shameful. Just look at him!"

I wanted to push the phone away, but I couldn't bring myself to
be that rude. I looked at the screen, against my better judgement.
The picture on display showed Cooper in the act of turning away
from the camera, but the photo had still captured most of his
face. He did indeed look rough. His face was pale and drawn, and

his hair stood on end, as if he'd run his hands through it several times. What concerned me the most was the exhaustion and stress showing in his blue eyes.

Worry and annoyance battled for dominance within me. "Where did you find this photo?"

"One of the ladies from bridge club sent it to me," Delphi explained. "She got it off the Internet."

"Apparently, it's posted all over social media," Luella added.

The only positive about the Gossip Grannies was that they didn't have an Internet presence. I shuddered to think how far their crazy rumors would spread if they ever upped their tech skills to that level.

"He clearly didn't consent to having that photo taken," I said, keeping my voice calm. "We all look rough when we're not made up and are caught off guard."

"Speak for yourself," Delphi said with a harrumph.

I barely managed to stop myself from rolling my eyes.

"Turning a blind eye won't help matters," Luella chided.

Angela came to my rescue at that moment. Probably because she could see I was about to lose my grip on politeness.

"Shall I ring up those purchases for you now?" she asked Delphi and Luella.

Both ladies looked at the boxes of chocolates in their hands as if they'd forgotten they were there. Before the women had a chance to say anything, I was already heading for the kitchen.

"I've got to get back to work," I called out over my shoulder. "Have a nice day, ladies."

Once in the sanctuary of the kitchen, I had to take several deep breaths to lower my blood pressure. While it bothered me when the Gossip Grannies made up wild stories about me and spread them around town, it upset me far more when they set their gossipy sights on one of my friends.

It wasn't the first time someone had taken surreptitious photos of Cooper and posted them online. That happened to pretty much all actors at some point, and a celebrity of his status had to deal with that on a regular basis. False rumors were also part of life for Hollywood stars, but I didn't like anyone making up stories about Cooper. He wasn't just a talented, good-looking actor; he was also a genuinely nice guy.

I did my best to shake off the encounter with the Gossip Grannies and got back to work. Although I'd spent seven years in Hollywood making my acting dreams come true, I'd returned home to Larch Haven just over one year ago, after a health scare made me reevaluate my life. While lying in my hospital bed, recovering from a ruptured appendix, I'd realized that I desperately wanted to get back to my hometown in Vermont. As much as I loved acting, working as a chocolatier in the shop owned by my grandparents, Lolly and Pops, felt like the perfect fit for me at this stage of my life. Of course, having a chance to take on an acting role in Larch Haven was like having the best of both worlds.

Coating molds with tempered chocolate and piping in delicious fillings helped to settle me down, and I put in a solid hour's work while the bell jingled above the shop's front door now and then, heralding the arrival and departure of customers.

I'd just finished off a batch of London fog truffles when Angie poked her head into the kitchen.

"Becca, can you watch the front for a minute while I pop over to the coffee shop?" she asked. "I've got a headache brewing, but I think I can cure it with a hit of caffeine."

"Sure. You caught me at a good time." I washed my hands at the sink. "You go on."

"Can I bring you back anything?"

"I'm fine, thanks," I said as I dried my hands.

"I'll just be a few minutes then."

"Wait a second, Angie," I said, stopping her as she was about to turn away. "Cooper invited me, you, and Dizzy to dinner at the Larch Haven Hotel tonight. Can you come?"

"He seriously invited me?" Angie asked with surprise and delight.

"Of course."

"Marco is taking Bella to her track meet after school," she said, speaking of her husband and daughter, "so I'll check with Lolly to see if Luca can have dinner with her and Pops."

Angie already had her phone out. "I'll let you know as soon as I've talked to Lolly."

I followed her out to the front of the shop.

She gave a squeal of happiness on her way out the door and turned back to me. "I'm so excited!"

She pushed her way out the door, the bell jingling overhead. As she set off along the cobblestone walkway, she put her phone to her ear.

I smiled as I watched her go.

Having *Love on the Canal* filmed in Larch Haven was bringing plenty of excitement to the town.

I remembered my earlier conversation with the Gossip Grannies but then pushed it to the back of my mind. Hopefully that little episode would be the end of any unnecessary drama attached to the production and its stars.

Chapter Two

MY HOMETOWN WAS A true gem and a magnet for tourists. Nestled in the mountains, Larch Haven was surrounded by green forests and rugged peaks. Instead of roads, the town had canals that wound their way through the neighborhoods, joining up with Shadow Lake to the west. Aside from golf carts, firetrucks, ambulances, and police cars, motor vehicles weren't allowed in Larch Haven and had to be left in the parking lot at the edge of town. Tourists and locals alike got around on foot, bicycle, or by boat.

Like Venice, Italy, Larch Haven was known for its gondolas, and whenever the canals weren't frozen, the iconic boats could be seen cruising along at any time of the day. Gondolas and whisper boats were available for tourists to rent, but we also had professional gondoliers who took tourists on leisurely tours of the canals.

I owned a whisper boat—powered by a quiet, electric motor—and that was how Angela, Dizzy, and I decided to travel from my cottage to the Larch Haven Hotel. Getting in and out of a small boat while wearing high heels wasn't an easy task and none of us wanted to risk falling in the canal, so we all wore ballet flats and carried our other shoes in our hands.

Once safely on board my boat, I shifted in my seat and tugged at the short skirt of my dress. My outfit wasn't exactly ideal for boating, but it would be a short trip. I'd opted to wear a one-shoulder, ruched, body-hugging dress in a shade of green that brought out the color of my eyes.

My best friend, Desiree Bautista (Dizzy for short), had met up with me and Angela at my cottage so we could get ready together. We'd done a lot of giggling as we dressed and did our makeup. I suspected that Angie was having the best time of all of us. She didn't often get to go anywhere without her kids in tow.

With my dress adjusted, I navigated the winding canals and got us to the main dock in under five minutes. Dizzy hopped out first, managing to do so gracefully despite the fact that she, too, was in a dress. Hers was dark blue with spaghetti straps, while Angie had opted for a black skirt and a shimmery top.

Once we had the craft secured to the dock, we changed into our high heels and left our ballet flats in the boat. Although Larch Haven saw its greatest influx of tourists during the summer months, especially during the annual gondola races, visitors came at all times of the year. Now, in April, the grass was a lush shade of green and flowers bloomed in beds, window boxes, and half barrels all around town.

A family of four climbed onto a gondola as we left the dock, and other tourists strolled along the wide walkway, chatting, snapping photos, and taking in the sights. The setting sun sent a pleasant warmth down on us, but I suspected that when it sank behind the mountains, the air would take on a chill. None of us had brought a coat or wrap, but we expected to be indoors most of the evening so we'd probably be fine.

When we left the main dock, the Larch Haven Hotel stood before us. Constructed from stone, it resembled an old English manor and had been built by the town's founder, Reginald Sutton-Maxwell. He'd come over to North America from England at the beginning of the twentieth century, bringing with him his Venetian bride. He'd designed the town to bring together the two worlds from which they came. The result was a canal town with charming cottages that looked like they belonged in the English countryside and colorful, timber-frame buildings that housed the local shops and restaurants.

The Larch Haven Hotel, once the private residence of Reginald and his Italian bride, was the fanciest hotel in town and was also home to a great restaurant. Not the best restaurant, in my opinion, because that honor belonged to The Gondolier, which was owned by my brother, Gareth, and his husband. Still, the hotel's restaurant was nothing to sneeze at.

Angie, Dizzy, and I started up the walkway that led to the hotel, but we slowed our pace when Officer Sawyer Maguire of the Larch Haven Police Department jogged down the front steps, wearing his uniform.

"Wow," he said as he approached us. "You three look amazing. What's the occasion?"

"Dinner with Cooper Graystone," Angie said, her eyes alight with excitement.

"I heard he arrived in town," Sawyer said, his dark eyes on me. "Filming starts tomorrow?"

I swore I could feel the heat of his gaze against my skin. "Bright and early," I replied, somehow sounding completely normal even though I was having difficulty drawing air into my lungs.

"Is there trouble at the hotel?" Dizzy asked.

When Sawyer turned his eyes her way, I could breathe again, but my skin still felt warm.

"No problem," Sawyer said. "I just stopped by for a chat with the security team. They've got extra people working while the production is in town."

Like Cooper, the other cast and crew were staying at the Larch Haven Hotel. Everyone in town knew that, so it wasn't surprising that the hotel had beefed up security. Cooper had mentioned being waylaid by fans in the lobby earlier, and I didn't doubt that similar incidents would occur all over town for the next three weeks. As long as everyone remained respectful, that shouldn't be much of a problem, but the hotel staff would understandably want to make sure that their celebrity guests weren't overly troubled onsite.

"Anyway," Sawyer continued, "I'd better get going. Enjoy your dinner."

"We definitely will," Angela said.

She and Dizzy started walking again. I was about to follow them when Sawyer touched my hand briefly. I hung back, letting the others go ahead.

"You really look amazing, Becca," Sawyer said.

Again, I could feel the heat of his gaze against my skin. Warmth filled my chest too. His compliment meant more to me than it would have from anyone else. "Thanks. We should get together soon. I haven't seen enough of you lately."

"Back at you, but I'm guessing you'll be busy for the next few weeks."

"I'll have some time off here and there. I'm not filming every day."

"We'll work something out then." His gaze lingered on me. "Have a good evening, Becca."

"You too."

I stood watching as he walked away, until I realized that Dizzy and Angie were waiting for me at the base of the hotel's front steps. I hurried to catch up with them.

"Are you okay, Becca?" Angie asked when I joined them. "You're a bit flushed."

"I'm fine," I said, shooting a subtle glare at Dizzy, who was fighting a smile.

She smoothed her expression into one of innocence, but her eyes still danced with silent laughter.

Dizzy and I had been friends with Sawyer since our preschool days. Since I'd returned home from my years in California, something had changed between me and Sawyer, though I hadn't been eager to acknowledge that, even to myself. Then, at Christmas, we'd shared an all-too-brief kiss under a sprig of mistletoe. Ever since, it had been harder to pretend that everything between us was just as it had been when we were growing up. It probably would have been even more difficult if I'd spent much time alone with Sawyer in recent weeks, but circumstances had worked against us in that respect.

I'd told Dizzy about the kiss under the mistletoe and she was very aware of the reason why my face was currently flushed. That wasn't something I wanted to dwell on at the moment, though, so I opened the hotel's front door and held it to allow Dizzy and Angela to go through ahead of me.

In the lobby, a huge chandelier hung from the high ceiling. The reception desk was located to our right and a seating area to the left. Straight ahead, a broad staircase led up to a wide landing, where the staircase then split into two, continuing up to the second floor in opposite directions. A suit of armor stood sentry on the landing, one of the relics that Reginald Sutton-Maxwell had brought over from England.

Beyond the seating area, a door led to the hotel's restaurant. Cooper came through that door and raised a hand in greeting when he spotted us. I waved back, but then my attention strayed to a man and woman who'd met up on the landing after coming down opposite branches of the staircase.

I recognized the blonde woman as Sonja Jepsen. She was the production's script supervisor and I'd met her at the table read of the script for *Love on the Canal*. I didn't recognize the man with her, but he had dark, curly hair and his otherwise light complexion was currently flushed with anger as he had a hushed and hostile conversation with Sonja on the landing.

Sonja shook her head at something the man said and turned away so she could continue down the stairs to the lobby.

"You're a thief, Sonja," the man shot after her with disgust.

She paused two steps down and looked back at him. "I'm sick of your false allegations, Tony. You're making a fool of yourself."

She resumed walking down the stairs, her head held high.

"We'll see who the fool is," Tony muttered.

He stayed on the landing, arms crossed over his chest as he glowered at Sonja's back. The light from the chandelier glinted off his wristwatch and the gold chains around his neck.

I exchanged uneasy glances with Angie and Dizzy as we made our way over to meet up with Cooper. Sonja passed him on her way into the restaurant, exchanging a quiet greeting with him without pausing.

"You clean up nice," I said with a smile before giving Cooper a kiss on the cheek.

He'd exchanged his jeans and T-shirt for khakis and a blue, button up shirt that matched his eyes.

"I could say the same about you three, but that would be a terrible understatement. You all look incredible."

I reintroduced him to Dizzy, whom he'd met only briefly during a video call a couple of years earlier, and he hugged her and Angie too.

"What's with the dark-haired guy?" I asked in a whisper as we made our way into the dining room.

Cooper glanced back in time to see the man storm across the lobby toward the hotel's front door.

"That's Tony Fleet," Cooper said. "Our props master."

"He was arguing with Sonja when we arrived."

Cooper rolled his eyes. "Not for the first time and I'm sure not for the last."

I was curious to know more, but we cut off our conversation as the restaurant's hostess led us to our table.

I spotted some familiar faces as we crossed the room. Sonja and producer Phil Chalupnik sat at a nearby table with director Jasmine Singh, whom I'd also met when I'd flown to Los Angeles for the table read of the script. I waved at them before taking my seat at the table for four that Cooper had reserved for us.

The food we ordered was delicious, but the company was even better. We chatted and laughed all through the meal. We were too full to indulge in dessert after our main dishes, so we stayed and talked a little longer over cups of tea and coffee instead.

Eventually, we reluctantly got up from the table. Cooper and I had to be up bright and early the next morning and didn't want to stay up too late.

Sonja was on her way out of the restaurant at the same time as we were heading for the lobby. I introduced her to Dizzy and Angela and we stopped beneath the crystal chandelier to chat for a minute.

"This town is so charming," Sonja gushed. "And so quiet! I'm such a light sleeper, but with no traffic noise here, I slept like the dead last night."

"It's definitely the polar opposite from Los Angeles," I said.

"Like a different planet," Sonja agreed. "I might have to move here."

"Same," Cooper chimed in. "Ready for some new neighbors, Becca?"

"Of course," I said with a smile.

We shared some parting words with Sonja before she headed up the stairs to her room and Cooper walked us out of the hotel.

Darkness had fallen while we ate our dinner and a sliver of a moon hung above the mountains to the north. Stars dotted the clear sky like glinting diamonds and the breeze smelled faintly of flowers. As I'd predicted, the air had grown chilly after the sun disappeared and I suppressed a shiver as we made our way down the front steps.

A group of giggling girls in their late teens melted out of the shadows on the hotel's front lawn and surrounded Cooper. They spoke over each other, asking for selfies and autographs.

Cooper dealt with it with good grace, smiling and happily acceding to their requests. He was signing the back of one girl's T-shirt when a woman who appeared to be in her late twenties came running down the hotel steps. She had fair skin that contrasted with her dark hair, which was cut in a chin-length bob with blunt bangs.

"Ladies, please," the new arrival said to the teens as she pushed up her black-framed glasses. "Mr. Graystone needs to leave now."

"It's fine, Geneva," Cooper said to her. "I've got time."

While the rest of us hung back, Cooper posed for selfies with each girl in the pool of illumination cast by the hotel's bright exterior lights.

Calling their thanks, the girls went on their way a few minutes later, giggling and looking at the new photos on their phones.

Geneva stood at the base of the steps, frowning and practically radiating disapproval.

"I'll walk my friends to the dock," Cooper said to her. "Then I'm heading to bed. No need for you to stick around."

Geneva's frown deepened, but she didn't make a move to follow us when we started along the walkway.

"My personal assistant," Cooper said in a low voice for Dizzy's and Angela's benefit. "She's a temp while my usual one is off for medical reasons."

"Does she double as a bodyguard?" Dizzy said in jest.

Cooper laughed. "She is a bit overprotective." His expression grew more serious. "But there's a reason for that. There's been a bunch of photos of me showing up on the Internet lately. I guess you'd call them unflattering. That always happens from time to time, but lately there's been a lot more. I don't know if it's one person responsible or what, but some of the pictures have been taken on sets where the public has little to no access."

I recalled the photo that the Gossip Grannies had shown me. "So you think someone on the inside has been taking surreptitious photos of you?" I asked.

Cooper shrugged. "Like I said, it could be more than one person. I ended up with food poisoning one day on set. Someone got a photo of me mid-puke."

"And they posted it online?" Angie asked with horror. "Who would do such a thing?"

"A lot of people, unfortunately," I said.

Cooper nodded. "It just goes with the territory."

Although he sounded nonchalant, the crease across his forehead and the look in his eyes told me that he was more troubled than he was letting on.

I didn't think he'd want to talk about it further in front of Dizzy and Angie, so I let the matter drop for the moment.

He walked us as far as the main dock and waited there as we putted away in my whisper boat. When I turned back to wave at him, I saw Geneva standing up the steps from the dock, keeping a close and watchful eye on Cooper.

Chapter Three

"DON'T GET USED TO me being up at this hour," I warned my two cats, Truffles and Binx, as I rolled out of bed the next morning, "because I'm not going to make a habit of it."

I was typically an early riser and liked to be at work in the kitchen at True Confections no later than seven in the morning, but getting up before five o'clock wasn't something I did for kicks. Today, however, I had to report to hair and makeup at six o'clock, and I wanted to get my day off to a good start with my usual yoga and Pilates routine.

Truffles and Binx didn't mind getting woken up early. The felines went from sound asleep to wide awake within a couple of seconds, and they led the way downstairs to the kitchen with sprightly steps, eager to get their breakfast. With my hair in a ponytail, I doled out some food for the cats, got through my exercise routine, took a quick shower, and got dressed. Then I was out the door.

The birds were awake and twittering in the trees, but I didn't see many other humans out and about as I walked along the canal. The sun hadn't yet risen up over the mountains, but the sky had lightened, with a few puffy, pink-tinged clouds drifting here and there.

The production's trailers had taken up a section of the large parking lot at the edge of town. When I arrived there, I found the trailer reserved for me and stepped inside, shutting the door behind me. There was a small sitting area with a loveseat, a chair, and a table. There was also a tiny washroom that wasn't much bigger than a coffin standing on end. I didn't know how much I'd use the trailer, since my cottage wasn't far away, but I appreciated having the space to retreat to nonetheless.

I heard something brush against the outside of the door and expected someone to knock. Instead, hurried footsteps faded away into the distance. Checking the time on my phone, I decided I shouldn't linger, so I exited the trailer and shut the door behind me. As I did so, a piece of paper fluttered in the light morning breeze. Someone had attached a note to the trailer door with a single piece of tape.

I reached for the note and then stopped without touching it.

My empty stomach twisted as I read the words scrawled on the piece of paper.

I hope you break a leg. Literally.

Who would leave a message like that?

I whirled around, trying to spot the note's author in the pre-dawn darkness, but the only person in sight was a production assistant wearing a headset and holding a clipboard. She was walking in my direction with brisk strides. I yanked the paper off the door. It must have been meant for me. My name was right there on the trailer door.

When the production assistant reached me, I asked her if she'd seen anyone near my trailer, but she hadn't. She'd been busy elsewhere. I assured her that there wasn't a problem and she directed me to the hair and makeup trailer. Still feeling unsettled, I stuffed the note in my pocket and headed in the indicated direction. I tried to shake off the incident, but my brain wanted to scroll through possible suspects. That was a pointless exercise, though, because I couldn't think of anyone who would direct such hostility toward me.

The door to the hair and makeup trailer opened as I approached, and Felicia Blessing emerged. Felicia was playing the lead role in *Love on the Canal*. We'd worked together briefly on the soap opera *Passion City*, and I'd had a small role in another film she'd starred in. She was lithe and elegant, with smooth, light brown skin and a blonde afro. She already had her makeup done and she wore a puffy, knee-length coat to protect her against the morning chill. The coat looked more suited to a Vermont winter than spring, but she'd grown up in Southern California and probably found the cool April morning too close to winter for her tastes.

Her beautiful face lit up when she spotted me. "Becca! Good to see you!"

"You too, Felicia." I returned the smile and the air kisses that she aimed at my cheeks.

"I hear you're a chocolatier now. Chocolate is my main weakness."

"Mine too," I said, still smiling. "Come by the shop sometime while you're here."

"You can count on it."

Her smile faded into a frown when she noticed something over my shoulder. I turned to see what had caught her eye and spotted the props master, Tony Fleet, walking beneath the parking lot's security lights toward the end of the line of trailers.

"I'll need a lot of chocolate if I'm expected to put up with him," she muttered.

Tony disappeared into one of the far trailers and Felicia's smile returned.

"I need to get to wardrobe," she said. "But I won't be leaving town without visiting your shop."

She hurried off toward the wardrobe department's temporary digs.

Mindful of the fact that it was nearly six o'clock, I entered the hair and makeup trailer. Cooper was there, seated in front of the makeup artist, while Diego Martinez was having his hair styled. I'd met Diego for the first time at the table read in LA a week ago, when all of us actors read through the script together. I figured I'd be getting to know him a lot better over the next three weeks. My character, Addison, was the best friend and confidant of Felicia's character, Journey. The main story followed the romance of Journey and Connor, Cooper's character, but one of the subplots involved a blooming romance between Addison and Enrique, played by Diego.

After I greeted everyone, Diego vacated his chair, and I took his place. Diego stayed in the trailer, lounging in a spare seat while drinking coffee from a takeout cup. Alex Skye, the hairstylist, released my dark brown hair from its ponytail, letting it fall down my back.

I'd never met Alex before, but I took an instant liking to him. His own hair was a mix of blue and purple, worn in a pompadour, and he had mermaid and other colorful, ocean-themed tattoos all up and down his fair-skinned arms. He had an upbeat and friendly demeanor that immediately put me at ease.

"I'm so lucky I get to work with such gorgeous hair today," he gushed as he fluffed up my hair, assessing it from different angles. "First Felicia's and now yours, Becca."

"Hey, what about mine?" Diego asked, pretending to be hurt.

"You didn't exactly leave me much to work with, hon," Alex said.

Diego hid his grin with his coffee cup as he took a drink.

Diego's black hair was indeed cut very short, but it was neatly styled, so Alex had clearly done well with what was there.

"I ran into Felicia on my way here," I said. "She didn't seem happy about Tony Fleet being part of the crew."

"That's probably an understatement," Michaela, the makeup artist, said as she put the finishing touches on Cooper's face.

"Why's that?" I asked, unable to help being curious.

"Ooh, girl, you haven't heard that story?" Alex asked, his tone suggesting that it might be a juicy one.

"They were married," Cooper said.

"And they divorced about four years ago," Alex added.

"Tony had a wandering eye," Michaela chimed in as she whisked the protective cape off Cooper.

Alex let out a snort of laughter. "It was more than his eye that wandered."

"I knew she was married and divorced a few years back," I said, feeling sorry for Felicia, "but I didn't know who the husband was or what led to their separation."

Alex shook his head as he started using a curling iron to style my hair into loose waves. "Felicia deserves so much better. You know that fancy watch Tony wears and all that bling around his neck? All paid for with Felicia's money."

"She has to pay him alimony," Cooper explained as he got up from his chair. "I'd better get going. See you all later."

We called out our goodbyes as he headed out of the trailer and Diego followed him a moment later.

"Tony's not known for endearing himself to people," Michaela said a few minutes later when I moved from Alex's chair to hers.

"Except to certain women," Alex amended. "Temporarily, anyway."

Michaela shook her head with disbelief. "I don't know what anyone sees in him."

"I'm with you there," Alex agreed.

"I heard he argued with Sonja again yesterday," Michaela said as she got started on my makeup.

"Again?" I echoed. "I heard him call her a thief last night at the hotel."

"That must be the umpteenth time," Alex said. "Sonja's been dipping her toes into the screenwriting pool. She had one of her scripts optioned last month."

Michaela took up the story as she applied my eyeliner. "Tony claims she stole his idea."

"I thought you couldn't copyright an idea," I said when Michaela stepped back to survey her work.

"You can't," she confirmed.

"Try telling Tony that." Alex took a drink from a travel mug. "He's threatened to take her to court, but he's never done it, probably because he knows he'd lose."

One of the other supporting actors arrived at the trailer and the conversation shifted, with Alex talking about how he and his boyfriend were saving up to get in on the LA property market.

A while later, with my hair and makeup done, I moved on to the wardrobe trailer, where I dressed in the jeans and soft, light sweater provided for me. I exchanged my sneakers for the high-heeled boots I was given and, once I received the green light, I climbed into a waiting golf cart with Diego. As the sun rose above the mountains to the east, the driver took us to Venice Avenue, Larch Haven's main shopping area.

Colorful timber-frame buildings lined the canal, with a cobblestone walkway between the stores and the water. One of the shops was True Confections. It felt strange not to be heading there to get to work in the kitchen, but I knew my grandmother would be there soon, standing in for me as chocolatier. That had been her job for decades since she and Pops founded the store. My grandparents had finally retired, but they still helped out now and again.

For the film, the local bakery—currently closed as it changed ownership—had been transformed into a flower shop, the business owned by Felicia's character. The first scenes of the day would be filmed outside the shop, followed by more scenes filmed inside.

When I climbed out of the golf cart, careful not to snag my clothing on anything, I spotted Dizzy walking toward the local coffee shop, Gathering Grounds. I glanced around to make sure I wasn't needed immediately, and then hurried over to meet up with her.

"I'm so excited!" she enthused as she looked over my shoulder at the crew members getting ready to film the first scene. "How are you feeling?"

"Nervous," I confessed.

That brought her full attention to me. "What? Why?"

I shared the concern that had hit me in the middle of the night. "What if I've forgotten how to act?"

"Not possible, Becca. It's part of who you are. Besides, you told me the table read went well."

"True, but that's not quite the same."

"Becca, you've got this," Dizzy said without a shred of doubt.

Her confidence helped to wash away some of my nerves. "Thanks, Dizzy."

She wiggled her fingers. "I'd hug you, but I don't want to mess up your hair, so you'll just have to imagine a virtual hug."

I smiled. "Done."

I glanced over my shoulder, knowing I should get back.

"If I can watch some takes before I go to work, I will," Dizzy said. "But either way, tell me everything later."

"Definitely," I promised.

As Dizzy disappeared into the coffee shop, I took a deep, steadying breath, and got ready to work.

Chapter Four

DIZZY WAS RIGHT, OF course. I fell back into acting like I'd never taken a break from it. I filmed two scenes that morning, one with Diego and another with Felicia and Cooper. I had a long break before my third and final scene of the day, so I wandered over to craft services for some lunch. The catering truck set up to feed the cast and crew was stationed at the corner of Venice Avenue and Amsterdam Avenue. The truck had been parked in such a way as to provide a semiprivate eating area between it and the wrought iron railing along the edge of the canal. A security guard stood nearby, no doubt to ensure that people unattached to the production didn't wander into the area and hassle the cast.

Felicia was currently busy filming a scene with the actress who was playing her mother, but Diego and Cooper had arrived at craft services ahead of me. They were both making their way through plates of tasty-looking food while standing around chatting.

"The pasta salad is delicious," Diego told me as I passed them on my way to the craft services truck.

"And make sure you try the spring rolls," Cooper added.

The spring rolls were vegetarian, so I took the advice of both guys. By the time I had a plate of food of my own, they'd taken seats in the chairs set out nearby. I grabbed a vacant chair and pulled it closer so I could join them.

"One more scene, then we're done for the day," Diego said to me, holding out his fist.

I bumped it with my own before sitting down.

"Slackers," Cooper joked. "I've got three scenes this afternoon."

Sonja came hurrying over to craft services from the direction of the faux flower shop. I figured she was taking advantage of a break in filming. As the script supervisor, Sonja oversaw the continuity of the film, tracking everything from props to makeup, lighting to hairstyles, from take to take and scene to scene. She worked closely with the director and stayed in communication with all the different departments. She was vital to the production and I'd heard that she was very good at her job.

"Man, he's at it again," Diego said with a shake of his head, pulling my attention away from Sonja.

I followed Diego's line of sight. Props master Tony stood by the corner of the catering truck with Chanel Yearwood, a local woman in her late forties. Her shoulder-length hair was dyed honey blonde and she was currently fluttering her false lashes at Tony as they stood close together, talking quietly.

As I watched, Tony fingered Chanel's necklace, saying something I couldn't hear. Her face brightened and she leaned in closer to him, resting a hand on his chest as she whispered something in his ear. Then she turned and flounced off.

I knew from one of my earlier scenes that Chanel was working as a background performer for the film. I also knew that she was married. Maybe Tony wasn't aware of that, but I wasn't sure if he'd care even if he had that information.

Tony pulled his phone from the back pocket of his jeans and tapped away at it. Alex, who'd styled my hair that morning, appeared and approached Tony. The props master barely looked up from his phone as Alex spoke to him. I couldn't hear anything Alex said, but he had a beseeching expression on his face.

The conversation between Cooper and Diego—which now had something to do with football—faded into the background as I focused on the other two men.

Tony shook his head and tucked his phone back in his pocket. His next words were loud enough to reach my ears.

"Forget it," he said in a dismissive tone before walking away.

"I need it back, Tony," Alex called after him, sounding desperate.

Tony laughed, a cruel note underscoring the sound, as he continued walking without glancing back.

Alex's face flushed with anger and his fists clenched at his sides. Then he seemed to gather control of himself and strode off in the opposite direction.

My attention snapped back to my immediate surroundings when Cooper's phone buzzed. He checked the screen and jumped out of his seat.

"Sorry, I've got to take this." He ditched his now-empty plate as he moved off to the edge of the canal, where he would have some privacy, and answered his call.

Sonja glanced his way as she approached Diego and me, carrying a plate of food.

"He needs to be back on set in half an hour," she said, her eyes on Cooper.

"I'm sure he'll be there," Diego assured her, unconcerned. His plate empty now too, he got up from his chair. "I need to stretch my legs. See you in a bit, Becca."

He set off along the cobblestone walkway, heading farther away from set.

Sonja sat down in the chair Diego had vacated, but she focused on her phone as she balanced it on her lap while she ate. From where I sat, I had a good view of True Confections, farther down Venice Avenue. While filming was underway, pedestrians were allowed to pass by the bakery-turned-flower-shop between takes so they could visit any of the nearby businesses. Shoppers could also access the stores from the other end of Venice Avenue, where the canal joined up with Shadow Lake.

I still had half an hour to kill before I was needed on set again, so I decided to stop by the chocolate shop once I was done eating.

The pasta salad was indeed delicious, as were the veggie spring rolls. I washed everything down with a cold drink of iced tea as I enjoyed the view of the canal and the feel of the midday sun on my face. Larch Haven really was a charming and beautiful town. Hanging baskets bursting with colorful flowers hung from the old-fashioned lampposts that lined the cobblestone walkway and the water of the canal reflected the brilliant blue sky and the few puffy white clouds that drifted across it. The bright daylight made the colors of the timber-frame buildings on Venice Avenue seem even more vivid and striking. It was a postcard-perfect scene and the ideal setting for a sweet love story.

A gondola cut smoothly through the water, steered by one of the town's professional gondoliers, easily identifiable by his blue-and-white striped shirt. A family of four sat in the craft, pointing out the sights to each other and snapping photos.

As the gondola glided along the canal, I got up and disposed of my plate and cup. Sonja, her break evidently over, ditched her own plate and grabbed a cookie from craft services before hurrying back to set. I followed at a slower pace, but still managed to slip past the fake flower shop before filming resumed.

When I opened the door to True Confections, the delectable scent of chocolate greeted me. I breathed in deeply, as was my habit each morning when I first arrived at the shop. The familiar, heavenly smell—and all the memories and warm feelings it conjured—was like a balm to my soul.

I smiled when I saw Pops behind the counter, bagging up boxcs of chocolates for the only two customers currently in the shop: a woman with a young girl in tow. I lingered off to the side until the customers left. Then I hurried around the counter to greet my grandfather.

"I see Angie's got you hard at work today," I said after kissing him on the cheek.

He smiled, the crinkles at the corners of his eyes deepening. "No rest for the wicked, and all that." He gave me a hug. "How's my Hollywood star?"

"Not really a star," I said, as I usually did when he called me that. Still, the way he said it with so much pride always made me glow with warmth on the inside. "But I'm doing great, Pops. My first two scenes went really well."

"I never doubted that they would."

"Is that my film star of a granddaughter I hear out there?" Lolly's voice rang out from the kitchen.

A second later, she joined us in the front of the store.

I greeted her with a hug. "How are things here at the shop?" I asked. "Is business slow with the production blocking access at times?"

"Business isn't bad," Pops said. "So Angela tells me. She just popped out to get some lunch."

"Customers are coming in more pronounced waves and lulls, that's all," Lolly said.

I made a move to head for the kitchen. "And the chocolates?"

Lolly blocked my path. "You're not to worry about that today, Rebecca. All you have to focus on is being an actor again."

I looked around at my family's beloved shop. "I miss this place when I'm not here," I said. "But I'm having a great time on set."

Lolly patted my cheek. "Good. Whenever you have a chance to enjoy both worlds, you should."

I was happy she felt that way. When I was first offered the role of Journey's best friend, Addison, I worried that my family might think I was neglecting my duties if I took time off to revisit my acting career, however briefly. I should have known better. Lolly, Pops, Angie, and the rest of my relatives living in Larch Haven had supported me all the way.

I chatted with my grandparents for another minute or two, until Angie returned and several customers arrived right on her heels. With a wave goodbye, I left the shop. Outside, I had to stop short to avoid running into a woman with long, dark hair and gray eyes. She had an oversized purse hooked on one elbow and held a paper shopping bag in her other hand.

"Sorry," I apologized, though I didn't actually bump into her. When I got a good look at her face, I recognized her as one of my high school classmates. "Daniela, hi! I didn't know you were back in Larch Haven."

Daniela's neutral expression changed into a decidedly un-friendly one. "I guess it's hard to know what other people are doing when you're wrapped up in yourself."

"Sorry?" I said, taken aback by her bitterness.

Now she smirked at me. "That's a lot of makeup, Becca. What are you trying to hide?"

I stared at her, speechless.

Her mother emerged from the shop next door and spotted us together.

"Come on, Daniela," she called to her daughter while sending a suspicious glance at me. "Let's go get some lunch."

With one last smirk in my direction, Daniela flicked her hair over her shoulder and walked off with her mother.

I stood there in shock for another second or two before making my way back toward craft services. By the time I neared the catering truck, I'd mostly shaken off the encounter. Perhaps I shouldn't have been surprised by Daniela's attitude. She'd always acted haughty and sometimes downright mean back in our school days, but I'd hoped that the passage of more than a decade would have matured her and made her a nicer person. Apparently, that hadn't happened.

Trying to forget about my former classmate, I checked my phone. Almost time for me to return to set. My final scene of the day would be filmed inside the flower shop. Tomorrow, we'd move to a new location in one of the residential neighborhoods.

I spotted Diego off in the distance, crossing a bridge on his way back to Venice Avenue. He would be in the next scene along with me, Felicia, and Cooper.

I considered getting myself a drink of water before retracing my steps along Venice Avenue, but then my attention shifted to Alex as he hurried my way.

"Just need to check your hair, Becca," he said before sizing me up and adjusting a few of my wavy locks.

Cooper still stood over by the edge of the canal, talking on his phone. He took his job seriously and was always punctual, so I didn't doubt that he'd wrap up his phone call soon.

Cooper's personal assistant, Geneva, sat in one of the chairs near the catering truck. She was staring at something near the canal, her eyes narrowed. I realized she was watching Tony, who was standing near a small dock where gondoliers could stop to pick up or drop off passengers. He was holding up his phone and looking in Cooper's direction. Cooper was too focused on his phone conversation to notice, but Geneva got up from her chair, her gaze still fixed on Tony.

As Diego approached, Alex waved him over, wanting to check his hair as well, even though it didn't appear to have changed at all since that morning.

I was about to ask Diego how he'd enjoyed his walk when I heard Cooper swear, his voice filled with uncharacteristic anger.

I turned his way just in time to see him charge toward Tony and knock the props master into the canal.

Chapter Five

TONY HIT THE WATER with a splash a second after his phone clattered to the cobblestones. He disappeared beneath the surface, but reappeared almost immediately, spluttering and flailing.

"Get me out of here!" he yelled when he saw the small crowd of onlookers that had gathered by the canal.

The security guard who'd been stationed near the catering truck earlier jumped down to the small dock and reached a hand out to Tony.

"I was having a private conversation!" Cooper yelled as the security guard hauled a dripping and bedraggled Tony out of the water.

Diego grabbed Cooper's arm and tugged him away from the canal. "Hey, man, settle down."

Cooper shook his arm free, still glowering at Tony. "You're the one who's been taking photos of me for months. You even sold some to the tabloids!"

Tony sneered at him. "Try and prove it."

Cooper took a step toward him.

Before he could get any closer to Tony, I grabbed one of his arms and Diego took the other.

"Seriously, man," Diego said. "He's not worth it."

Cooper let us guide him away from the dock, but his eyes remained stormy, his jaw tense.

"Hey, give that back!" Tony yelled.

We turned around to see him heading for Geneva, who had his phone in her hand. She swiped the screen and tapped at it.

"Once I've deleted the video." She tapped the screen again and held the phone out.

Tony snatched it away from her.

The security guard hovered next to Tony, watching everyone closely. More people had gathered nearby to see what was happening. I recognized most of the onlookers as part of the production, but a few passersby had stopped as well.

Phil Chalupnik hurried over our way. Diego clapped Cooper on the shoulder and then met up with Phil, presumably to bring him up to speed on what had transpired.

"I'm going to change," Tony grumbled before storming off, his clothes still dripping.

Chanel Yearwood emerged from the small crowd of onlookers and hurried after Tony.

Geneva came over to where I stood with Cooper.

"Forget about Tony," she advised him. "I'll take care of things."

Cooper ran a hand through his hair, a mixture of anger and regret in his blue eyes.

Phil finished talking with Diego and came over our way to see if Cooper was all right. Cooper just wanted to get back to work, so we all returned to set and tried our best to shake off the incident.

· · · · ● · ● · · · ·

LATER THAT AFTERNOON, I arrived home at my cottage to find my gray tabby cat, Truffles, waiting for me just inside the front door. I kicked off my shoes and scooped Truffles up into my arms, nuzzling my nose into her soft, furry cheek as she purred.

"Where's your brother?" I asked as we made our way down the hall toward the family room and kitchen at the back of the cottage.

Truffles only purred harder in response to my question, but I found my black cat, Binx, in the family room, rolling around on the rug as he batted at his catnip banana.

When he saw me, Binx leapt to his feet and gave the toy a swat so it skittered across the floor. Then he had the zoomies and tore around the room, leaping on and off the furniture and literally bouncing off the wall at one point. Eventually, he flopped at my feet and looked up at me with his green eyes.

I'd laughed all the way through his display of silliness and I still had a smile on my face as he lay there, swishing his tail back and forth. I set Truffles down and picked up Binx.

"You have lots of energy," I said before kissing the top of his head. "Want to go for a walk?"

He responded by wriggling in my arms until I set him down. Then he trotted to the back door.

"I'll take that as a yes," I said.

I clipped both cats into their harnesses and attached their leashes. Then I took them out for a walk, which was really more of a slow wander while they sniffed at interesting scents and occasionally pounced on passing insects.

Once Binx and Truffles were satisfied with their outing, I put them in their catio, the outdoor enclosure Pops had helped me build for them. Then I returned indoors to wash the makeup off my face. As I did so, I remembered Daniela's snide remarks and the message left on my trailer door. Was Daniela responsible for the mean note? Probably. She definitely harbored plenty of animosity toward me, for whatever reason.

Trying to let all thoughts of my former classmate wash away like my makeup, I finished cleaning my face. I was patting my skin dry with a soft towel when I heard a knock on the front door.

I hurried to answer it and stepped back to let Dizzy inside. We'd arranged to meet for dinner at my place before she had to head back to work at the local library. This was the one day of the week when the library stayed open into the evening, and an author was coming to give a talk and sign books.

Dizzy held up a paper bag as she crossed the threshold into my cottage. "I hope you're ready to eat, because these smells have been making my stomach grumble all the way here."

"Definitely ready," I said. "And thanks for bringing the food."

She'd stopped at a restaurant on the way to pick up fish tacos.

It didn't take us long to get the food out on the kitchen table and our plates filled. Dizzy wanted to know about my day on set, so I filled her in, finishing with the skirmish between Cooper and Tony that had ended up with the props master in the canal.

Dizzy's brown eyes widened as I told the story. "Cooper did that? Is he known for losing his temper?"

"No way," I said between bites of delicious taco. "I've never seen him like that before."

"Is he all right now?"

I took a drink of water before answering. "He seems to be. I think he really regrets what happened."

Dizzy speared some of her salad with her fork. "Will he get in trouble?"

"I don't think so," I said, hoping he wouldn't. "As long as nothing like that happens again."

"What about Tony?" Dizzy asked. "Shouldn't he lose his job if he's been taking photos of actors on set and selling them to the tabloids?"

"You'd think so, but I guess it depends on whether or not there's any evidence to back up Cooper's claim."

Dizzy shook her head. "Tony sounds like a real jerk."

"I've never worked with him before, but he doesn't seem very popular." I finished up my tacos before changing the subject. "I ran into Daniela Roumeliotis today."

Dizzy made a face. "Was she her usual charming self?"

"As always," I said with a sigh.

I told Dizzy about my brief and somewhat baffling conversation with Daniela outside True Confections.

Dizzy shook her head in disbelief. "Does she not know that actors wear makeup? And you wrapped up in yourself? That's totally not true!"

I shrugged. "I don't know what her problem is. I was hoping she'd be nicer now, but apparently not."

"She was always jealous of you," Dizzy said, pushing her empty plate aside.

"Why would she be jealous?" I asked. "I know she was upset that time in junior year when I got the lead role in the school play, but is that really worth holding a grudge over?"

"To her it is," Dizzy said. "Just forget about her, Becca. She's not worth worrying about."

"I won't let her get to me." I stacked up our plates. "I didn't even realize she was back in Larch Haven."

"Neither did I." Dizzy grabbed our empty glasses and carried them over to the sink. "She must have returned recently, otherwise we would have heard about it before now."

"Didn't she move to New York after we finished high school?"

Dizzy shrugged. "I remember her mom saying Daniela was modelling in New York, but I heard from Teresa Hernandez that she was waitressing in New Jersey and trying to land a rich husband. I don't know how much of that is fact and how much is fiction, though."

I told Dizzy about the note I'd found on my trailer door, and produced the crumpled piece of paper from my pocket to show her. I shared my suspicion that Daniela was behind it.

"That's going too far," Dizzy said, fire in her eyes. "You should show this to Sawyer."

"It's not worth bothering him about it." I stuffed the paper back in my pocket. "Besides, I can handle Daniela."

"What if the note was left by someone else?"

"You think there could be a second person in town who dislikes me that much?" I had trouble believing that. I didn't make a habit of rubbing people the wrong way.

"Okay, no," Dizzy conceded. "I'm ninety-nine percent sure it was Daniela."

"Me too, so please don't mention it to Sawyer. There's no point."

Dizzy agreed to my request, though not entirely without misgivings. We didn't spend any more time discussing Daniela that evening, to my relief. Dizzy had to get back to the library, so I shooed her out the door, not letting her stick around to help me clean up. Once I had the kitchen tidy, I texted Cooper to see how he was doing. His uncharacteristic loss of temper had me concerned, especially since I got the sense that there was something more going on with him lately.

He texted back right away, telling me he was fine and inviting me to join him for a drink at the hotel bar. I didn't have to get up quite so early the next morning, so I told him I'd be right over.

When I arrived in the lobby of the Larch Haven Hotel, my shoulders tensed. Tony was on his way down the stairs from the second floor and I hoped he wasn't about to start trouble. I glanced around, but Cooper was nowhere in sight. My shoulders relaxed. As long as Tony stayed out of the bar, maybe we could avoid any more drama that evening.

On my way into the bar, I glanced back at Tony. He'd stopped on the landing and was checking out the suit of armor stationed there. He lifted the visor and peeked inside. A middle-aged couple climbing the stairs looked his way.

"Pretty cool, huh?" Tony said of the suit of armor.

The couple nodded and smiled, continuing up to the next floor.

I carried on into the bar and found Cooper tucked in a booth near the back of the dimly lit room. I slid into the seat across from him.

I barely had time to greet him when a server showed up to take my order. I checked the menu and asked for one of the mocktails. The server disappeared and I turned my full attention on Cooper. He had a glass of beer in front of him and the napkin that sat on the table next to his drink looked as though it had been folded and refolded many times over.

"Are you really okay, Cooper?" I asked with concern.

He noticed me looking at the napkin and let out a sigh. "I screwed up this afternoon."

"Those photos that have shown up online and in the tabloids have been bothering you more than you've let on, haven't they?"

He shrugged one shoulder. "I thought I was doing fine with it, but when I saw Tony filming my phone call...." He let out an irritated breath. "I get that I'm in the public eye, but some things should still be private."

"They should," I agreed. "Is there something else going on?"

He stared into his beer for a moment before answering. "I haven't told this to anyone except Wes and Geneva, but I've been seeing a therapist lately. That's who I was talking to on the phone this afternoon."

No wonder he didn't want Tony capturing any of that conversation on video.

"Remember how I told you a few years back that I struggle with anxiety?" he asked.

"I remember." We'd talked about it now and then when we were filming *Twilight Hills* together. I also struggled with anxiety at times, especially back when I was living in Hollywood, so it was something we had in common.

"For some reason, it's been getting worse," Cooper continued. "I feel like there's pressure on me all the time. Like I can never measure up, but I've got to keep pretending that I am."

"I get that," I said.

He nodded and gave me a grateful half smile. "I know you do. That's why I know I can tell you this." He turned his glass in a slow circle. "Anyway, I guess that's why I've been on edge more than usual. And when those photos started showing up, with me looking like a wreck in some of them...." He took a second to gather his thoughts. "It's like someone was kicking me in the gut while I was at my most vulnerable."

I reached across the table and gave his hand a squeeze. "I'm sorry, Cooper."

The server appeared with my drink, so we broke off our conversation.

Cooper let out a breath and took a sip of beer. "Enough about that," he said when we were alone again.

"Are you sure?" I asked. "We can talk more about it if you want."

"Thanks, Becca," Cooper said with sincere gratitude. "I might take you up on that sometime, but tonight let's just enjoy the fact that we get to hang out together again."

I touched my cocktail glass to his pint glass. "It really is great to see you."

It turned out that we wouldn't have had a chance for more private conversation anyway. One of the camera operators for *Love on the Canal* came into the bar with Sonja. When they spotted Cooper and me, we invited them to join us.

The four of us chatted about the film and life in general while we enjoyed our drinks. After nearly an hour had passed, Sonja's phone chimed. When she checked it, her forehead furrowed in puzzlement.

"Everything okay?" I asked her.

Sonja slid out of the booth. "I need to check on something. See you all in the morning."

"I should get going too," Cooper said shortly after Sonja's departure. "I'm pretty beat."

"Same." Greg, the camera operator, got up from the booth and said good night.

After Cooper and Greg left, I was about ready to go on my way as well, but then Phil and the film's first assistant director joined me at my booth. I decided to stick around a little longer and ordered another mocktail. By the time I'd finished my second drink, I knew I needed to call it a night.

I said good night to the others and made my way out of the bar.

As I entered the lobby, Chanel slipped in the front door of the hotel and made a beeline for the stairs. A security guard emerged from a shadowy corner of the lobby and strode in her direction. I recognized the man as a local, but I didn't know his name. I did, however, know that he liked the salted caramels we sold at True Confections. I'd seen him in the shop purchasing a box on more than one occasion.

"Mrs. Yearwood," he called out.

Chanel stopped halfway up the first flight of stairs, a guilty expression on her face.

Reluctantly, she retraced her steps to meet up with the security guard.

"Sorry, Mrs. Yearwood," he said. "With all the actors staying here, we're trying to keep people away from the upper levels."

"I just need to visit a friend." She spoke quietly, so I almost didn't hear her.

"I could walk you up to your friend's room," the security guard offered. "Sorry for the inconvenience. Like I said, it's just because of the actors being here."

"I understand." She checked her phone and then gave a forced little laugh. "Silly me. I should have checked my messages. My friend is actually at the pub."

She was already on her way out the front door when she waved to the security guard. "Thanks for your help, Kyle."

I followed her out the door and saw her scurry off in the general direction of the pub. I turned for home, heading for the arched stone bridge that would take me over the first of the canals I'd have to cross to get to my cottage. My phone chimed in my pocket so I pulled it out to find a new text message from Dizzy.

Any idea what's happening at the parking lot? her message read. I paused on the bridge to send a reply. *No clue. Why?*

Her response came seconds later. *Lots of emergency lights flashing. I'm just leaving the library. I might take a look.*

I'll see you there, I wrote back.

Turning around, I broke into a jog and followed the cobblestone walkways toward the parking lot at the edge of town. As I drew closer to my destination, I caught sight of red and blue lights flashing in the darkness. A few other curious people were also heading in that direction.

When I reached the first in the long line of trailers parked at one end of the lot, I spotted Dizzy approaching from my left.

"Hey," I greeted when I met up with her. "I hope nothing terrible has happened."

"Same," she said, looking worried, "but there must be at least three police cars, judging by all those lights."

When we neared the props trailer, I realized that was where the police had converged. Several officers were on the scene, including Sawyer. He was talking to one of his colleagues, but when he spotted Dizzy and me approaching, he broke away from the other officer and quickly strode toward us.

"Don't go any closer," he cautioned, blocking our path. "You don't want to see this."

But it was too late.

Before he'd stepped in front of me, I'd caught a glimpse of Tony sprawled on his back on the cobblestones, the front of his shirt dark with blood.

Chapter Six

I KNEW FROM DIZZY's loud gasp that she'd seen Tony too.

The parking lot's security lights, along with the red and blue flashes and a spotlight set up by the police, made the scene all too clear.

Regret flickered across Sawyer's face as he put an arm around each of us and moved us farther away from the props trailer.

"Let's get a screen set up," he called over his shoulder to his fellow officers.

I didn't want to see Tony like that again, but for some reason I glanced over my shoulder as Sawyer ushered us away. Fortunately, Officer Ollie Nyberg stood between Tony and me now, using a pair of tweezers to grab a scrap of black-and-white silk fabric that had snagged on the corner of the trailer. Officer Nyberg placed the fabric in a plastic evidence bag and I faced forward again.

The other curious townsfolk I'd passed on my jog over to the parking lot came toward us. Sawyer asked them to stay back and ignored their questions when they wanted to know what was going on.

"I'm sorry you saw that," he said to Dizzy and me after he'd quieted the others down.

"Is he dead?" Dizzy asked, a single tear running down her cheek.

"I'm afraid so," Sawyer said.

I hooked my arm through Dizzy's.

"Was he working on the film?" Sawyer asked me. "Did you know him?"

I nodded, fighting off the wave of nausea that had crashed over me at the sight of Tony's body.

After swallowing hard, I found my voice. "Tony Fleet. He's the props master. Was," I corrected myself. "Who found him? Does Phil know? What about Jasmine?"

"Nyberg found him," Sawyer said. "Who are Phil and Jasmine?"

"The producer and director."

Sawyer shook his head. "We haven't notified anyone yet. Do you know if Tony had any family?"

It was my turn to shake my head. "I didn't really know him. This is the first time I've worked on a production with him and we never talked. I know he was once married to the star, Felicia Blessing, but they divorced several years ago."

"And Felicia, the producer, and the director are all staying at the Larch Haven Hotel?" Sawyer checked.

I nodded.

"When did you last see Tony?" he asked.

"Shortly after seven this evening," I replied. "I went to meet Cooper at the hotel. Tony was coming down the main staircase when I arrived."

"Okay, thank you, Becca," Sawyer said. "You two head on home."

"Could he have died in some sort of accident?" Dizzy asked me, flashing blue and red lights reflecting off her dark hair as we walked slowly away from the scene.

"An accident would be better than the alternative," I said, "but I didn't see anything around that could have caused him to bleed like that."

The door to the props trailer was standing open—I'd noticed that much—and Tony had been sprawled at the foot of the fold-down steps that led up to the door. I'd seen Tony's body for only a handful of seconds, but I hadn't observed any potential dangers in the area. The open door had blocked my view of the trailer's entrance, but I couldn't think of any accident that could have struck Tony down like that.

"Do you think the movie will be shut down?" Dizzy asked. "Maybe it's terrible that I'm even thinking about that."

"I don't know," I said. "Tony had an assistant working with him. I guess it depends on whether or not she can take over his role."

I walked with Dizzy to her apartment, located over Hooked on Books, the local bookstore. I gave her a hug before she headed up the exterior stairs to her door.

"I don't know if I'll be able to sleep tonight," she admitted as she hugged me back.

"Same." If I did manage to sleep, I feared I'd be plagued with nightmares.

"Text me so I know you're safe at home?" she requested.

"For sure," I promised.

On my walk home, I couldn't help but feel on edge. I usually enjoyed the symphony of croaking frogs and chirping crickets after nightfall, but nature's music provided cover for potentially more frightening noises to hide behind, and I found myself glancing around and listening for footsteps. The darkness held an ominous weight that, while a product of my imagination, nevertheless sent a chill over my skin.

I walked briskly, with my phone clutched in my hand. Once I left Amsterdam Avenue for my residential neighborhood, I didn't see another soul. After crossing the final bridge on my route, the night seemed to close in around me and I jogged the rest of the way to my front door. As soon as I got inside, I locked up behind me.

Finally breathing more easily, I kicked off my shoes and sent a quick text to Dizzy so she'd know I was home. A few minutes later, with my cats winding around my legs as we headed upstairs to bed, most of my nerves had eased.

But I still couldn't rid my mind of the memory of Tony lying dead on the ground.

· · · ● ● · ● ● · · ·

ALL MEMBERS OF THE cast and crew for *Love on the Canal* were summoned to an emergency meeting at a conference room at the Larch Haven Hotel early the next morning. When I arrived, I found most people already there, standing in groups and whispering about Tony. Clearly, the news of his death had already spread.

A continental breakfast had been set out on a long table at one end of the room, with coffee and tea available to drink. Even though I'd skipped breakfast to get to the meeting on time, I couldn't bring myself to eat anything at the moment. Instead, I fixed myself a cup of tea with cream and sugar and then edged my way around groups of people to reach Cooper at the other side of the room. He sat slumped in a swivel chair, his face pale and his hair messy, like he hadn't tidied it after rolling out of bed. He stared across the room, but I suspected he wasn't seeing much of anything.

Geneva stood beside him like a sentinel, arms crossed over her chest as she viewed the room through her thick-framed glasses.

When I nudged Cooper's arm to get his attention, his blue eyes snapped out of their stare to look at me.

"You doing okay, Coop?" I asked, worried.

He scrubbed a hand down his face. "I'm all right. I just can't believe someone killed Tony."

"The police haven't officially stated that he was murdered," Geneva said.

"I heard he got shot." Cooper sounded confused. "Is that what happened, Becca?"

"I have no idea," I replied. A gunshot definitely could have caused all the blood I'd seen, but I didn't mention that. "Hopefully someone will tell us in a minute."

"Maybe a prop gun misfired when he was handling it," Geneva speculated.

Cooper frowned. "Why would he have a prop gun? There aren't any guns in this film."

Geneva was about to say something more, but she didn't get the chance.

At the front of the room, Jasmine Singh clapped her hands to get everyone's attention.

"Thanks for getting here so early, everyone," the film's director said to the room at large. "As I'm sure you've all heard by now, Tony died last night. The police haven't officially released any details about his death yet, but I'm told that early indications point toward foul play."

That information sent a ripple of shocked murmurs through the room.

Jasmine waited for everyone to quiet down before continuing. "I ask that you refrain from posting anything about Tony's death online for the time being, as the police are still in the process of contacting his relatives. We're going to have a grief counselor brought in and we expect her to arrive here in Larch Haven tomorrow morning. She'll be available to any members of the cast or crew who need someone to talk to about this terrible tragedy."

I glanced around the room, checking to see if anyone appeared particularly distressed about Tony's death. Most people looked upset to some degree, but no one seemed bereft. Not outwardly, anyway.

"As for the production," Jasmine continued, "the show must go on, as they say. Thankfully, Tony's assistant, Maggie, is more than capable of stepping in to take over Tony's duties."

Maggie, a tall and slender woman with shoulder length blonde hair and fair, freckled skin, gave a faint smile and a brief wave.

The people standing next to her gave her pats on the back.

"Now," Jasmine said, "before we get started for the day, the local police would like to speak to each one of us in turn."

Several people sent curious glances toward the room's open door. I followed their gazes to see Detective Naomi Ishimoto standing in the doorway, wearing a gray pantsuit with a burgundy blouse, her expression professionally neutral. Officer Fiona Mc-Nally stood on one side of the detective, and Sawyer on the other, both of them dressed in their uniforms.

A few feet in front of me, Sonja hurriedly tucked her phone into the back pocket of her jeans. Then she proceeded to gnaw on her thumb nail.

I winced at the sight and then met Sawyer's gaze from across the room. He gave me the barest hint of a nod before I returned my attention to Jasmine.

"Please remain in this room until you've spoken with Detective Ishimoto or one of her colleagues. Once you've all been questioned, we'll get back to work. Thank you, everyone."

Detective Ishimoto took over then, asking to speak with Felicia Blessing first. Felicia rose from her chair to follow the detective. As she passed me, I saw apprehension in her brown eyes, but no grief. Of course, not everyone showed their grief in an outward fashion, but I wondered, given her history with Tony, if his death saddened her or came as a relief.

After Detective Ishimoto left the conference room with Felicia, Sawyer and Officer McNally each left with a member of the crew. The rest of us stayed behind to wait for our turns.

I hoped I'd get to speak with Sawyer, but it was Officer McNally who pulled me away half an hour later. She took me to a small office, where she proceeded to ask me all I knew about Tony. I didn't have much to tell. As I'd done with Sawyer the night before,

I explained that I'd heard about Felicia's past marriage to Tony, but I didn't know what else to say until she asked more questions.

"Who all did he have contact with here in Larch Haven?" McNally asked.

"The cast and crew, of course." I thought carefully, trying to remember if I'd seen him with anyone else. "I saw him speaking with Chanel Yearwood yesterday morning. Chanel's working as a background performer."

"Do you have any idea what they were talking about?" Officer McNally asked.

"No. I didn't hear a word of their conversation."

I didn't know if I should add my speculations. Chanel was married, after all, and I didn't want to cause any trouble for her if I'd misinterpreted what I'd seen.

"Is there something more?" McNally asked, noticing that I was weighing something in my mind.

"It looked like Chanel and Tony were flirting, but I don't know for sure if that's what was happening," I said, deciding that I should be completely open with the officer.

McNally made no comment on that. She jotted something down in her notebook and asked me if I had anything further to share.

I didn't, so she told me I could go.

Instead of leaving the hotel, I returned to the conference room. A couple of crew members were still waiting for their turn to talk to the police, but I wasn't the only one who'd returned after being questioned. It seemed gossip was high on everyone's list of priorities.

Now that more time had passed, my appetite was slowly making an appearance. I selected a croissant from the table and nibbled on it as I wandered through the room.

I was wondering who to talk to when I spotted Cooper returning to the room. Geneva immediately latched onto him and followed him to the food table, talking quietly the whole way. While Geneva spoke in his ear, Cooper surveyed the breads and pastries. In the end, he bypassed all the food and got himself a cup of coffee.

I wandered over to join him and Geneva.

"I take it you've talked with the police," I said to Cooper.

"The detective," he confirmed, worry clouding his blue eyes.

"What did she ask you?" Geneva's question sounded like a demand.

Cooper shrugged. "How well I knew Tony. That sort of stuff." He stared down into his coffee cup for a second before adding, "She wanted to know about yesterday's incident."

"When you pushed Tony into the canal?" I asked before finishing off the last bite of my croissant.

He nodded. "She wanted to know what that was all about."

Geneva let out a noise of disdain. "Surely the cops don't think you killed Tony because of the photos and videos."

"I'm pretty sure it's crossed their minds," Cooper said, his knuckles turning white as he clutched his mug of coffee.

"Ridiculous!" Geneva fumed. "Don't talk to the police again without a lawyer present."

"What lawyer?" Cooper asked. "All my lawyers are in LA."

Geneva whipped out her phone and started scrolling through her contacts. "Then I'll get one to come to Vermont."

She tapped a contact and walked off to a corner of the room so she could speak on the phone privately.

Cooper shook his head as he watched her go. "I'm looking forward to Wes coming back. Geneva means well, but she goes a little overboard at times."

"Are you in any trouble, Cooper?" I asked. "If Tony really was murdered...." I let the sentence hang, not sure how to finish it.

He sighed. "It doesn't help that I don't have an alibi."

"You were with me for part of the evening."

"But then I left," he said. "On my own. Becca, I didn't kill Tony."

"Of course you didn't!" I'd never even entertained that as a possibility.

"But there's no one who can vouch for me after I left the bar." His shoulders sagged. "Maybe Geneva's right. Maybe I do need a lawyer." He drank down the last of his coffee in one big gulp.

"I doubt it'll come to that," I said, hoping I was right. "But having a lawyer here to advise you probably isn't a bad thing."

Cooper stared across the conference room, his gaze unseeing, just like it had been earlier that morning.

"Really, Cooper," I said in a whisper, "how are you holding up?"

He refocused on me. "You mean with my anxiety?"

I nodded.

"I'm coping, but being under police scrutiny doesn't help." He almost tried to drink more coffee, but remembered at the last second that his mug was empty. He set it on the corner of the conference table.

"You're not the only person they're interested in," I said, certain that must be the truth. "I'm sure they're asking Felicia lots of questions. She was married to the guy, after all."

"And didn't like that she was paying him alimony," Cooper added. "But Felicia's not a killer."

I hoped he was right about that.

Chapter Seven

SAWYER RETURNED TO THE conference room while Geneva was still on the phone, trying to arrange for a lawyer to come to Vermont to help Cooper. When Sawyer looked my way, I gave Cooper a quick hug.

"Hang in there," I told him. "I'll see you later. You can text me anytime, day or night."

Cooper hugged me back. "Thanks, Becca."

I wound my way around the other cast and crew members to reach Sawyer.

"You spoke with McNally?" he asked when I stopped before him.

I nodded. "I'm on my way out now."

Sawyer's gaze shifted to Cooper, then back to me. "I guess it's nice to be reunited with Graystone."

"It is," I agreed, "though the circumstances aren't exactly ideal anymore." I lowered my voice. "Jasmine said it was probably foul play. Is that true?"

"Unfortunately," Sawyer confirmed. "I can tell you that because Detective Ishimoto's releasing an official statement to that effect in about half an hour."

"Was he shot?" I asked, remembering what Cooper had said earlier.

Sawyer's forehead furrowed. "No. All I can say is that it was an incident involving a knife."

That struck me as an odd way to phrase it. "You mean he was stabbed?"

"I can't go into details, Becca."

I let that drop for now. "Tony didn't seem like the nicest guy, but why would anyone kill him?"

"That's what we're going to find out," Sawyer said. "And by 'we' I mean...."

"You and your fellow officers," I finished, having heard the same caution before. "Not me."

One corner of his mouth turned upward. "You're catching on."

It took effort not to roll my eyes, but even with that reaction to what he'd said, I was hit with a kick of emotion in my stomach. I missed spending time with Sawyer. I hadn't seen him nearly enough lately.

"I wrap early today," I said. "Will you be working late or can you come over to my place for a while?"

"I'm not sure about the working late part yet. Can I let you know this evening?"

"Sure." I rested a hand on his arm as I passed him. "Talk to you later."

Outside the conference room, I followed the hallway toward the front of the hotel. On my way, I passed a couple of staff offices, including the one where McNally had spoken to me earlier. The door to that office stood open a crack, and I paused just after I passed it.

Sonja's voice drifted out into the hallway. "I was having drinks with some of my colleagues at the hotel bar."

I recognized Officer McNally's voice next. "What time was that?"

"Around eight," Sonja replied.

"And how long did you stay at the bar?"

"Maybe thirty or forty minutes."

That fit with what I remembered.

"Then where did you go?" McNally asked.

"Up to my room, and that's where I was until I woke up this morning."

"Can anyone confirm that?"

"No," Sonja said with a huff. "I was asleep. Alone."

McNally continued the conversation with another question. "So you didn't see Mr. Fleet at all that evening?"

"Not after we wrapped for the day, just before seven o'clock."

"All right," the officer said. "Thank you, Ms. Jepsen."

I jolted myself out of my eavesdropping and hurried to get farther down the hallway before McNally or Sonja emerged from the office. Sawyer wouldn't be impressed if he found out that I'd been caught listening in on a police interview.

I didn't find it surprising that McNally had questioned Sonja about her movements around the time of Tony's death. She'd asked me the same questions, and I figured all the cast and crew members were getting asked to provide those details. After all, Tony wasn't from Larch Haven and, as far as I knew, he didn't have any previous connection to the town. So, if someone killed him, it made sense to look for the culprit among those connected to the movie production.

That thought sent a shiver up my spine.

As I crossed the lobby, I spotted Jasmine standing next to a potted plant by the seating area. She was busy on her phone, but she looked up when I approached her.

"Becca," she said warmly, "how are you doing with everything that's been happening?"

"I'm all right," I assured her. "It's terrible, but I didn't know Tony well. How about you?"

She pressed her lips together. "It's been a terrible shock and a bit of a nightmare to deal with, but I'm okay. I've known Tony for a few years, but we were never close. He wasn't really the type of person to get close to."

"He certainly didn't seem like the most charming guy," I said.

Jasmine gave a murmur of agreement. "He was good at his job, but he could be difficult. Clearly, someone really had it out for him."

"You don't think his murder could have been a spur of the moment crime?" I asked.

"It doesn't sound like it," she replied. "The police asked me who among the cast and crew might have the ability to set up a booby trap. I said Tony, and maybe Maggie or the stunt coordinator. Other than that, who knows?"

"A booby trap?" I echoed with surprise.

Jasmine lowered her voice, perhaps somewhat belatedly. "The police wouldn't give me many details, but it sounds like the trap was rigged so that a knife came swinging down when the door to the props trailer was opened."

I winced at the mental picture that brought to mind. "That's horrible."

"And premeditated."

"But Tony was the intended victim?" I checked.

Jasmine thought about that for a second. "It had to be him or Maggie, but Tony was in and out of the props trailer the most. Besides, who would want to kill Maggie?"

That was a question I couldn't answer. I knew Maggie even less than I knew Tony.

Jasmine had to get going, so she hurried out of the hotel ahead of me. Cooper and Geneva came down the hall from the conference room just as I was about to follow in the director's footsteps. I waited for them and together we headed over to the trailers at the edge of town. The police had taped off the props trailer, but we were able to access all the others.

As we approached the hair and makeup trailer, Maggie was jogging in the opposite direction, looking stressed.

"Are you doing okay, Maggie?" Cooper asked.

She stopped, short of breath. "Just scrambling to make sure we have all the props we need for the day. The police won't let me into the trailer until later today, so we might have to do some schedule juggling. I'm on my way to talk to Jasmine."

With a wave, she jogged off.

The schedule did indeed get shifted around for the day, although it didn't affect me too much. I didn't even have my hair done when I found out that my one scene of the day had been moved from the middle of the morning to early afternoon.

Since I had some time on my hands, I walked over to the library to check on Dizzy. When I entered the building, the place was quiet, even for a library. An elderly man sat reading a newspaper and a woman browsed the romance section, but I couldn't spot any other patrons from where I stood near the front door. One of Dizzy's colleagues sat behind the circulation desk, working at a computer, but I didn't see my best friend.

I made my way quietly past the shelves until I found Dizzy in the biographies section, reshelving books from a cart.

I gave her a hug and asked how she was doing.

"It took me ages to fall asleep last night," she said, "but I'm okay. What about you?"

"The same, really." I'd tossed and turned for a couple of hours before finally drifting off to sleep the night before.

As Dizzy continued to shelve books, I filled her in on everything I'd heard that morning, keeping my voice to a whisper.

"A booby trap," she said when I got to that part. "I wasn't expecting that."

"Neither was I."

Dizzy pushed the cart farther down the aisle. "Ew. Really?" She peered at the underside of one of the upper shelves.

Someone had stuck their chewed wad of gum there.

"Gross," I said, making a face.

"I've seen worse in this job, believe me," she said with a sigh. "Still, I can't say I enjoy this part." She shook her head and placed one of the books from the cart on the shelf above the gum. "I'll come back for it when I'm done with these books."

"A booby trap means it was premeditated," I said, getting back to our conversation. "And alibis could be trickier."

Dizzy nodded. "Since we don't know when the trap was set. It could have been rigged long before Tony was killed."

"But not too long," I said. "He and Maggie would have been in and out of the trailer while filming was still going on."

"Good point. That must narrow it down." Dizzy turned her cart down the next aisle and I followed along with her. "Did you hear about Tony and Heller Yearwood?" she asked.

"No," I said, my curiosity piqued. "Is that Chanel's husband?"

"That's him. Apparently, Heller heard a rumor that Tony was flirting with Chanel while she was working as an extra on the film."

"I saw them together," I said. "It looked like the flirting was going both ways."

"Well, Heller was up at the pub in Snowflake Canyon yesterday afternoon," Dizzy continued. Snowflake Canyon was a ski resort town up the mountain from Larch Haven. "He had a bit too much to drink, which I gather is normal for him. He was overheard ranting and raging about Tony going after his wife."

"So there was some jealousy there," I commented.

"That might be an understatement," Dizzy said as she slipped a book onto the shelf. "At one point, Heller said he was going to tear Tony to pieces."

Chapter Eight

"I'M WORRIED ABOUT COOPER," I confessed to Dizzy after we'd finished talking about Heller Yearwood and his drunken threats. I'd already told her about Cooper being questioned about his fight with Tony.

Dizzy shelved another two books. "Is he really a suspect?"

"I hope not, but I'll ask Sawyer later." I sighed. "Not that he'll tell me anything."

"You're seeing Sawyer later?" Dizzy asked with a mischievous smile as she pushed her cart farther along the aisle.

"Don't start with that," I warned as I followed her. "Just as friends. Like always. Unless he has to work. Then I won't see him at all."

She shook her head as she slid more books into place on the shelves. "One of you needs to make a move."

"The mere thought terrifies me," I confessed as anxiety swirled unpleasantly in my stomach.

Dizzy stopped her work and faced me. "Which is scarier: taking a chance and seeing where things go, or dancing around your feelings forever?"

The anxious swirling in my stomach grew more vigorous. "They're both equally frightening." I closed my eyes for a moment, trying to settle my nerves. "What should I do, Diz?"

"I think your heart knows the answer to that question," she said.

I wasn't sure that any part of me knew the answer, but I hoped Dizzy was right.

Nevertheless, I did what I'd been doing ever since Sawyer had kissed me under the mistletoe at Christmas: I pushed all thoughts of changing our relationship to the back of my mind and pretended that everything was as it always had been between us.

I left Dizzy to attend to the chewing gum on the bookshelf and spent a couple of hours in the kitchen at True Confections, helping Lolly make London fog truffles—featuring white chocolate ganache infused with Earl Grey tea. We also made more chocolate gondolas and filled boxes with the salted caramels Lolly had made earlier that morning.

Later, on my way to report to the hair and makeup trailer, I spotted Chanel Yearwood's husband, Heller, ahead of me. He was a stocky man with thick brown hair, bushy eyebrows, and a scar that cut across the weathered, lightly tanned skin of his cheek.

When he turned into the local travel agency, I followed him to the door of the business, without really knowing why. Okay, maybe I did know why. If he was angry at Tony for flirting with his wife, he had a motive for killing the props master. Maybe I should have kept on walking to the hair and makeup trailer, but instead I entered the travel agency before I had time to question the wisdom of that decision.

I stationed myself in front of a rack of brochures near the door. As I flipped through the shiny pamphlets, feigning interest in them, I listened in on Heller's conversation with travel agent Claire Walters.

"I need to book a trip," he told Claire after she greeted him and offered him a seat in front of her desk. "Preferably somewhere warm."

"When were you hoping to get away?" she asked.

"As soon as possible."

The hint of urgency in his voice made me wonder why he was so eager to get out of town. Maybe he was concerned about getting caught by the police.

I sized him up out of the corner of my eye as Claire started going over potential travel destinations with him. There was something pugnacious about his look and demeanor, and I had no trouble picturing him punching someone in a moment of anger. But would he go to the effort of setting up a booby trap to kill a man who'd flirted with his wife?

Of course, I didn't know that Chanel and Tony had stopped at flirting. Maybe Heller knew more about what had transpired between the two than I did.

The other agent who worked at the office emerged from the back room and smiled at me.

"Hello. Can I help you with anything?" she asked me.

I grabbed two random pamphlets off the rack and held them up with a smile. "No, thanks. I've got what I need."

With a cheery wave, I made a quick exit and continued on in the direction of the trailers. As I walked, I took my first good look at the brochures I'd grabbed. Both were for overseas guided tours for seniors. I folded them up and stuffed them in my pocket.

Once seated in the stylist's chair, I watched Alex in the mirror and noticed that he had dark rings under his eyes that weren't there yesterday. His blue-and-purple hair was tied up in a topknot rather than styled in a pompadour like the day before. He was also quieter and more subdued than he had been the last time I sat in his chair.

"Are you doing okay, Alex?" I asked as he started styling my hair into waves. "Did you know Tony well?"

The two men must have known each other to some degree, I figured, considering the hushed argument I'd witnessed between them. Still, even if what I'd seen suggested that there was some bad blood between them, maybe that didn't tell the whole story about their relationship.

Alex came to life at my question. "Did I know him well? Thank heavens, no." He shook his head. "My grandma would be horrified to hear me speak like that of the dead, but the truth is, I wasn't a Tony fan."

"So you knew him well enough not to like him," I surmised.

Alex paused in his work. "I guess you could say that. Our paths crossed professionally now and then, but we weren't pals."

I wanted to ask him about the argument I'd witnessed, but I didn't want him to know that I was aware of it. I liked Alex, but I'd just met him and didn't know him well. Someone had murdered Tony, and quite possibly someone from the cast or crew, so I needed to be careful what I said.

"A lot of people seem to have complaints about Tony," I said. "Did you have any specific ones?"

"Nope." Alex's jaw tensed. "I heard he wasn't the nicest guy, so I steered clear of him as much as possible."

"Except you weren't too successful at that," Michaela, the makeup artist, said as she organized her supplies.

Diego had left her chair as I arrived and had since exited the trailer, leaving me alone with Alex and Michaela.

"Didn't you have an argument with Tony the other day?" Michaela asked Alex.

I yelped and jumped half out of the chair when the hot curling iron brushed against my ear.

"I'm so sorry!" Alex cried, horrified. "Oh, Becca, I can't believe I did that to you!"

"It's okay. It's okay." I sank back down into the chair, putting one hand to my ear. It still hurt, but not nearly as badly as during the moment of contact with the curling iron. "What's the damage?"

Alex carefully lifted my hair away from my ear to inspect it. "It's a little red," he said, chagrined.

Michaela moved next to him to take a look. "I've seen far worse. It might not feel great, but there's no real damage done. It just looks like a bit of sunburn."

I relaxed into the chair. "That's a relief."

Alex looked close to tears as he rested a hand on my shoulder. "I'm so sorry, Becca."

I met his eyes in the mirror and patted his hand. "It's all right, Alex. I'm fine."

He got back to work, more carefully this time. I couldn't relax completely, at least not until he'd finished with the curling iron, but I tried not to let my apprehension show. I didn't want Alex feeling any worse about the incident than he already did.

I wanted to bring up his argument with Tony again, but Alex looked so worried that I didn't have the heart to steer the conversation back to that topic. Not at the moment, anyway. Hopefully I'd have a chance to do so another time.

When Alex finished up with my hair, I moved over to Michaela's chair. She'd just started in on my makeup when the trailer door flew open and Felicia rushed in, out of breath.

"I'm so sorry, but I need my makeup fixed," she apologized. "I'm due back on set in ten minutes."

I moved back over to Alex's chair to make room for Felicia in front of Michaela.

"No worries," the makeup artist told Felicia. "I've got you covered."

As Felicia sank down into the chair, I noticed that her eye makeup was smudged and she had tear tracks running down her cheeks.

"What's the matter, Felicia?" I could have slapped myself for asking that question. "I'm sorry. You must be upset about Tony."

Felicia sniffled as Michaela got to work, obliterating the tear tracks on her cheeks. "It's upsetting that somebody I once loved was murdered," she agreed. "But you might think I'm a terrible person, because it's my second conversation with the police that made me cry."

"They talked to you again already?" Alex asked with surprise.

"That detective came to talk to me on set with another officer," Felicia said. "She wanted to ask me more questions. It felt more like an interrogation than an interview. I never would have wished Tony dead, but our divorce definitely wasn't amicable. He was a real thorn in my side when he was alive and even still now that he's dead." She winced before smoothing out her expression so Michaela could keep working. "That must make me sound awful, but Tony really was difficult."

"Girl, you don't need to explain," Alex said. "We know what Tony was like. It's awful that someone murdered him, but I'm glad you don't have to deal with him any longer."

Felicia sniffled again. "Thanks, Alex."

"Why did the questions upset you?" I asked, wondering what, exactly, had driven her to tears.

Felicia tipped her chin up as Michaela worked at repairing her eye makeup. "I think I'm a suspect. *Me*! Can you believe that?"

Alex shook his head. "That's nuts."

"At first, the detective asked routine questions. Like, did I know of anyone who might have wanted to hurt Tony. I told her I didn't. Tony wasn't exactly known for making friends everywhere he went, but I can't think of anyone who would actually want to kill him.

She paused for a moment, but I stayed quiet, hoping she would continue. She soon did.

"I asked the police if it could have been a robbery gone wrong. Instead of answering, they asked me if he had any valuables with him that a robber might have taken. I mentioned Tony's watch—he paid thousands for that stupid thing—and those gold chains." She rolled her eyes. "He always liked showing off."

"What did the police have to say about that?" I asked.

"They were surprised when I said Tony always wore the watch and chains. Apparently, he wasn't wearing any of them when he was found."

I thought back to the moment when I'd seen Tony lying on the ground. I hadn't noticed that the jewelry was missing, but I hadn't seen his body for long, and the blood had distracted me.

I swallowed hard, trying to banish the vivid picture in my head.

"And then they turned everything around on me and interrogated me some more," Felicia continued, her voice rising in pitch. "Like they thought I'd killed Tony, stolen those things from him, and then brought up the possibility of a robbery gone wrong to make myself seem innocent."

Alex and Michaela both scoffed at that.

"Why would you need to steal from Tony?" Alex asked. "That's ridiculous. You make way more money than he ever did."

"Exactly." Felicia calmed down when she realized she had someone on her side.

With her makeup now fixed, Felicia jumped up from the chair and called out her thanks before dashing out of the trailer.

I followed a couple of minutes behind her, after Michaela put the final touches on my makeup. As I rode in a golf cart to the day's filming location, my thoughts whirred in my head.

Sure, Felicia made more money than Tony did—probably way more—but I wondered if the police knew that Felicia had been paying Tony alimony ever since their divorce. If they didn't know that by now, they would soon. The disparity in their incomes didn't get Felicia off my suspect list and likely not off Detective Ishimoto's list either. After all, Felicia could have killed Tony to get him out of her life permanently, so she no longer had to pay him or deal with him in any way. She might have taken the watch and jewelry to make the crime look like a robbery gone wrong, or out of spite, since—if the rumors were true—Tony paid for them with the money she'd been required to give him.

As the golf cart came to a stop and I climbed out, thanking the driver, I felt a rush of sympathy for Felicia. If she was innocent—which I hoped she was—life would likely be difficult for her until her name was cleared. If the media found out that she was a suspect in her ex-husband's death, that could turn into a public relations nightmare. She had people to help her with those things, but that didn't mean it wouldn't be stressful for her.

Even though I felt bad for Felicia, I was relieved that Cooper wasn't the only suspect under scrutiny by the police. Hopefully, whoever had really killed Tony would get caught sooner rather than later.

In the meantime, I silently vowed to do all I could to help Cooper.

Chapter Nine

THAT AFTERNOON, I FILMED a scene with Felicia and Diego in the flower shop. Felicia's character, Journey, owned the flower shop and my character, Addison, was her employee and best friend. Journey had given up on finding true love for herself, but was determined to get Addison and Jorge—Diego's character—to finally act on the feelings that had been brewing between them since well before the story started. Of course, along the way, Journey would fall head over heels for Cooper's character, Connor. After a big misunderstanding, which would leave Journey and Connor temporarily heartbroken, everything would get resolved and both couples would live happily ever after.

In the current scene, Addison and Journey were talking about Connor, the new man in town, when Jorge came into the store to buy a bouquet of flowers for his mother's birthday. In a not-so-subtle way, Journey pretended to be busy, forcing Addison to serve Jorge. Some awkward but sweet interaction followed before Jorge went on his way.

Once we'd finished filming that scene, I was done for the day. I stopped by True Confections to find Angela with my sixteen-year-old cousin, Milo, who worked in the store for a few hours each week.

Three customers were browsing the shelves when I arrived, but it wasn't long before they headed out the door with bags filled with chocolates.

As soon as the shop was empty of customers, Angie came rushing out from behind the counter, practically bursting with excitement. She gave me a hug that nearly crushed my ribs.

"Easy!" I protested. "I need oxygen to live!"

Angie released me with a sheepish smile. "Sorry! I guess I'm a little excited."

"Yep. Just a little," Milo said wryly, though there was a twinkle in his eyes.

"What's going on?" I asked.

Angie's smile brightened so much it could have lit up the entire planet. "You're not the only one who's going to be in *Love on the Canal*!"

"You got the call?" I asked with building excitement.

Angie had signed up to work as a background performer, but had been waiting to hear if she'd get chosen or not.

"Yes!" She did a little happy dance. "They want me for at least two days, starting the day after tomorrow. And...." She turned and gestured at Milo like she was a game show host.

Milo grinned. "Me too."

I grabbed Milo by the arm and tugged him out from behind the counter so we could have a group hug.

"I'm so excited you both get to be part of this," I said, ruffling Milo's brown hair.

"Hey!" He darted out of my reach and tried to fix the damage I'd done to his hairstyle.

He had it short on the sides and long in the front and kept it swooped back. He was wearing his usual outfit of jeans with a button up shirt and a waistcoat. That had been his go-to ensemble for a while now. I thought Milo looked like he belonged in a boy band, and he actually had started a band with some friends over the winter. Milo was the most talented member of the group, in my opinion, but I could have been biased.

"My mom is going to come in and look after the store on those days," Milo said.

His mom, my aunt Kathleen, often helped out at True Confections whenever we were in need of an extra set of hands.

"And Lolly will continue to look after the kitchen side of things, with help from my mom," Angie assured me.

Her mom, my aunt Elizabeth, was the oldest of my dad's siblings.

Some of Angela's happiness faded away. "We heard about the death. Was it someone you knew well?"

"Hardly at all. It's still sad and unsettling, though."

My cousins likely would have asked more questions about Tony's death, but a rush of customers came in through the door, putting an end to our conversation. I tried to head for the kitchen, but Angie insisted that I go home. Everything was taken care of, she assured me, so I didn't argue. After my less-than-stellar sleep the night before, I was ready to return home.

After cuddling with Binx and Truffles and washing the makeup off my face, I spent some time lounging on my patio, reading a book. Birds twittered in the trees and every now and then a gondola glided by. Eventually, when my stomach rumbled, I set the book aside and made vegetarian quesadillas for dinner.

I checked my phone repeatedly, hoping for word from Sawyer. I still didn't know if he'd be working late or if he'd have a chance to stop by for a visit. Finally, when the quesadillas were almost ready, I received a text message from him, letting me know that he was on his way over.

I smiled, glad that we'd get to spend the evening together. At the same time, nervousness skittered along my skin.

"Stop it," I ordered myself out loud. "Everything will be fine."

I didn't want to let my worries about my feelings for Sawyer get in the way of enjoying my time with him.

A few minutes later, he knocked on the front door and I hurried to open it, happy anticipation replacing my nervousness. I hadn't spent nearly as much time with Sawyer as I would have liked over the past few months. His mom had come to Larch Haven in January and she'd stayed for several weeks. Although I got together with her and Sawyer a couple of times, I didn't spend more than a few minutes alone with him that month.

When February arrived, the Valentine's Day rush hit True Confections and I had to work long hours to keep up with the demand for chocolates. Just when things were settling down again, Sawyer's great aunt passed away in Mexico City, his mother's birthplace and current home. Sawyer had traveled to Mexico to attend the funeral and be with his relatives. By the time he returned to Vermont, I was deep into preparations for the Easter rush. Then I'd flown to Los Angeles for the table read of the script for *Love on the Canal*. What little time we'd spent together over the past couple of months had been only in passing, and that wasn't enough for me.

I smiled when I saw Sawyer standing outside my door in jeans and a black hoodie. He held a bakery box with a familiar logo.

"Love at First Bite?" I stepped back to let Sawyer into the cottage. "Didn't it close hours ago?"

Love at First Bite was a cake shop owned by my friend Stephanie Kang. Stephanie made the most delicious cakes and cupcakes, and the mere sight of the box and logo made my mouth water.

"I stopped by on my lunch break," Sawyer said as I shut the door behind him.

"And there's still something left in the box?"

"I exercised great restraint," he said. "And I stored them at home. Every last crumb would have disappeared if I'd left them unattended at the station."

"Cops would steal cake?" I asked, pretending to be shocked.

"Cake, doughnuts, and cookies are never safe."

He handed me the box, but I set it aside on the hall table so I could give him a hug.

"It's really good to see you," I said as I wrapped my arms around him and leaned against his chest.

Maybe I held on a little longer than necessary, but so did he.

"You just saw me this morning," he pointed out, speaking into my hair before I reluctantly stepped back.

I picked up the bakery box so I wouldn't be tempted to hug him again. "That's not the same."

He held my gaze, his dark eyes intense. "No, it's not."

The longer we stared into each other's eyes, the harder I found it to breathe, so I forced myself to look away. I turned down the hall and led Sawyer to the kitchen at the back of the cottage. Truffles and Binx woke up from napping on the couch and jumped down to greet Sawyer.

I set the bakery box on the counter and grabbed two plates. "Do you want quesadillas first or do you want to go straight for the cake?"

"Quesadillas," he said. "They smell amazing."

"Hopefully they taste good too." I slid the quesadillas out of the frying pan and onto two plates. When I turned around, Sawyer had a cat in each arm.

"Sorry, guys," he said to Binx and Truffles as they purred. "Those quesadillas are calling to me."

He set the cats down and washed his hands at the kitchen sink. Truffles and Binx, having already eaten, padded off toward the foyer, probably to sit in one of the front windows. They loved to watch the world outside.

As we ate our dinner, I got Sawyer to catch me up on his family and everything he'd been up to since he returned from Mexico. He, in turn, wanted to know all about my life.

"How are things going with the movie, aside from the unfortunate incident from last night?" he asked once we had slices of chocolate mousse cake in front of us.

"It's been great," I said with a smile. "Having a chance to act while here at home in Larch Haven is almost too good to be true."

"Best of both worlds?"

"Exactly." My smile faded. "Of course, it's hard to think about the movie now without thinking about what happened to Tony."

Sawyer's face had grown more serious too. "I'm sorry you saw him the way you did."

"And I'm sorry you've got another murder to investigate."

We fell quiet as we enjoyed our cake slices.

"You're not going to pepper me with questions about the case?" Sawyer asked once we'd finished our dessert.

"Would I do that?" I asked with mock innocence.

Sawyer rolled his eyes. "I'm surprised you didn't start as soon as I stepped in the door."

I gathered up our plates and carried them to the sink. "All I want to know is whether Cooper is really a suspect."

He joined me by the sink. "Most of the cast and crew who don't have alibis are suspects at this point." He took each plate as I rinsed it and placed it in the dishwasher.

"Including me?" That was an unsettling thought.

"You're covered," Sawyer said, to my immense relief, "thanks to Dizzy and everyone who saw you at the hotel bar that night."

That relief was short-lived. "But how is that possible? I get that you can narrow down the time of death, but what about the time the booby trap was set?"

Sawyer's gaze snapped to mine. "How do you know about the booby trap?"

"Jasmine Singh, the director. She told me the police asked her questions about who might have the skills to set it up."

Sawyer didn't look impressed. "She wasn't supposed to share that information."

"I don't know who else she's told, but nobody will hear it from me. Well, except Dizzy," I amended. "I already told her."

Sawyer raised his eyes toward the ceiling. "Of course you did."

I tried to steer the conversation back on course as something occurred to me. "What about security cameras? Didn't the ones at the parking lot catch anything incriminating?"

"The camera near the props trailer was damaged the night before the murder."

I digested that disappointing news. "The killer was planning ahead."

Sawyer nodded his agreement.

"How far up the suspect list is Cooper's name?" I asked.

"I can't tell you that," he said as he closed the dishwasher.

I turned my back to the counter and leaned against it. "He didn't do it. Cooper wouldn't hurt anyone."

"He shoved Tony into the canal," Sawyer reminded me.

"Okay, sure," I conceded, "but he'd never do anything worse."

Sawyer didn't appear convinced. "For your sake, I hope you're right about that."

"I am," I said with conviction. "I want you to meet him while he's here in Larch Haven."

"I met him this morning while Detective Ishimoto was interviewing him."

"In an unofficial capacity," I clarified.

He averted his gaze from mine. "I saw the two of you in the conference room this morning. You seem close."

"We are." When I caught a flicker of uncharacteristic uncertainty in Sawyer's eyes, I quickly added, "In a completely platonic way."

He met my gaze again. "That's good to know."

The intensity in his eyes left me breathless and scrambling for something to say or do.

I crossed into the family room and grabbed the script I'd left on the coffee table. "Do you want to run lines with me?"

"I can't act," Sawyer said.

"You don't need to act. All you have to do is read Jorge's lines and tell me if I get any of mine wrong." I flipped to one of the scenes I'd be filming in the coming days.

"All right," Sawyer said as I handed him the script. "I can probably manage that."

We ran through the first few lines, which were innocuous enough. As we got farther along, I wondered if I'd made a mistake in asking him to read this particular scene with me.

"Do you want me to feed you your line?" Sawyer asked.

I realized I'd fallen silent. "No," I said quickly, forcing my mind back on track. "I've got it." I took a breath and got myself back in character before speaking my next line. "I thought you were busy tonight."

Sawyer raised his eyes from the script before saying, "I took the evening off because I had to see you. I had to tell you...."

"Tell me what?" I asked, my pulse quickening.

He stepped closer to me. Once again, he looked up from the script before reciting his line. "That I can't stop thinking about you," he said, his eyes on mine. "I haven't been able to stop thinking about you for months. For years." He stepped even closer, the distance between us now down to mere inches. He took one of my hands in his, intertwining our fingers. "Addison, I really need you to know...."

He trailed off, just as the script instructed.

I drew in a shaky breath and tried to clear the buzzing in my head. "And that's when we're interrupted by the smell of burning cookies."

Sawyer didn't move and neither did I.

"I don't smell burning cookies," Sawyer said, his thumb running back and forth over my hand, leaving trails of tingles in its wake.

We were so close that I could see the varying and mesmerizing shades of brown in his eyes. I drank in the details, unable to look away.

I could have sworn that electricity crackled in the sliver of air between us.

"You were very convincing," Sawyer said.

"So were you. I thought you said you were no good at acting."

He kept his eyes locked on mine. "Who says I'm acting?"

My pulse raced and the buzzing in my head now ran through my entire body. He was so close. If I moved just a little....

A loud knock made me yelp with surprise.

Someone was at the front door.

The buzzing in my bloodstream faded away and I landed back in reality with a soundless but jarring thud.

"Our burning cookies," Sawyer said with a hint of humor and a lot more regret.

I slid my fingers from his and let out a sigh.

On my way to the foyer, I gave myself a mental shake, trying to clear my head of the pleasant fuzziness that had taken over during that moment with Sawyer. My mind cleared, but my pulse continued to race. I'd come so close to throwing caution to the wind and kissing him.

Now, I didn't even want to think about that. So, instead, I did my best to put that charged moment behind me and opened the door.

Chapter Ten

ANGELA'S HUSBAND, MARCO, WAS the one at the front door. My laptop had been acting up recently, and Marco—who worked with computers for a living—had offered to fix it for me. As Marco handed over my laptop, Sawyer made his excuses and slipped out into the night. A mixture of disappointment and relief swirled around inside of me as he disappeared along the canal path.

Marco stayed to chat for a few minutes, but then he, too, went on his way. It was getting late by then, so I started my nighttime routine. Soon, Binx, Truffles, and I were curled up in bed. Fortunately, I was tired enough that I drifted off to sleep with only minimal mental replaying of what had happened between Sawyer and me that evening.

In the morning, I filled a travel mug with chai tea and sipped at it as I wandered along the canals to the line of trailers in the parking lot. I was on my way to report to hair and makeup when I noticed Alex and Felicia together, standing between two of the trailers. They were in the middle of a hushed and apparently serious conversation. When Alex spotted me, his eyes widened and he quickly said something to Felicia. She whipped her head around my way, and I knew I didn't imagine the wariness in her eyes, even though she quickly banished it and smiled at me, calling out a greeting.

Alex scurried into the hair and makeup trailer ahead of me, while Felicia returned to her private trailer.

"Everything okay with Felicia?" I asked as I settled into Alex's chair a minute later.

"Of course. She's fine," Alex said, the words a little too fast and his tone a little too chipper. "I mean, it's not easy, what with Tony dying, but she's okay."

After adding that amendment, he changed the subject, chatting enthusiastically about Larch Haven and all its charm.

I smiled and answered all the questions he asked about the town, but I couldn't shake a vague sense of unease. Alex didn't want me knowing what he and Felicia had talked about, of that I was certain. That didn't necessarily mean anything. They were entitled to have private conversations. If a murder hadn't happened recently, I probably wouldn't have thought much of it at all. But a murder had been committed, and that had the suspicious part of my brain working overtime.

After filming two scenes that morning, I had a break of at least two hours ahead of me. I wandered over to craft services and sat down in one of the available folding chairs, trying my best to relax as I enjoyed the sight of the water rippling on the canal, causing the reflections of the leafy trees and grassy banks to waver and undulate.

The main shopping area of Larch Haven consisted of three avenues which together formed a U shape. Venice Avenue made up the southern arm and Giethoorn Avenue the northern arm. Amsterdam Avenue—where the Larch Haven Hotel and the town's main dock were located—formed the gentle curve at the base of the U. In between Venice and Giethoorn Avenues, numerous smaller canals curved and crisscrossed, the little islands in between home to cute cottages, including my own. At the mouth of the U, the various canals opened out onto Shadow Lake.

Today's scenes—all exterior ones—were being filmed either on Giethoorn Avenue or outside one of the cottages on the other side of the canal. The craft services area was set up at the corner of

Giethoorn Avenue and Amsterdam Avenue, giving me a good view of the crew as they moved all their equipment across the nearest bridge to the front lawn of the cottage being used as the home of Felicia's character, Journey.

Part of me wished that the production team had chosen my cottage to showcase in the movie, but another part of me was relieved that they hadn't. The owners of the chosen cottage had vacated their home for the next couple of weeks and were staying at the Larch Haven Hotel, with the production company footing the bill. I was glad to be able to return home each evening to my beloved cottage and my cats, so things had probably turned out for the best, even if I did—in my very biased opinion—have the cutest cottage in all of Larch Haven.

As I lounged in my chair, watching the crew, Cooper came over and slumped into the chair next to me. I'd seen him first thing that morning, before he had his makeup done, and I hadn't failed to notice the dark rings under his eyes. Now, with his face made up for filming, those dark smudges were no longer visible, but his posture and expression told me that he still felt just as tired and ragged, despite how wide-awake he'd appeared while acting out his scenes.

"Did you have a rough night?" I asked him.

He almost ran a hand through his carefully styled hair, but thought better of it at the last second. "I didn't sleep much. I spent over an hour at the police station yesterday evening."

I sat up straighter at that news. "Why?"

He shrugged. "Detective Ishimoto wanted to ask me more questions."

Apprehension settled heavily in my stomach. "Did you have a lawyer with you?"

He gave me a brief, humorless smile. "Geneva made sure I did. She was there too. Well, she wasn't in the interrogation room, but she waited outside."

"Interrogation?" I echoed, not liking the sound of that word. "Is that what it was?"

"That's what it felt like." His troubled eyes scanned the gently rippling water of the canal. "I think I'm in a lot of trouble, Becca. A family was out walking their dog the night Tony was killed and they told the police they saw me near the trailers before I met you at the hotel bar."

I digested that information. "Were they telling the truth?"

He gave me a grim nod. "I was in the area. I went out for a walk, but I didn't see Tony, and I didn't go in the props trailer."

"And you never told the police about your walk before they heard about it from the witness?"

"Of course not. It was bad enough that I fought with Tony before he died. If I told the cops I was near the scene of the crime that night, I probably would have become suspect number one."

"But now they've heard it from somebody else," I said.

"And that makes things worse for me," Cooper finished the thought. "I know. I should have told them everything right from the start."

This time he did run a hand through his hair, leaving several strands sticking up. No doubt Alex would be horrified when he saw what Cooper had done, but at the moment, that was the least of our worries.

"I don't know what I'm going to do, Becca," Cooper confessed. "It's like my life is spiraling out of control." He turned his blue eyes on me. "I didn't kill Tony."

"I know you didn't," I assured him, reaching out to squeeze his hand.

"But the police think I did. Or they at least think there's a good chance I did." He pulled out his phone. "And look at this." He navigated to a website and handed me the device. "The tabloids are tearing me apart."

The website showed a blurry picture of Cooper with a hand to his face. He could have been brushing a fly away from his eyes, but the frozen moment also could have been interpreted as one of anguish. The blazing headline declared that Cooper was now a falling star and a murder suspect, on his way to rehab for a drug and alcohol addiction.

I closed the webpage and handed him his phone. "Cooper, don't look at those things. They're ridiculous and it's not healthy for you to pay them any attention."

"You can say that again. Every time I see something like that, my anxiety goes up another notch." He closed his eyes. "Everything's falling apart, Becca."

I wanted to give him a hug, but Geneva marched over to us at that moment, her gray eyes flashing.

"Make sure you don't talk to anybody about what happened last night," she said to Cooper, eyeing me with disapproval.

"I'm not about to broadcast the fact that the cops questioned me again," he said, exasperated. "But Becca is my friend. I can tell her whatever I want."

Geneva's face took on a miffed expression. "I'm just trying to help."

Cooper sighed. "I know. I'm sorry."

His apology seemed to mollify her. "The cops will figure out that you had nothing to do with the murder," she said to Cooper. "It's not like they don't have a whole pool of other suspects to choose from. Like Felicia Blessing. Talk about motive. She doesn't have to pay Tony alimony anymore. Hey," she added, her eyes lighting up. "Maybe she even inherits from Tony."

"They divorced years ago," I pointed out. "And they didn't have an amicable relationship. I doubt he left anything to Felicia."

"You don't know for sure," she said to me, clearly annoyed.

"I don't," I conceded. "But Felicia earned way more than Tony ever did anyway."

Geneva wasn't ready to let go of her theory. "But maybe Tony was independently wealthy."

"Then why would Felicia have to pay him alimony?" Now Cooper was the one sounding annoyed. He got up from his chair. "Take a walk with me, Becca?" he requested, his eyes pleading with me.

When I got up, Geneva took a step to follow us.

"Sorry," Cooper said to her. "I want to speak to Becca alone for a while. I'll see you later, Geneva."

She frowned, but stayed put as we walked away.

A couple of supporting actors and a few crew members migrated toward the craft services food truck, so I quickly decided that wasn't a good destination for us.

"Come on," I said. "I know where we can go to talk privately."

Cooper followed me without question. I led him farther along Giethoorn Avenue, in the direction of Shadow Lake. Where the cobblestone walkway ended and the canal opened out onto the lake sat The Gondolier, the restaurant owned by my brother, Gareth, and his husband, Blake. The Gondolier wouldn't open until later in the day, and the front door was locked, but I knocked anyway, knowing that Blake wouldn't be far away.

Sure enough, a shadowy form emerged from the back of the restaurant and crossed the dimly lit dining room toward us. As he came closer, the shadows faded and I could see Blake clearly. Once he realized who was at the door, he unlocked and opened it.

"Hey, Becca." Blake's blue gaze landed on my companion. "You must be Cooper Graystone."

"This is Blake, my brother-in-law," I said to Cooper.

"Good to meet you, man." Cooper shook the hand Blake offered him.

"We need a quiet spot to sit for a while," I told Blake. "Is it okay if we hang out here?"

"Of course." Blake stood back so we could enter the restaurant. "Gareth's in the kitchen, but no one else is here yet. Sit wherever you like." He shut and locked the door behind us. "Can I get you anything?"

"No, thanks," I said. "We don't want to be any trouble. We just needed to get away for a bit."

Blake nodded, but looked at me like he was wondering what might be going on between Cooper and me. He didn't question us, though. Instead, he told us to holler if we needed anything and then he disappeared into the back.

I poked my head into the kitchen to say hi to my brother, who was in the midst of checking his inventory of ingredients. That done, Cooper and I sat down at a table for two, far enough away from the windows that we wouldn't be visible to anyone walking past the restaurant, unless they pressed their face up to the glass.

"I think you should stay off social media, at least for a while," I said once we'd settled into our seats. "You need a break from all the negativity and ridiculous rumors that are going around."

"You're right," Cooper agreed with a heavy sigh. "My therapist told me the same thing. I feel bad when I don't interact with my fans because most of them are good people, but maybe I'll hand my accounts over to Geneva for a while."

"That's a good idea."

"Do you know what else people have been saying about me?" he asked.

"If it were something truthful, it would probably be that you're an amazing, talented, kind person," I said.

He flashed me a ghost of a smile. "Thanks, Becca. People do say a lot of positive things, but...."

"The negative things sound the loudest in your head?" I guessed.

"You totally get it."

"I really do. You know things were getting to me when I was living in LA."

He nodded. "You're doing a lot better now that you're back home?"

"Way better," I said. "I get bouts of anxiety now and then, but not as frequently and not as badly as I did before."

Cooper leaned back in his chair, his shoulders slumped. "Maybe I need a change of scenery too."

"I'm a little afraid to ask," I said, "but what is it that people have been saying about you?"

"That I'm washed up because I'm doing made-for-TV movies now."

Indignation heated my blood. "That's ridiculous. That doesn't make you washed up. Besides, that's not all you're doing."

He'd just spent the winter filming several episodes for the second season of a popular television series. He played one of the lead characters and he'd already received plenty of praise from critics and viewers for his performance.

Cooper nodded. "I know. Like you said, I just need to step back from the Internet so I don't see or hear those things."

"Please do."

He released a breath. "It's not just the rumors and the murder investigation that are feeding my anxiety. I've got two days before I film the scene where I take Felicia on a gondola ride. I've never rowed a gondola in my life. I'm worried I'm going to end up falling into the canal. Then I'd really make a splash on the front page of the tabloids." One corner of his mouth turned upward. "Pun intended." All humor faded from his face. "Of course, that'll be the least of my worries if I end up in jail."

"You're not going to jail," I said firmly.

"But I don't know how to clear my name," Cooper said, dejected. "I didn't kill Tony, but I can't prove it."

"I'm going to do whatever I can to help you with that," I promised. Then I paused to think for a moment. "When's your call time tomorrow?"

Cooper consulted his phone. "Not until nine o'clock."

I formulated a plan in my head. "I might not be able to clear your name by that time tomorrow, but I know someone who can help with your other problem." I regarded Cooper from across the table. "Do you trust me?"

"Of course," he said without hesitation.

"Then meet me at the dock in front of the Larch Haven Hotel at six o'clock tomorrow morning."

Chapter Eleven

THE BENEFIT OF TAKING on one of the supporting roles in *Love on the Canal*, rather than playing a lead character, was that I didn't have to spend as much time on set. I loved being part of the movie, but I also found it hard to be away from True Confections. The shop had always been part of my life, but now it was such an integral part of my daily existence that I missed it if I was away for more than a day or two at a time.

That's why I woke up the next day looking forward to having the day off from filming, so I could spend time making chocolates in the kitchen at True Confections. First, however, I was meeting Dizzy and Cooper at the town's main dock.

After getting dressed and feeding my cats, I set off on foot. The branches of the leafy green trees swayed in the gentle morning breeze and birds twittered and sang like there was an avian convention going on in the treetops. The rising sun—not quite up over the mountains yet—had tinged the clear sky with a light shade of pink, casting a rosy glow over the town and the water in the canals.

As I crossed the final bridge on my path to the main dock, I spotted Cooper chatting with two young women dressed in spandex running outfits. They had their phones out and Cooper posed for selfies with each woman before they thanked him and jogged off, bright smiles on their faces. I was glad to see a smile on Cooper's face too.

"More fans?" I guessed as I reached him.

"They were great," he said. "They're fans of *Valley of Fury*."

Valley of Fury was a feature film Cooper had starred in last year.

I noticed Dizzy walking toward us along Amsterdam Avenue. I waved and then approached a little wooden booth which had just opened for the day. I'd paid the attendant the rental fee for a gondola and signed the necessary paperwork by the time Dizzy reached us.

"Hey, Dizzy." Cooper offered her his fist and she bumped it with her own. "Are you in on this plan of Becca's?"

"She basically is the plan," I said.

Dizzy grinned. "I hear you need to learn how to pilot a gondola."

"By tomorrow," Cooper said.

"Don't worry," Dizzy assured him. "I've got you."

"So you're my teacher?" Cooper asked. He looked to me. "Not you, Becca?"

I laughed. "Dizzy's far better at it than I am. But I'm here for moral support."

The truth, which I didn't see any point in mentioning, was that I'd only learned to pilot a gondola the previous summer. I'd spent most of my life terrified by the thought of falling into the canal. Although I'd gone boating and swimming in Shadow Lake regularly as a young child, my brother had tried to scare me with stories of a dangerous lake monster lurking beneath the surface. I hadn't believed him—not entirely, anyway—until one day while I was swimming, something large and scaly had brushed against my leg.

After that, I avoided going in the lake at all costs and even had outriggers added to my kayak to reduce the risk of capsizing. As far as I was concerned, the canals were just as dangerous as the lake. After all, the monster might have been slim enough to work its way through the channels.

Last year, however, I'd had a change of heart. I still believed that a large and mysterious creature resided in the depths of Shadow

Lake, but I no longer thought it meant any harm. There had never been any reports of people being injured, killed, or even chased by such an animal. There had hardly even been any sightings of something that might be a lake monster. So, I figured the creature most likely wanted to be left alone and, if anything, might actually be gentle.

While swimming to shore in an effort to flee a killer the summer before, a wave had swept up behind me, giving me an extra push to safety. I couldn't say for sure, but I had later wondered if my so-called lake monster had given me a little helping hand. Or a helping fin.

Although I sometimes still experienced a shiver of unease at the thought of willingly submerging myself in the water, I'd been building up my resolve all winter. When summer arrived, I was determined to start swimming in the lake again.

As my opinion of the lake creature had started to change last summer, I'd taken Sawyer up on his offer—more like a challenge, really—to let him teach me how to row a gondola. I'd caught on fairly quickly, but I still didn't have the years of experience that Dizzy had. She'd never shared my fear of the water. So, now, even though I knew how to navigate a gondola through the canals, I figured Cooper would be in better hands with my best friend.

"We'll start with a demonstration," Dizzy decided once we'd descended the steps to the dock.

Cooper and I climbed onboard the gondola and settled onto the seats. Dizzy untied the line and hopped onto the stern without a single wobble or hesitation. I relaxed while Dizzy began navigating the canal, with Cooper watching her every move. She explained what she was doing, demonstrating how to move forward and turn left and right.

"All right. Your turn, Cooper," she said as we glided back to the main dock.

Dizzy hopped off the gondola so she and Cooper could switch places.

Cooper wasn't quite as surefooted as Dizzy, but he still managed to step onto the stern without losing his balance.

Once Dizzy was satisfied with the way Cooper had placed his hands on the oar, she gave him the go-ahead and coached him along. He got off to a bit of a bumpy start, hitting the bank of the canal with the bow of the gondola and then losing his balance when he leaned too far forward. That sent the gondola rocking back and forth. I gripped the sides of the craft, hoping we wouldn't end up in the water, but I needn't have worried. Cooper regained his balance and the boat settled.

After that, he caught on quickly. Within minutes, Dizzy and I were able to relax and enjoy the mostly smooth ride along the canal.

"So how come Dizzy is so much better at this than you are, Becca?" Cooper asked as he continued to keep us moving through the water.

"She's had a lot more practice," I said, hoping to leave it at that.

Dizzy laughed. "Ask her why," she told Cooper.

I groaned with embarrassment. "No, don't ask."

Cooper grinned. "Oh, I'm asking. Tell me, Dizzy. What's the story?"

Dizzy proceeded to tell him the entire tale about my fear of the lake monster and how I'd refused to learn how to pilot a gondola until the previous year.

Cooper had a good laugh at the story, but when he settled down, he said, "Becca, as funny as it is that you were such a scaredy-cat for so long, I believe you when you say there's something big and mysterious living in the lake."

"You do?" I asked with surprise. I thought he'd think I was a nut.

"Sure," he said. "There's so much we don't know about what happens in deep lakes or at the bottom of the ocean. And there are plenty of documented instances of divers and other people discovering weird, gigantic creatures that we either never knew existed or hardly ever see."

"Yes!" Dizzy agreed, brimming with enthusiasm. "Like the oarfish found off the coast of Southern California in 2013. That thing was eighteen feet long, and oarfish can get as long as fifty feet."

I nodded, remembering the first time Dizzy had told me about that discovery. "That one from California totally looked like a sea serpent."

"And there are some really old and really huge sturgeons out there," Cooper added.

"Who knows what else is down in the deep," Dizzy said.

"I'm glad you don't think I'm crazy," I told Cooper.

"No way. I guess this is something we've never really talked about before, but I have an open mind when it comes to the mysteries of the universe. I saw a crazy UFO when I was fifteen. I tried to find some rational, down-to-earth explanation for the way that thing moved in the sky, but I came up empty. Even if it was a top-secret military craft, I swear it had to have been made with some sort of alien technology." He took his eyes off the canal ahead of us long enough to give us both a quick look. "Now maybe you think *I'm* crazy."

"Not even close," I said. "But don't get Dizzy started on UFOs and alien lifeforms. Not today, anyway."

"She's right on both counts," Dizzy agreed. "I would love to sit down and chat UFOs and paranormal activity for hours, but we've got more important things to deal with today."

"Maybe that's something we can do another day," Cooper suggested.

Dizzy appeared taken aback, but not for long. "Sure," she said with a smile.

I looked from Dizzy to Cooper, sensing that something in the air between them had just shifted.

That definitely caught my interest. For now, however, I had to concentrate on other things.

"All right," I said as we slid beneath a stone bridge. "Now that the gondola problem is taken care of, it's time to tackle the job of clearing Cooper's name."

"Let's start with our suspects," Dizzy said as she kept an eye on Cooper, ready to critique his technique, if needed.

Cooper stopped rowing and nearly lost his balance again. "You mean, you'll help too, Dizzy?"

She gestured at the oar. "Focus." When he got back to rowing, she answered his question. "Of course I'll help."

"But you don't know me well enough to know that I'm not a killer," Cooper pointed out as he navigated a bend in the canal like he'd been doing it for years.

"Becca has known you for ages," Dizzy said. "She trusts you, and I trust Becca, so I'm all in. Besides," she added with a proud smile, "I'm Becca's trusty sidekick. She'd be lost without me."

"That last part is very true," I said, "but you're more than a sidekick. You're my partner in crime solving."

"Sidekick fits better," Dizzy said to Cooper before addressing me. "But I appreciate the attempt to promote me."

"Whatever our imaginary job titles are, we need to get down to business," I said.

Cooper steered the gondola around a bend in the canal. "I never knew you were a Veronica Mars."

I smiled up at him. "I'm just an actor and chocolatier who's trying to help a friend."

"And that," Cooper said with a grin, "is the Becca Ransom I know and love."

Chapter Twelve

"LET'S START WITH OUR suspects," I suggested as Cooper continued to take Dizzy and me on a gondola ride along the canals. "Felicia Blessing has to be on the list, since she had a history with Tony, and I'm guessing she doesn't have an alibi, considering how the police questioned her a second time."

"The cops questioned her again?" Cooper kept rowing. "I guess that means I'm not the only suspect, but the police are barking up the wrong tree. Felicia's a sweetheart."

"Her name still needs to go on the list," Dizzy insisted, "until we have some evidence to the contrary."

"Don't worry," I told Cooper. "She's not our only suspect. As much as I like him, Alex Skye needs to go on the list too."

"Alex is harmless," Cooper protested.

"I hope you're right about that." I took out my phone and started making notes, wishing I had a notebook and pen with me. Somehow writing things out by hand always made them clearer in my head. Maybe later I could transfer my notes onto paper.

"Who's Alex and why is he on our list?" Dizzy asked.

"He's the production's hairstylist," Cooper replied. "And I have no idea why he'd be on the list. Becca?"

I looked up from my phone. "He seemed upset when I saw him talking to Tony the other day."

"Upsetting people was practically a sport for Tony," Cooper pointed out.

"Maybe so, but this happened shortly before Tony died so I don't think we can ignore it."

"Any idea what it was that upset Alex?" Dizzy asked.

I thought back, visualizing the scene I'd witnessed by the catering truck. "Alex wanted something from Tony, but I have no idea what. I only know that he seemed desperate. Tony told Alex to forget it and walked off, laughing. It was cruel, obnoxious laughter, not like he thought they were sharing a joke."

"That sounds like Tony," Cooper remarked.

"What do you think Alex might have wanted from Tony?" I asked Cooper.

"I have no clue," he said.

"Then we need to talk to Alex," Dizzy declared. "And add Heller Yearwood's name to our list."

I did as she suggested.

"Hella?" Cooper said with confusion.

"Heller," Dizzy corrected. "He lives here in Larch Haven."

"And his wife, Chanel, is working as a background performer," I added. "I saw her with Tony and they looked like they were flirting."

Dizzy told Cooper what she'd shared with me about Heller's outburst at the pub in Snowflake Canyon.

"It's kind of surprising that an angry husband didn't do Tony in earlier," Cooper said when Dizzy had finished. "The guy was always flirting with women, single or married. And often doing more than just flirting. That's what broke up his marriage with Felicia."

"I heard something more about Heller yesterday afternoon," Dizzy said. "I would have texted you, Becca, but I knew I'd be seeing you first thing this morning."

"Don't keep us in suspense," I prodded.

"Apparently Heller went to the Larch Haven Hotel, looking for Tony, not long before the murder happened," she said.

"Where did you hear that?" Cooper asked.

"At the library." Dizzy smiled. "It's amazing what you can learn there, and not just from the books."

"Aren't libraries supposed to be quiet?" Cooper asked.

"People are just as good at gossiping in whispers as they are at normal volume," Dizzy said.

"Do you know the source of the rumor?" I asked Dizzy, knowing we had plenty of untrustworthy sources in our town. The Gossip Grannies, for example.

"I heard it was Consuelo Díaz who saw him at the hotel," Dizzy said, referring to a local café owner who was also an avid reader. "When Consuelo came in to return a book at the end of the day, I asked her about it—subtly of course—and she confirmed the rumor. She was at the hotel restaurant for dinner that night. Apparently, Heller was asking around, trying to find out Tony's room number because the hotel staff wouldn't give it to him."

"That reminds me," I said. "I saw Chanel at the hotel too. She tried to sneak upstairs, but got stopped by a security guard. She claimed she was there to meet a friend."

"And you think Tony was that friend?" Cooper asked.

"He definitely could have been."

"Okay," Dizzy said. "So Heller might have committed the murder because he was upset about his wife's relationship with Tony."

"But would he have gone to the effort of setting up a booby trap?" I asked.

"I don't think we know enough about him to say yes or no," Dizzy said.

"You're right," I agreed. "And there's something else about Heller."

I told Dizzy and Cooper about following Heller into the travel agency and how eager he'd been to book a trip to get away from Larch Haven.

"Sounds like he wants to go on the run," Dizzy remarked.

"Or at least leave town until the dust settles," Cooper said.

"All right." I added some notes to my phone. "So we've got three suspects so far. What about Chanel Yearwood? Should we add her name? Maybe she was getting attached to Tony and then saw him flirting with another woman? And maybe she went to the hotel to see if he was still alive because she didn't know if her trap had worked?"

"I wouldn't disregard that possibility," Cooper said.

Dizzy tipped her head to one side as she considered the idea. "Since we don't know that she had any reason to feel jealous, I think her motive is pretty flimsy right now. Maybe put her name at the bottom of the list."

I did just that, adding a question mark after her name.

"I could really use some breakfast," Cooper said. "And coffee. Being a gondolier is hungry work."

"Let's take the gondola back to the main dock," I suggested. "Then I'll treat you both to breakfast."

"You know how much food I can put away at breakfast time, right?" Cooper asked.

"I remember," I assured him with a smile. "And my offer still stands."

We returned the gondola to the dock with the craft none the worse for wear. Cooper appeared much happier and more relaxed than he had the day before. I knew he wouldn't have a problem with his gondola scene, and I hoped everything else would go well for him too. Of course, for that to happen, the police would either have to realize on their own that Cooper had nothing to do with Tony's murder, or we'd have to figure out how to prove that to them.

"We have one more suspect to add to our list," I said to Cooper and Dizzy once the three of us were seated at an outdoor table at the Rialto Café.

The small restaurant had opened just as we'd arrived at the door, so we were the first customers of the day. That meant we didn't have to worry about other diners overhearing our conversation.

I did, however, wait to continue sharing my thoughts until after the waiter had taken our orders.

As he'd warned me, Cooper had a big appetite and ordered the Hungry Gondolier's Breakfast Sandwich. The jalapeño cheddar bagel was loaded with a sausage patty, gooey cheese, bell peppers, mushrooms, fried eggs, and crispy bacon. He also ordered extra bacon and eggs on the side, and a fruit salad. He finished up his order with coffee.

Dizzy and I had more modest requests. She asked for buttermilk pancakes and orange juice, while I ordered waffles with strawberry sauce and a cup of tea.

"Okay, so who's our other suspect?" Dizzy asked in a low voice once our waiter had taken our orders and left us alone again.

"Sonja Jepsen," I replied.

Cooper nodded. "Of course. Again, I don't think Sonja is a killer, but I can see why you want her name on the list."

Dizzy waved at us. "Fill me in, please. I don't even know who Sonja is."

"She's the script supervisor," I explained. I second-guessed what I'd said moments before. "Or maybe Tony was more likely to kill her than the other way around?"

"I could see it working both ways," Cooper said. "If Sonja were capable of murder, which I don't believe."

"Fair enough." I added Sonja's name to the growing list on my phone.

Dizzy waved again. "Hello! I'm still in the dark here."

"Right. Sorry, Diz," I apologized. "Tony accused Sonja of stealing an idea he supposedly had for a screenplay."

"He never actually wrote the script," Cooper added. "And Sonja probably didn't steal anything, but Tony had been mad about it for weeks. He even threatened to take her to court, but I don't think he ever acted on that threat."

"But maybe he had Sonja worried," Dizzy said. "She definitely has a motive then."

"And no alibi, at least for part of the evening." I filled Dizzy and Cooper in on what I'd overheard when Officer McNally was questioning Sonja.

"Alone in her room," Dizzy repeated when I'd finished recounting the story. "That won't be easy to prove or disprove."

"My thoughts exactly." I noticed a crease of confusion cutting across Cooper's forehead. "What's wrong?"

"Sonja claims she was in her room all evening?"

I confirm that with a nod.

"After I left you in the bar, Becca, I knocked on Sonja's door on the way to my room. She lost her phone charger and borrowed mine that afternoon. I wanted to see if she was done with it."

"And she didn't answer the door?" Dizzy guessed.

Cooper shook his head, his forehead still furrowed. "Maybe she was sleeping." His face cleared. "That's probably it. She was sound asleep."

"Except," I said slowly, remembering something, "she mentioned to me that she's a really light sleeper. That's why she likes how quiet it is here in Larch Haven."

We all let that sink in.

"So she likely lied about her alibi," Dizzy concluded.

"Unless she was in the shower when I knocked on her door," Cooper said.

"That's a possibility," I conceded.

"But she's got a motive and possibly had the opportunity to set up the booby trap," Dizzy said.

"We definitely need to take a closer look at her." I added a couple of notes next to Sonja's name and then tucked my phone away as the waiter approached with our meals.

Cooper looked ready to drool when the waiter set his loaded plate in front of him. "This looks amazing."

"It'll taste amazing too," Dizzy assured him. "The food here is great."

"So let's not spoil it by talking about murder while we eat," I suggested.

Dizzy and Cooper readily agreed, and for the rest of our time at the café we simply enjoyed our food and each other's company.

Chapter Thirteen

AFTER DIZZY LEFT THE café for the library and Cooper headed off to the hair and makeup trailer, I turned my steps toward True Confections. A few early-rising tourists strolled along the canals, but the town was still quiet. The day's scenes for *Love on the Canal* would be filmed inside and around the cottage used as the home of Felicia's character, so there were no signs of the production on Venice Avenue that morning.

As was typically the case on days that I worked at True Confections, I was the first to arrive at the shop. I breathed in the delicious scent of chocolate as I made my way into the kitchen and got ready to make bonbons and truffles. It didn't take long for me to get immersed in my work. The familiar routine helped to settle my mind, which had been spinning in circles ever since Cooper, Dizzy, and I had chatted about our suspects.

As I coated balls of Earl Grey ganache with shredded white chocolate, I realized I'd forgotten to ask Cooper about Felicia's connection to Alex Skye. Maybe there was nothing to the furtive conversation I'd witnessed between the actress and the hairstylist, but with an unsolved murder case hanging over the town, it held my interest.

I hoped Felicia and Alex had nothing to do with the crime, but if I was going to help Cooper, I couldn't leave any stone unturned, no matter what might creep out from underneath. I considered texting Cooper to ask him what he knew about Felicia and Alex's relationship, but I changed my mind at the last moment. Maybe it was best to raise that question in a private, face-to-face conversation. I didn't want anyone accidentally seeing text messages that revealed my suspicions about my colleagues.

I'd been working for nearly an hour when I heard someone unlock the front door and enter the shop. I figured it was Angela, so it took me by surprise when Milo appeared in the kitchen doorway.

"Hey," I greeted. "Shouldn't you be on your way to school?" I checked the clock on the wall. "Did you miss the bus?"

Larch Haven didn't have a high school of its own, so kids of that age took a bus up to Snowflake Canyon to attend classes there.

"Dad's giving me a ride this morning, so I don't have to leave quite so early," Milo replied. "And he wanted to get a coffee from Gathering Grounds."

That was the local coffee shop, located a few doors down from True Confections.

"And you simply couldn't pass up an opportunity to see your favorite cousin?" I teased.

"If any of my other cousins heard me agreeing to that statement, I'd be in trouble."

I laughed. "That's okay. I know I'm your favorite."

"Sure." He drew out the word.

"So why are you really here?" I asked.

He stuffed his hands in the pockets of his jeans, suddenly hesitant. I piped mint chocolate ganache into molds coated with milk chocolate as I waited for him to speak. After a few seconds, he did.

"I've been thinking...."

"Uh oh," I said. "That could be dangerous."

Milo rolled his eyes. "You sound like Pops."

"I come by it honestly." I went back to piping. "What have you been thinking about?"

"I'd like to learn how to make chocolates."

I looked up from my work with surprise. "For the shop? You want to be a chocolatier?"

He shrugged. "Maybe. I'm not sure yet. I just know I want to give it a try."

A smile spread across my face. "I'm happy to show you the ropes. Unless you'd rather learn from Lolly?"

He shrugged again. "Maybe from both of you? But mostly you. I know Lolly's supposed to be enjoying her retirement."

I set my piping bag aside. "I'd love to teach you, Milo. And if it's something you enjoy, it would be great to have an extra pair of hands here in the kitchen sometimes."

"Cool. Thanks, Becca." He remained standing in the doorway.

"Is there something else?" I asked, sensing that he had more to say.

"Don't hate me for asking this, but are you and Cooper Graystone a thing?"

The question took me by surprise. "Where did you get that idea?"

Milo looked a bit sheepish. "Camille heard that you were a couple. She wanted me to ask you if it's true."

Camille was Milo's girlfriend. They'd started dating a few weeks earlier.

"I didn't want to bug you about it," he said quickly. "But then I wondered...."

"Wondered what?" I prodded when he trailed off.

"If you'd really be around to teach me about making chocolates."

"Ah," I said, finally understanding. "You're wondering if I'm moving back to California to be with Cooper?"

Milo shrugged one shoulder and nodded.

"Don't worry. You're going to get your chocolate lessons. I'm not moving anywhere, and you can tell Camille that Cooper and I are definitely not a couple. We're very close friends, but it doesn't go beyond that." I started packing a few imperfect bonbons—which I called misfits—into a small paper bag. "Where did Camille hear that, anyway?"

"I don't know," Milo admitted. "She just said that the rumor's been going around town."

I added one last bonbon to the bag and held it out to Milo. "For you to share with your friends. And rumors in this town are usually heavy on the fiction and light on the facts."

"Don't I know it." Milo accepted the bag of chocolates from me. "Thanks for this. I'd better run."

"Have a good day at school!" I called as he disappeared, heading for the front of the shop. A few seconds later, the bell jingled above the door.

I smiled after he'd gone. Whether or not Milo actually wanted to be a chocolatier as a career, the fact that he was interested in learning how to make the bonbons and truffles we sold in the shop brought me a glow of happiness. True Confections was more than just a business, it was a major part of our family, a place where I—and my brother and cousins—had spent many happy hours while growing up, hanging out, working, and spending time with Lolly and Pops. I knew our grandparents would be pleased with his interest too, even if he didn't choose to make it his full-time job in the future.

I wasn't as happy with the rumors about Cooper and me being a couple. At least I'd already set the record straight with Sawyer in that regard. I wouldn't have wanted him to hear the rumor and not know that it wasn't true.

The fact that I was worried about Sawyer thinking I might be dating someone else gave me pause. Maybe it didn't really mean anything, I told myself, even though I knew that was a lie.

How would I feel if I learned that Sawyer was dating someone?

Even posing the question to myself made my heart hurt and my stomach swirl unpleasantly.

I didn't need more of an answer than that.

Angela arrived then, interrupting my thoughts, to my relief. After I chatted with her for a few minutes, I refocused on my work, pushing thoughts of Sawyer aside. As I coated my custom-made gondola molds with tempered milk chocolate, my mind strayed to the new truffle and bonbon flavors I wanted to try in the near future. I was thinking of creating a bonbon inspired by one of my favorite flavors of bubble tea—brown sugar milk tea—and I also wanted to add lilac truffles as a seasonal product. I had a recipe written out for the lilac confections, but I wouldn't be able to test it until the flowers bloomed, which would happen soon. Fortunately, Lolly and Pops had lilac bushes in their garden, and there were many others around town, so I'd have plenty of blooms to work with when the time came. Hopefully, the lilac truffles would taste as good in reality as they did in my imagination.

Once the store opened for the day, I heard customers coming and going, but I continued to work. I wanted to get as many types of chocolates made as I could, so Lolly wouldn't have to work too hard the next day when I was back on set.

When I had finished batches of mint melty truffles, London fog truffles, peanut butter pretzel truffles, and salted caramels, I placed a variety of the confections in the chocolate gondolas I'd made, and then wrapped the treat-filled boats in cellophane, tying each package closed with a purple bow. Then I filled several boxes to put on the store's shelves. Finally, I carried a tray of assorted bonbons and truffles out to the front of the shop so I could refill the display case.

"Perfect timing," Angela said as I made my way behind the counter. "I was just about to tell you we needed to restock."

"Looks like business has been brisk this morning," I remarked when I saw the many empty spaces in the display case.

"It's been busy," Angela confirmed. "The London fog truffles are a real hit."

"I'm glad to hear that." The Earl Grey-infused truffles were my latest addition to the menu.

Although I'd meant to go straight back to the kitchen after refilling the display case, I changed my plans when Heller Year-wood entered the shop. I didn't remember seeing him in True Confections before and he hesitated just inside the door, as if he wasn't quite sure where to browse first.

"Welcome to True Confections, Mr. Yearwood," Angela said in greeting. "Is there anything I can help you with?"

"Do you have any dairy free chocolate?" he asked as he gazed around the shop.

I jumped in to help. "Right over here." I set my empty tray aside and hurried out from behind the counter to lead Heller over to a display of dairy-free chocolate bars. "We have a few different flavors: dark chocolate, chili, orange, and hazelnut."

He chose two each of the dark and orange chocolate bars.

"I saw you at the travel agency the other day," I said, keeping my voice casual. "Are you going on vacation?"

Heller's bushy eyebrows drew together. "Just thinking about it," he mumbled before turning toward the sales counter.

Angela rang up his purchases while I wandered behind the counter to retrieve my tray. After Heller had paid for the chocolate bars, he headed out the door. I watched him go, pondering what he'd said. When I saw him at the travel agency, he'd sounded as though he was doing more than just thinking about going away. He'd seemed quite adamant that he wanted to book a trip, and quickly.

Maybe he'd downplayed his desire to get away just now because he didn't want word getting out that he was planning to flee. Then again, if he wanted to avoid getting caught by the police for murdering Tony, wouldn't he have left already? Perhaps not, if he didn't want to make it too obvious that he was leaving because of the murder.

I shook my head, wishing that my thoughts about the murder wouldn't get so jumbled. I was having trouble finding any clarity.

"Everything okay?" Angela asked. She must have seen me shaking my head.

"Everything's good," I assured her, but then I wondered if I'd jinxed myself.

The bell above the door gave a cheerful jingle as it opened to admit the Gossip Grannies, Delphi and Luella.

"Hello," Delphi said as she led the way into the store. "I guess we won't be seeing much more of you, Rebecca."

"Why is that?" I asked, confused by the comment.

"Because you're heading back to Hollywood, of course," Delphi said, as if I should have known the answer.

"The lure of the bright lights is just too much to resist," Luella added.

Angela shot me a glance and raised her eyebrows.

"I'm not moving back to California," I said firmly.

Luella patted my arm on her way past me. "Right. We understand that you want to keep the news quiet."

"Why would she want to keep it quiet?" Angela asked.

Delphi shook her head. "It'll be such a disappointment to Oona and Ernest," she said, referring to Lolly and Pops. "It really isn't fair to Oona to force her out of retirement because you're having a fling, Rebecca, but young people are so headstrong these days."

Luella nodded in agreement. "And selfish." She clicked her tongue in disapproval.

"What fling?" I asked, and then wished I hadn't.

"With Cooper Graystone." Luella looked to Angela. "Perhaps she thinks it will last, but those Hollywood men aren't the marrying type."

"I'm staying in Larch Haven," I said, raising my voice a notch in the hope of actually getting Delphi and Luella to listen to me. "And I'm not dating Cooper Graystone."

Delphi turned her attention to the boxes of assorted bonbons sitting on a shelf, acting like I hadn't spoken. So much for getting them to accept the truth.

When the Gossip Grannies had their backs to us, I shared a look with Angela and rolled my eyes. I decided I should get back to the kitchen before Delphi and Luella got my blood pressure up any higher than they already had.

"Oh, Rebecca," Luella said as I turned toward the hall that would take me to the kitchen.

I stopped, drawing on my acting experience to hide how much I regretted not making a hastier escape.

"You're friends with Sawyer Maguire," Luella continued.

"Yes," I said slowly, wondering where the conversation was going.

Delphi chimed in as she selected a box of bonbons from the shelf. "When do you think he and his colleagues are going to catch on?"

"Catch on to what?" I asked.

"What really happened with that actor who supposedly died," Delphi said.

"Supposedly?" I echoed.

"Wasn't he the props master?" Angie asked.

I nodded. "Tony Fleet."

Delphi waved off what Angela and I had said. "Close enough. The point is, it was an act of revenge."

Angie spoke up while I was still processing everything. "Who killed him out of revenge?"

"Nobody!" Luella said with glee.

"I'm confused." Angie looked my way.

All I could do was shrug at her.

Delphi shook her head, as if she thought my cousin and I were terribly slow on the uptake. "Don't you see? He set up a fake murder so that fancy actress would go to jail for the crime."

"You mean Felicia Blessing?" I asked.

"She's the one," Luella confirmed.

Angela looked more confused than ever, and I couldn't blame her.

"Are you saying that Tony Fleet faked his death so that Felicia Blessing would go to jail for killing him?" she asked.

"I'm pretty sure Tony is really dead," I said.

Luella let out an exasperated sigh. "That's what he wants everyone to think."

"He's probably in Bermuda now," Delphi added.

"The police found Tony's body," I said, not sure that I should really be continuing the conversation. "How could he fake that?"

"Movie people can fake all sorts of things," Delphi said, as if that should have been obvious.

"But not DNA," I pointed out.

"I wouldn't be so sure," Delphi said. "You'd be amazed what people can do these days."

Luella nodded her agreement.

"Okay." I had no idea what else to say. I turned to the kitchen once again, eager to get away this time.

"You'd better fill Sawyer in," Delphi called after me. "The police might never clue in otherwise."

I hurried into the kitchen, where I released a heavy sigh.

I might not have solved the mystery of Tony's death, but the one thing I felt I could be certain of was that the Gossip Grannies hadn't either.

Chapter Fourteen

By the middle of the afternoon, I'd made enough bonbons and truffles to keep True Confections well stocked for the next couple of days. Even though I'd heard the Gossip Grannies leave the shop hours earlier, I still peeked out the kitchen door before venturing into the front of the store. I appreciated the fact that Delphi and Luella purchased chocolates from True Confections on a regular basis, but I preferred not to be around when they did so. I didn't know if the ladies truly believed the stories they spun, but they certainly had some avid followers in town who did.

To my relief, the only customers in the store were an elderly couple and two young mothers with babies in tow. I helped Angie serve the customers and the store fell quiet once they left.

"You don't need to hang around here any longer," Angie said once we were alone. "You've put in a long day already."

"Thanks, Angie." I tugged at the elastic holding my ponytail together and released my hair to fall down my back. As I did that, I formulated a plan in my head. "Does Chanel Yearwood still work at that boutique near Hooked on Books?"

"She owns it now," Angie replied. "Why?"

I decided to keep my answer vague. "I just wanted to ask her something."

"Isn't she working as a background performer for *Love on the Canal*?"

"She is," I confirmed. "Maybe I'll see her on set tomorrow."

Except, I wasn't sure I wanted to wait that long to talk to her. Besides, I didn't know how many days she'd be working as an extra. If I couldn't find her at the clothing boutique, I'd put my plan on hold for a day or so, but I was hoping I wouldn't have to do that.

"I'll see you on set tomorrow too," I said with a smile.

Angela's face lit up with excitement. "Yes, you will!"

I slipped my apron off, hoping to get away without any further questions. After I'd tossed my apron in the laundry hamper in the back, I passed through the front of the store on my way out. Unfortunately, my cousin picked up our conversation again.

"What do you need to ask Chanel? I didn't think you knew her."

"I don't, really," I admitted.

I wasn't sure what else to say. I didn't want to tell my cousin that I was looking into Tony's murder. She knew I'd done something similar in the past, but I didn't want her worrying about me, and I didn't want word of my activities spreading to other members of our family, like Lolly, Pops, and my brother.

Luckily, two customers entered the store at that moment, saving me from having to provide any further explanation. After saying hello to the shoppers, I waved at Angela and hurried out of the shop. What I hadn't told Angela was that I wanted to have a chat with Chanel to see if she harbored any bitterness toward Tony. I didn't actually know if she had a motive for killing the props master, but I hoped that talking with her would give me an idea of how she felt about him at the time of his death. I also wanted to see if I could find out more information about her husband, Heller.

As I walked along Venice Avenue, heading for Chanel's clothing boutique, I realized that I needed to focus on alibis as well. When I'd seen Chanel at the Larch Haven Hotel on the night of Tony's murder, she said she was heading off to the pub to meet her friend. Although I strongly believed that the "friend" she wanted to see was Tony, I didn't know that for certain. If Chanel really had gone straight to the pub from the hotel and met up with someone there, maybe that meant I was wrong about her looking for Tony that night.

Maybe I should have focused on stronger suspects than Chanel, but most of the other people on my list were busy with filming *Love on the Canal* at the moment, so I decided it made sense to focus on the Yearwoods. Tomorrow, when I was back on set, I could try to dig up some more information on the other suspects Cooper, Dizzy, and I had put on our list.

When I arrived at the clothing boutique, I realized that luck was with me. The shop was open and when I peeked through the large front window, I could see Chanel inside, talking with a customer. I entered the boutique and said hello when Chanel called out a greeting to me. Since she was still chatting with a gray-haired woman I recognized as a local, I began browsing, pretending that I was interested in the skirts and dresses hanging on a rack along one wall.

After several minutes, the other customer paid for a few items and left the shop. Chanel came over my way as I took a dress off the rack for a closer look.

"It's Rebecca, isn't it?" Chanel asked. "You're one of the stars of *Love on the Canal*."

"A supporting actor," I amended with a smile. "But yes, I'm Rebecca Ransom. You've been working on the film too, haven't you?"

Chanel ran a hand down her hair with a smile. "Just as an extra, but it's been fun."

"I think I saw you with Tony Fleet one day," I said. "It's terrible what happened to him. Were you two friends?"

Chanel's smile slipped from her face. "No, we weren't friends," she said, a little too quickly. Her fingers strayed to the base of her throat, as if reaching for a necklace, but there was nothing there. She dropped her hand. "I met him once on set, but that's all. I can't believe someone killed the poor man."

I was certain she was downplaying her relationship with Tony, but I didn't want her to know that.

"My friend and I happened upon the scene of the crime shortly after the police got there," I said. "It was a sight I'd rather forget. I hope you didn't see it."

"No, I didn't, thank goodness. I was having dinner and drinks with friends all evening."

I pretended to accept that as the truth. "That's a relief."

"Would you like to try that dress on?" Chanel asked, turning her attention to the garment in my arms.

For the first time, I took a good look at the dress I'd removed from the rack. The color—a deep shade of purple—had caught my eye. Now that I had a full view of the garment, I realized I didn't have to feign interest in it. The dress, made from a jersey cotton fabric, had long sleeves and a boat neckline.

"I would, yes," I answered truthfully.

"The fitting room is just back here." Chanel led the way to the back of the shop and into a room with a bench, a full-length mirror, and two cubicles.

The bell above the shop door announced the arrival of another customer, so Chanel left me alone to try on the dress. The fabric felt wonderfully soft against my skin, and I was pleased to discover that the dress fit me perfectly. I checked the price tag and decided I would buy it. That made me feel a little less guilty about coming into Chanel's store under false pretenses.

By the time I changed back into my clothes and returned to the front of the shop, the other customer had left and Chanel was on her own.

She smiled brightly when I told her I wanted to buy the dress and she quickly set about ringing up the purchase.

"Did I hear something about you and your husband going on a trip soon?" I asked, acting like I wasn't sure of what I was saying.

"No," Chanel said as she worked the cash register. "We don't have any travel plans."

"I must be confusing you with someone else then."

Two more customers entered the shop, so I paid for my purchase and thanked Chanel before making my exit. Although I was happy about my new dress, I felt like I was leaving empty-handed in terms of solid information.

I knew that Chanel hadn't told me the truth, not entirely, anyway. She hadn't spent the whole evening in question at home, because I'd seen her at the Larch Haven Hotel. Maybe she'd gone straight home from there, but if so, that meant she'd lied to the security guard about heading for the pub. Why would she have done that if she didn't have something to hide? She could have changed her mind on the way, or received a text from her friend, canceling their plans to meet up, but I felt certain that she'd really been at the hotel to see Tony, or to check if he was still alive. I didn't know how to prove that, though, so I didn't think I'd made much headway with my investigation.

I didn't think Chanel had lied when she answered my question about having plans to travel in the near future, but I wasn't sure that helped me out much. Maybe Heller was planning to flee on his own because he killed Tony, or maybe he changed his mind about going away.

There were too many possibilities. Somehow, I needed to narrow down my list of suspects, but I didn't know what steps to take next.

Feeling frustrated, I stopped by the side of the canal to send Dizzy a text message, asking if she wanted to meet up. Her shift at the library would end soon and I wanted to tell her about my attempt at sleuthing, even though it was mostly a failed attempt.

Dizzy texted back right away and agreed to meet me at the local pub, The Oar and Anchor. Since she had to stay at the library for a few more minutes, I wandered home for another visit with Binx and Truffles. I gave them each a cuddle and fed them their dinners before heading out again, leaving my new dress on my bed.

I was walking across a bridge that would take me to Giethoorn Avenue when I spotted Sawyer up ahead. That would have made me happy, if not for the company he was in. He stood on the cobblestone walkway, not far from The Oar and Anchor, with the Gossip Grannies facing him and Daniela Roumeliotis standing a little too close to his side, her body angled toward his. He wore his police uniform and was clearly on duty, but I somehow doubted the three women were talking to him about crime prevention, especially considering the way Daniela kept giggling and flipping her hair over her shoulder.

My steps slowed as I crossed the bridge, and I considered changing my route so I could avoid the Gossip Grannies and Daniela. After all, I'd already had one dose of Delphi and Luella that day, and I wasn't sure if I could handle a second. As for Daniela, my last encounter with her didn't leave me eager for another.

As I stepped off the bridge, I was still wondering if I could sneak around the group without being spotted, but then Sawyer caught sight of me over Luella's head. Daniela latched onto his arm and moved even closer to him. I fought the urge to roll my eyes and took perhaps a little too much pleasure in the fact that the tense set of Sawyer's jaw suggested he wasn't enjoying himself.

He said something to the women that I couldn't hear and peeled Daniela's fingers from his arm. After another couple of words, he dodged around the women to head my way.

I waited for him at the foot of thc bridge. Delphi and Luella glanced my way and then walked off, their heads together as they chatted away. I had a bad feeling that I was the subject of their conversation. Daniela shot me a glare over her shoulder and then flounced off toward Amsterdam Avenue.

"You're a popular man," I commented as Sawyer approached.

"If that's popularity, I don't want anything to do with it." He glanced over his shoulder, as if making sure the Gossip Grannies and Daniela hadn't decided to follow him.

"Do I even want to know what the four of you were talking about?" I asked.

Sawyer came to a stop in front of me. "No. Definitely not."

I groaned. "That means you have to tell me." I held up a hand to stop him before he had the chance. "Was it about my fling with Cooper Graystone?"

Sawyer regarded me through narrowed eyes. "You said the two of you were just friends."

"We are," I said quickly. "Maybe I should have said my *nonexistent* fling."

"Got it in one." Sawyer shook his head. "Don't make me repeat the details."

"Don't worry," I reassured him. "I don't want to hear them."

"That's because you're smart," Sawyer said. "Where are you headed?"

"To meet Dizzy at the pub."

"I'll walk with you."

We fell into step together.

"What about Daniela?" I asked, even though it probably would have been better for my blood pressure not to raise the question.

Sawyer's dark eyes grew stormy. "She was happy to jump in and suggest that you should move back to Hollywood, where—in her words—you would no doubt leech off Cooper's fame and fortune."

I made a face. "What's her problem?"

"I was going to ask you that."

"Dizzy says it's jealousy left over from high school."

"Well, whatever the case, I told her that you don't need to do any sort of leeching because you're a successful and independent woman."

"You said that to her?" I asked, pleased by his words.

"Why not? It's the truth. And I couldn't exactly say the other things that wanted to come out of my mouth."

"Like what?"

"Let's just say if my mother heard me say them, she'd wash my mouth out with soap, even though I'm a fully grown adult."

I smiled at Sawyer, a warm glow spreading through my chest. "I appreciate you standing up for me."

He looked my way. "I always will, Becca."

Butterflies danced in my chest as my cheeks grew warm.

"I wish I could ticket those Gossip Grannies," Sawyer said as we strolled slowly along the canal. "Or better yet, toss them in lockup for excessive gossiping."

I laughed. "It's probably best that you can't do that. If you did, you'd no doubt become the subject of their craziest rumors."

"Better me than you."

His words sent another rush of warmth through me. "The Gossip Grannies don't bother me." When Sawyer raised an eyebrow, I amended my statement. "Much."

We drew to a stop outside The Oar and Anchor.

I considered sharing with Sawyer what I'd learned during my conversation with Chanel, but then I thought better of it. I really hadn't learned much, and telling Sawyer that I'd been looking for clues would only make him worry and want to lecture me.

Approaching footsteps caught my attention and I turned to see Dizzy jogging over our way.

"Sorry, Becca," she said as she reached us. "It took me a little longer to get away from the library than expected."

"No worries," I assured her. "I just got here myself."

"What trouble are you two planning to get up to this evening?" Sawyer asked, regarding us with suspicion.

"Trouble?" Dizzy echoed with mock innocence. "When have we ever caused any trouble?"

Sawyer shook his head as he started to walk away. "Just make sure I don't have to arrest you for anything."

"Don't worry," Dizzy called to him. "Whatever we might get up to, we're too smart to get caught."

Sawyer stopped and turned to fix us with his most intimidating glare.

Dizzy and I both burst into laughter.

Judging by the way he grumbled under his breath as he stalked off, that wasn't the reaction he'd wanted.

"Any progress?" Dizzy asked as we entered the pub.

I sighed. "Not really. I talked to Chanel, but didn't get much out of her."

"I meant with you and Sawyer," Dizzy clarified, "but if you'd rather talk about murder, we can do that."

"I'd rather talk about murder. What does that say about me?"

Dizzy tucked her arm through mine as we made our way through the pub. "It says you're a scaredy-cat with a thirst for solving mysteries."

"Yes," I said as we slid into a vacant booth. "That pretty much sums me up."

Chapter Fifteen

AFTER A WAITRESS HAD taken our orders and brought us our drinks, I told Dizzy about my visit to Chanel's boutique.

"I'm sure she was downplaying her relationship with Tony," I said as I wrapped up, "and I know for sure that she lied about being at home all evening on the night Tony died, but I still don't have anything that will help me clear Cooper's name."

"You'll get there," Dizzy said before taking a sip of her daiquiri.

I let out a sigh. "I'm not so sure, Diz." I took a drink of my mango flavored mocktail. "Jessica Fletcher would be so disappointed in me. If she were actually alive."

"Jessica Fletcher will always be alive," Dizzy declared, "so long as books, DVDs, and TV reruns exist."

That brought a smile to my face. "You're right. And that's amazing."

Dizzy held up her glass and I clinked my own against it.

"Now," Dizzy said once we'd set down our drinks, "let's put our heads together and come up with a sleuthing strategy."

We hashed out our plan—a very simple one, really—as we ate our food. Basically, it consisted of Dizzy looking into the lives of Chanel and Heller Yearwood while I poked around on set to see if I could turn up any clues or find out if any of our other suspects had alibis.

As we ate and chatted, I noticed Maggie, the new props master, sitting at the bar with a couple of other crew members.

I let out a groan as I looked her way.

"What's wrong?" Dizzy asked as she stabbed her fork into her pasta.

"I want to cross suspects off our list, not add more," I said quietly.

With the pub growing busier around us, I didn't want anyone overhearing our conversation.

"Who is it we need to add?" Dizzy asked.

I tipped my head in Maggie's direction. "If we consider who benefits from Tony's death, Maggie's got to be on the list. She was Tony's assistant. Now she's got his job."

Dizzy considered that. "Do you think that promotion is worth killing for?"

"*I* don't think so, but she might," I said. "I really don't know her."

"Add her to the list and see if you can find out if she got along with Tony or if she's really ambitious."

I made a mental note to do that.

"It might help if we knew who else benefits from Tony's death," I said before taking a sip of my drink.

"Like who inherits his estate?" Dizzy asked.

I nodded.

"We should look into his private life," she decided. "Find out if he has any family members or other close relationships."

I took another sip of my drink to wash down a bite of my veggie burger. "I'll ask around tomorrow."

"And I'll see what I can find out online."

With those plans made, we returned our attention to our meals. When we'd finished eating, our red-haired waitress came to clear away our plates. Her name was Emma Ireland, and she came into True Confections about once per month to buy hazelnut truffles.

"It's awful what happened to the guy who was murdered," Emma said as she stacked our plates. "I thought they might have to stop filming the movie, but that doesn't seem to be the case."

"No," I confirmed. "The victim's assistant was able to take over as props master." I nodded in Maggie's direction. "That's her at the bar. The one with the blonde hair."

Emma looked over that way. "Oh, Maggie, right? She's got wicked aim. She was here for the darts tournament we had the other night." Emma paused with our plates in her arms. "Come to think of it, that was the night of the murder."

Dizzy perked up. "She was here that evening?"

"Sure," Emma said. "She stayed for the whole tournament. Won it, actually. If she ever challenges you to a game of darts, definitely don't take her up on it."

"We'll keep that in mind," I said.

"What time did the tournament start and finish?" Dizzy asked like a sleuthing pro.

"Same as usual," Emma replied. "It started at seven and ended around ten." She smiled. "Would you like anything for dessert?"

We declined, and Emma hurried off with our plates.

"There you go," Dizzy said to me. "Maggie's got an alibi so you don't have to add her name to our list after all."

"I might do so anyway," I said. "Just so I can have the satisfaction of crossing it off."

· · • • · • • · · ·

I HAD TO REPORT to hair and makeup at six o'clock the next morning and I knew I had a long day ahead of me. I had several scenes to film, but there would also be long stretches of waiting around. Although determined to make the most of those spells of downtime, I didn't have much luck at first. I asked a few discreet questions about Tony and any family he might have, but nobody I spoke to knew anything about his private life apart from his marriage to Felicia and their subsequent divorce. Felicia probably knew something about his family, but I didn't have a chance to talk to her privately.

Fortunately, I got to chat with Cooper while we ate some lunch. The craft services truck was parked near Venice Avenue again, since the day's scenes would be filmed inside and outside the bakery-turned-temporary-flower-shop and on one of the picturesque stone bridges not far from the row of colorful timber-frame shops that lined the canal.

Geneva joined us for the first part of our meal, but then she took a walk as she made some phone calls. Once she was out of earshot, I shifted my chair closer to Cooper's.

"There's something I forgot to ask you about yesterday," I said in a low voice, so no one else would hear. A few other cast and crew members were grabbing a bite to eat, but everyone was spread out, giving us some privacy. "What can you tell me about Felicia's relationship with Alex Skye?"

"Not much," Cooper replied. "They've worked together before, so they might be friends, or at least friendly acquaintances. Why?"

Keeping my voice quiet, I told him how I'd seen the two of them having what appeared to be a furtive conversation.

"And you think that might have something to do with the murder?" Cooper asked.

"I really don't know," I admitted. "But anything even remotely suspicious is catching my attention these days."

"You and Geneva both," Cooper said with a note of exasperation in his voice.

"Everything okay with her?" I asked.

"Sure." Cooper leaned back in his chair as he watched Geneva wander along the canal, her phone to her ear. "She suspects everyone, except me, of killing Tony, and she's worried I'll be the next victim, for some reason. She wants to know my every movement. Doesn't want me to be alone, unless I'm in my hotel room." He let out a sigh. "She means well, though, and Wes will be back in a couple of weeks.

I patted his arm. "Maybe it's not such a bad idea to have someone looking out for you while there's a murderer on the loose."

Cooper's eyebrows drew together. "Do you think the killer might strike again?"

I suppressed a shudder at the thought. "I hope not, but when we don't know the motive for the murder, it's hard to be sure."

"Now I'll be looking for booby traps everywhere."

I winced. "Me too. For some reason it didn't occur to me to be worried before."

"Tony wasn't exactly skilled at making friends, so I bet we're fine. Most likely, he was the killer's one and only target."

"You're probably right," I said, but I couldn't help thinking that if the killer found out about us trying to solve the crime in order to clear Cooper's name, we might end up with targets on our backs. "It might be best not to talk to anyone about the murder, though. Except the police, of course, if they have questions for you."

"Thankfully, they've left me alone since that last interrogation. Maybe that means they're focused on other suspects."

"Hopefully."

As I finished off the last bite of my lunch, I spotted Sonja at the catering truck, getting a plate of food.

I nudged Cooper's arm. "Hey, tell me you didn't have hot water in your hotel room last night."

He stopped with a fork full of food halfway to his mouth. "Huh? I had hot water."

"But just tell me you didn't."

"I'm confused, Becca."

I spoke in a whisper. "I need to get some information out of Sonja and I'll feel better if I—technically at least—don't have to lie."

"Okay, I get it," Cooper said, catching on. "Becca, I didn't have hot water in my hotel room last night."

I smiled and patted him on the shoulder as I got up from my chair. "Thank you."

I left him to finish his lunch and disposed of my paper plate and wooden fork before joining Sonja at the craft services truck.

By the time I'd requested a cup of chai tea, Maggie had joined Sonja and I at the serving window.

When I had my takeout cup of tea in hand, I tried to strike up a conversation with Sonja, one I hoped wouldn't sound like I was fishing for information in relation to the murder.

"I hope you didn't get an icy shock last night," I said to Sonja as she stepped away from the catering truck with a drink in one hand and a plate of food in the other.

"What do you mean?" she asked, confused.

"Cooper told me he didn't have hot water in his hotel room last night," I explained. "It's not nice to find that out when you go to take a shower."

"I had hot water last night," Maggie said as she accepted a plate of food from the caterer. "At least I did whenever I turned on the water."

"Maybe it was just Cooper's room then." I inhaled the aroma of my hot tea, hoping the conversation wouldn't turn out to be a waste of time.

Sonja shrugged. "I wouldn't know. I shower in the mornings, and there was hot water when I got up today."

"That's good," I said with a smile. "I wouldn't want you thinking that Larch Haven isn't up to snuff."

Sonja shook her head, adamant. "No way. This town is the cutest."

"Right?" Maggie said.

The two women walked off together, chatting about work.

I watched them go, my thoughts spinning.

Since Sonja—a self-proclaimed light sleeper—showered in the mornings, she wasn't taking a shower when Cooper knocked on her door on the night of Tony's murder. That meant she likely wasn't in her hotel room.

And if she wasn't in her room, where was she?

Chapter Sixteen

BY THE TIME I was done on set that evening, exhaustion made my limbs feel heavy. Fortunately, my commute home consisted of only a few minutes of walking. Not so fortunately, an unpleasant sight greeted me when I reached my cottage.

A small piece of paper stood out like a beacon on my front door. I glanced around, but there was no one in sight. Dread slowed my steps, but then a rush of anger took over and I stormed the last few paces up my front path and ripped the note from the door.

As with the one I'd found on my trailer, this note had a short, scrawled message on it.

You're nothing but a has-been.

I crumpled the paper in my fist and unlocked the door. Once inside, I dropped the note on the hall table, smoothed it out, and took a quick photo, which I then sent to Dizzy. With that done, I vowed to forget about the note and Daniela's nastiness. I took some deep breaths, releasing my anger as I exhaled. As my irritation dwindled, my exhaustion returned.

I kicked off my shoes and then read an incoming text message from Dizzy.

Another one? You should tell Sawyer.

I know it's Daniela, I wrote back. *No point bothering Sawyer.*

Please tell him.

I sighed, but gave in.

I composed a short text message for Sawyer, telling him about the notes and the fact that I felt certain Daniela was the author. Then I sent him the photo I'd taken of the most recent message. That seemed to appease Dizzy.

After greeting my cats and feeding them dinner, I eyed my couch with longing, but I resisted the temptation to lie down. If I did that, I'd fall asleep within seconds, and I'd probably wake up in the middle of the night with my stomach complaining about the fact that I hadn't eaten any dinner.

I didn't have the energy or motivation to cook, so I hopped in my whisper boat and traveled the short distance to The Gondolier on Giethoorn Avenue. With the sun sinking behind the mountains to the west, the light spilling out of the restaurant's windows looked warm and inviting.

When I entered The Gondolier, I noticed that the place was about two-thirds full and I saw several familiar faces among the diners. Most of them were locals, but a couple of them were actors with minor speaking roles in *Love on the Canal.*

Three middle-aged women sat at the bar, but all the other stools were vacant. I nodded at Natasha, the hostess, and crossed the dining room to sit on the stool farthest from the other women at the bar.

"Hey, Becca," Trevor, the bartender, greeted. "Are you here to eat or to see your brother?"

"Eat," I said as my stomach rumbled.

The short trip along the canal had banished some of my sleepiness and, now that I felt more alert, I was hungrier than ever.

Trevor grinned. "What'll it be?"

"Whatever Gareth wants to give me."

Trevor nodded and disappeared into the back. He returned a minute later.

"It won't be long," he said before moving down the bar to check on the women sitting at the other end.

They chatted with Trevor for a minute before paying their bills and heading for the door.

Blake emerged from the back and said a quiet word to Trevor before coming over my way, the bar between us.

"Hey, Becca," he said. "How's filming going?"

"Great," I said with a smile. "But it's left me with an appetite."

"Gareth's putting together a tofu yaki udon bowl for you."

My stomach gave a fierce rumble and my mouth watered. "Yum."

"How about a drink while you wait?"

I accepted the offer and Blake poured me a glass of sparkling water flavored with passion fruit. He stayed and chatted with me for a couple of minutes and then disappeared into the kitchen, reappearing soon after with my yaki udon.

I inhaled the delicious aroma as Blake set my dinner in front of me. Then I dug in.

Blake left me alone so he could check on the other diners and attend to tasks in the office. I focused solely on eating, my stomach practically sighing with happiness now that it was getting food.

After I'd eaten a few bites, I slowed down, wanting to savor the delicious meal. I paused to take a drink of my sparkling water and when I set the glass down on the coaster again, someone slid onto the stool next to me.

"Hey, Becca," Trish Abernathy greeted.

Trish worked at the Larch Haven Hotel and had done so for years. She'd climbed her way up the employment ladder and now held the position of guest services manager. She was a few years older than me and she had long hair that was naturally light brown but had been dyed dark auburn.

"Hey," I returned. "I haven't seen you for ages. How are things?"

"Good. Well, except for the fact that one of our guests got killed," she amended. "That's really creepy and sad. He worked on the film, right? Did you know him?"

"Not well," I said. "I saw him around on set, but we didn't really interact."

"It's scary. I hope the cops catch the killer soon."

Trevor came over our way then. "What can I get for you, Trish?"

She glanced at my dinner. "Can I get what Becca has? But to go?"

"You got it. Anything to drink?"

"Well, if you're going to twist my arm," Trish said with a smile, "maybe a strawberry shake."

Trevor grinned. "Water while you wait?"

"Sure, thanks."

Trevor got her a glass of ice water and then relayed her order to the kitchen.

"Did the police seal off Tony's room as part of their investigation?" I asked once Trish and I were alone again.

"Yep." She took a sip of water. "They were in there for ages the morning after the murder. Searched the place and took a bunch of stuff with them. I thought maybe they were done with it, but then I heard they're keeping it sealed off for a while longer."

"Any idea what they took from the room?" I asked.

Trish shrugged. "No idea. Why do you think the guy was killed?"

"I'm not sure." I didn't add that I had several suspects and motives in mind.

Trish asked me about my role in the film and we chatted about my work on *Love on the Canal* until Trevor brought out her food. She paid him and then slipped off her stool.

"See you, Becca," she said as she left.

I called out a goodbye and then returned my full focus to eating. It wasn't until I was nearly finished my dinner that my attention strayed again. My phone, which I'd placed on the bar upon my arrival, vibrated, alerting me to the fact that Dizzy had sent me a text message.

I read the message as I finished off my yaki udon. Dizzy hadn't had a chance to do any research on the Yearwoods until she'd arrived home from work that evening. Since then, however, she'd scoured Heller's and Chanel's social media profiles.

Check this out, one of her messages read.

She followed it up with a screenshot of one of Heller's social media pages. The previous fall, Heller had posted a photo of himself with three other men. They had packed bags at their feet and stood on a dock, with a small floatplane behind them. A quick read of the caption Heller had written revealed that the men were heading off on a hunting trip.

I couldn't figure out the significance of the post until another message from Dizzy arrived on my phone.

Read the comments, her message said.

I returned to the screenshot and zoomed in on the comments below the photo. Nothing jumped out at me as significant until I reached the final comment.

Remember all the time we used to spend hanging out in the woods? Your traps were epic, man.

Traps? I wrote back to Dizzy, my dinner temporarily forgotten in front of me. *As in booby traps?*

Could be, right? Dizzy wrote.

Definitely, I texted back.

I didn't find anything useful about Chanel, Dizzy added. *And no mention of going on a trip on her profile or on Heller's.*

I praised Dizzy's online detective work and she told me she would pass the screenshot on to Sawyer.

I'd just returned my attention to my dinner when my brother appeared behind the bar, wearing his chef's coat.

"Wow. A visit from the chef himself," I said. "To what do I owe this honor?"

"I just wanted to see how you like your yaki udon."

"Really?" I asked, skeptical. "With all these diners still here, you ventured out of the kitchen to ask me that? You already know I love it." This wasn't the first time he'd cooked the dish for me.

He rested his forearms on the bar and leaned in closer to me, lowering his voice. "Okay, so maybe there's another reason."

I waited with a hint of apprehension.

He glanced around, as if making sure no one was close by. "I've been hearing things."

"Maybe you should get that checked out," I said, unable to keep the cheeky response to myself.

Gareth sent me a withering look. "I meant around town."

"Let me guess," I said with a sigh. "You heard something about me and Cooper."

"Is it true?"

"That I'm having a fling with him so I can mooch off him?"

Gareth's hazel eyes darkened. "You're not a moocher."

"No, I'm not, but that's what the Gossip Grannies and Daniela Roumeliotis are spreading around town."

"Those ladies need to learn to mind their own business."

"Never going to happen." I picked up my fork and stabbed a noodle. "So what, exactly, did you hear?"

"That you and Cooper are an item and you're thinking of moving back to California."

"That's just a kinder version of the same rumor. And it's not true," I added for clarity.

"Glad to hear it."

"Why?" I smiled. "Because you'd miss me if I moved away again?"

Gareth's face remained serious. "Because I've also heard that Cooper's been having some troubles, of the drug and alcohol variety."

My smile and good humor slipped away. "Again, untrue. You don't need to check up on who I'm dating. Or not dating. I can make good decisions all on my own."

"I know that," Gareth said. "You're smart and level headed, and not one to be blinded by good looks."

"Did you just compliment me?" I asked. "I should have recorded that for posterity."

His eyes narrowed. "Very funny."

"Are you done grilling me?" I twirled a thick noodle around my fork. "Because I'd prefer you do that to some meat in the kitchen."

He kept his forearms resting on the bar. "I'm not evil, you know. I just want to make sure you have all the facts so you don't get blindsided."

"I know you're not evil," I conceded. "You're just a big brother. And those aren't always the same thing."

"Wow." Gareth straightened up. "Now who's being generous with the compliments?"

I smiled and started eating again.

My brother took a step back from the bar. "I need to get back to the kitchen."

"Hey, Gareth," I said before he could walk away. I used my fork to point at my bowl. "It's delicious."

That brought a hint of a grin to his face as he turned for the kitchen.

Gareth and I liked to tease and needle each other, and sometimes he was a bit overprotective, but I knew he wanted what was best for me and it was nice to have someone looking out for me.

I wasn't so appreciative of the rumors, though. Maybe I needed to talk to Lolly and Pops. I didn't want them thinking I was getting ready to move back to California.

After making a mental note to visit my grandparents the next day, I refocused on my meal. I was just finishing up when two new diners arrived at the restaurant. I twisted around on my barstool to watch as Heller and Chanel followed the hostess to a free table.

As I started to turn back to the bar, I did a double take.

Chanel wore a black-and-white silk scarf around her neck.

On the night of the murder, I'd caught only a glimpse of the scrap of fabric that had snagged on the corner of the props trailer, but Chanel's scarf looked similar to what I'd seen.

As she walked past me, my heart rate ticked up.

Her scarf was torn along one edge.

Chapter Seventeen

BEFORE LEAVING THE GONDOLIER, I texted Sawyer about Chanel's scarf and the fact that I thought it was a match for the fabric found at the scene of the murder. I kept my phone in my pocket as I navigated the canals in my whisper boat, even though I wanted to check it for a response. As eager as I was to get a text message back from Sawyer, I didn't want to crash into the bank and end up in the water. Here and there, old-fashioned lampposts shed light on the canals and the walkways, but in the dark areas I had only the light on the bow of my boat to illuminate the path ahead of me, so I needed to keep my wits about me.

Once I'd arrived home safely, I pulled my phone from my pocket, only to feel a pang of disappointment.

Sawyer hadn't texted me back.

I considered phoning him, but decided against the idea.

Maybe he was working late, or maybe he'd gone to bed early. Either way, I decided not to bug him until the next day. Besides, if I called him and he answered, he'd probably lecture me about staying out of the murder investigation. I was fine with leaving that part of the conversation until morning.

Spotting Chanel's torn scarf, and realizing the potential implications, had left me wide awake. Instead of heading straight to bed, where I probably would have tossed and turned, I stayed up for another hour, finally writing on paper the suspect list that Dizzy, Cooper, and I had come up with. Next to the Yearwoods' names,

I added the information Dizzy had found on Heller's social media page. I also made a note about Chanel's scarf.

Binx and Truffles kept me company on the couch as I wrote, snoozing away.

When I shut my notebook, I yawned, my earlier sleepiness making a comeback.

I headed up to bed, my cats following on my heels. Fortunately, I drifted off to sleep without too much trouble and woke up feeling mostly refreshed the next morning.

I knew that Lolly would be at True Confections early, and I had some time to spare before I had to be on set, so I stopped by the shop and made sure that my grandmother knew the truth about me and Cooper and where I intended to live in the future. She hadn't yet heard the rumors started by the Gossip Grannies, but I had no doubt that she would soon. At least now she'd know that they were nothing more than rumors. She promised to fill Pops in and I left the shop feeling better about the situation.

Three hours later, I'd finished filming my first scene of the day. Felicia and I had walked through the local park for the scene, talking about the upcoming flower festival our characters were involved with, as well as our respective love interests. What I enjoyed the most was the fact that Angie and Milo were there as background performers. Angie even got to walk right past Felicia and me at one point. I hoped that both Angela and Milo would both be visible in the final cut.

After that scene, I had a break stretching ahead of me. I had a bite to eat and then wandered along the canal near the southern edge of the park. When I returned to the holding area, I found Angie and Milo chatting with some of the other background performers. Angie spotted me and excused herself from the group, rushing over my way.

"This is so much fun, Becca!" she enthused. "I know I'm just in the background, but it's cool to be right in the middle of the production and see how everything works."

"Careful," I teased. "Next thing you know, you'll be running off to Hollywood."

She laughed. "Not likely, but I'm going to enjoy this as much as possible for as long as it lasts."

I gave her a hug. "I'm glad you're having a great time. It's exciting for me to have you and Milo in the film." I glanced around at the other extras who were mingling in the shade of a cherry tree. "Is Chanel Yearwood working here today?"

"She was supposed to be, but she couldn't make it," Angie said. "I overheard a couple of people talking about it. Something came up last minute, apparently."

Angie was needed for the next scene, so she excused herself and hurried off.

I found a vacant chair and sank into it, watching the next scene unfold before me without really seeing what was happening. Maybe what had prevented Chanel from being on set was a trip to the police station.

I'd left my phone in my trailer earlier so I couldn't look at it right then. When I'd last checked it, I'd found a brief message from Sawyer thanking me for the information I'd sent, but he hadn't said anything more.

I was itching to text him again and ask if he or his colleagues were interrogating Chanel. Maybe it was for the best that I didn't have my phone on me. I didn't want to be a nuisance to Sawyer—or at least not more than I already was—and he likely wouldn't answer the question anyway.

Fortunately, I didn't have much time to speculate about Chanel and her whereabouts, because I had another scene to film in the park. Then, for the afternoon, the production moved to a new location, outside The Oar and Anchor on Giethoorn Avenue. I filmed a brief scene there with Diego and Felicia, and then I was done for the day. A golf cart driven by a production assistant carried me to my trailer, where I changed back into my own clothes before returning my day's outfit to the wardrobe department.

I was craving a bubble tea and some time with my bestie, but I knew Dizzy had to work for another half hour. I was contemplating what I should do in the meantime when I spotted Geneva standing near the end of the hair and makeup trailer. She had her back pressed up against the exterior wall of the trailer and was leaning slightly toward the far corner, as if she were trying to peer around it.

There was something decidedly furtive about her behavior and that kicked my curiosity into high gear. I walked toward her, trying to move quietly while not looking like I was sneaking up on her. I figured she was spying on someone, and I wanted to know that person's identity, but when I got within fifteen feet of Geneva, I accidentally kicked a pebble and it skittered across the pavement.

Geneva jumped and whipped her head my way. She pressed a hand to her chest, over her heart, and took hurried steps in my direction. "Becca! You startled me!"

I silently cursed the fact that she now stood between me and the far end of the trailer, so I had no chance of seeing who might be around the corner. Not without being obvious about it, anyway.

"What are you up to?" I asked, keeping any suspicion out of my voice.

"Nothing," she said quickly. "Excuse me. I've got a phone call I need to make."

She brushed past me and rushed off.

More curious than ever, I quietly made my way along the trailer until I reached the corner where Geneva had been stationed. A murmur of voices met my ears.

I peeked around the corner and then pulled back.

Felicia and Alex stood about ten feet away, deep in conversation.

Pulling out my phone to pretend I was sending a text message, I hovered near the corner and strained to hear what Felicia and Alex were saying. My pulse sped up when Alex spoke.

"I can't take the guilt," he said, sounding tortured. "I wish I'd never done it."

"We can't turn back time." A current of worry ran through Felicia's words.

"No," Alex agreed, "but maybe I can at least ease my conscience."

"I don't want my career to be over," Felicia said with desperation. "Please, Alex."

I chanced another peek around the corner. Alex put an arm around Felicia and gave her a squeeze.

"I'd never throw you under the bus, Felicia," he said. "Whatever I decide to do, you won't be implicated in any way."

They walked off and the rest of their conversation was too quiet for me to hear.

I tucked my phone into my pocket, questions swirling around in my head.

What did Alex feel so guilty about? Killing Tony?

And how was Felicia involved in what he'd done?

Had they set up the booby trap together?

I didn't want either one of them to be guilty, but I couldn't ignore what I'd heard.

I pulled out my phone again and sent separate text messages to Dizzy and Cooper, letting them know I needed to talk to them. Cooper had already wrapped for the day and texted back to say he was at the hotel. Dizzy would be finished working at the library shortly, so we agreed to meet at Cooper's hotel room in half an hour. On the way, I stopped at the local tea shop to pick up drinks for all of us. Cooper had never tried bubble tea before and I had informed him that I was determined to change that.

He told me to surprise him flavor-wise, so I ordered him a brown sugar milk tea with pearls. I added a taro slush with pearls for myself and a lychee oolong tea with lychee jelly for Dizzy. With the three drinks safely held in a cardboard tray, I carried them toward the Larch Haven Hotel, running into Dizzy as I left Venice Avenue for Amsterdam Avenue.

She took her drink from me with thanks and sipped at it as we walked.

"I'm dying to know what new information you have," she said between sips.

"Not that I'm trying to keep you in suspense, but I might as well tell you and Cooper at the same time."

"Fair enough," she conceded, "but let's move faster then."

We picked up our pace and reached the hotel within minutes.

"Cooper's room is on the second floor," I said as I led Dizzy toward the staircase.

Fortunately, no security guard stood in our way.

When we passed the suit of armor on the landing, I remembered Tony showing an interest in the relic. A wave of sadness hit me as we continued climbing the stairs. Tony might not have been the nicest guy, but that didn't mean he deserved to be murdered, and if he had family or other loved ones, his death was no doubt difficult for them.

The sooner the killer was caught, the sooner his family could have closure. Not to mention the fact that Cooper would no longer have to worry about being under suspicion.

Dizzy and I reached the second floor and started along the hallway. Ahead of us, a door on our left opened a crack and then slowly eased open another inch or two. I drew to a stop and put out an arm to keep Dizzy from moving farther forward. I pressed a finger to my lips and then pointed at the door. We pressed ourselves closer to the lefthand wall as the door opened a little more. Staying close to the wall, I crept along the carpeted hallway.

As a nose emerged from the room, I picked up my pace, eager to see who was being so stealthy.

I nearly crashed into Chanel Yearwood as she poked her head out into the hall.

Her eyes widened when she saw me. She jerked back into the room, but then realized Dizzy and I had already got a good look at her. Her eyes darted left and right. Then she forced a smile and gave a brittle, high-pitched laugh.

"You two startled me," she said quickly. "I was just here visiting a friend."

She tried to dart past us, but then the next door down opened and Cooper stepped out into the hall. He frowned when he saw Chanel closing the door behind her.

"Hey," he said to her. "What were you doing in Tony's room?"

Chapter Eighteen

CHANEL'S DEMEANOR CHANGED IN a flash.

"It's none of your business what I'm doing here," she snapped at Cooper.

"You were in a murder victim's room," Dizzy pointed out.

Chanel's face flushed. "It's not Tony's room anymore." She shoved the door open wide so we could see the room. "All his stuff has been cleared out and there's no crime scene tape sealing it off. It's just a hotel room. And, like I said, I was here visiting a friend."

She shut the door and marched off down the hallway.

"An invisible friend?" Dizzy asked as Chanel disappeared down the staircase. "Because it didn't look like anyone was in there."

Still frowning, Cooper knocked on the door Chanel had closed. He got no response. He knocked again, with the same result.

"Dizzy's right," he said. "There's no one in there."

"What do you think we should do?" Dizzy asked. "She was up to something shifty."

"We'd better talk to someone on the hotel staff," I said. "If the room has been given to someone else, maybe that person gave Chanel a key to meet them here but then didn't show up as planned."

"Good idea," Dizzy agreed. "I guess if she's having an affair or something, it's really none of our business."

"And if the room hasn't been assigned to another guest since Tony died?" Cooper wondered as we turned for the staircase.

"Then the police should know she was in there," I said.

By the time we reached the lobby, Chanel was nowhere in sight. She'd probably hightailed it out of the hotel as soon as she got down the stairs.

I recognized the hotel employee behind the reception desk as Ellen Smart, a fortysomething woman who was friends with Angela. She wasn't busy at the moment, so the three of us approached and quickly told her about what we'd witnessed.

Ellen's forehead furrowed with concern as she listened. "There shouldn't have been anyone in that room," she said when we'd filled her in. She reached for the phone. "I'd better contact the police."

She made the call and Dizzy, Cooper, and I waited in the lobby's sitting area for the police to arrive. Cooper took a cautious first sip of his bubble tea and quickly declared that we'd successfully converted him. Since there was no one else close by, I spoke in whispers, filling my friends in on what I'd seen and heard by the trailers earlier.

"Geneva was eavesdropping?" Cooper asked when I'd finished.

"It sure seemed like it," I said. "But I can't exactly criticize her for it when I did the exact same thing."

Dizzy nudged Cooper's arm. "Geneva's what you're worried about? Felicia and Alex practically confessed to killing Tony!"

"Not quite," I cautioned.

"They're guilty of something," Dizzy insisted.

"I agree with you there," I said.

Cooper had fallen quiet, his blue eyes troubled and distant.

"What are you thinking?" I asked him.

He blinked and seemed to come back to the present. "I hate the thought of Felicia and Alex being involved in Tony's death. I like both of them and I have to kiss Felicia in a few days. I'd like to think I'm a good actor, but kissing a killer and pretending I'm in love with her? I'm not sure I can handle that."

"I don't blame you," Dizzy said.

I rested a hand on Cooper's back. "Hopefully by that time we'll know who killed Tony and whether or not Felicia was involved."

Officer Nyberg arrived at the hotel then, so we filled him in on what we'd witnessed on the second floor. He thanked us and moved on to speak with Ellen. I considered telling Nyberg about Felicia and Alex's conversation, but decided I'd rather talk it over with Sawyer instead. Hopefully I'd have a chance to do that before long.

Since I'd already shared with my friends what I wanted to tell them, Dizzy and I decided to head home.

"Hey, Dizzy," Cooper said before we made it to the door. "We should exchange numbers so we can have that paranormal chat while I'm in town."

"Okay," Dizzy said with mild surprise. "We can do that."

I chewed on some tapioca pearls from my bubble tea while they exchanged phone numbers.

"Let's get together soon," Cooper suggested as he handed Dizzy's phone back to her.

She tucked the device into her pocket. "Sure. Let me know your schedule and I'll see how it works with mine."

Cooper walked us to the door, where we shared some parting words.

Dizzy and I continued to enjoy our drinks as we wandered away from the hotel, following a route that would take us to Dizzy's apartment above Hooked on Books. I'd decided to accompany her home before returning to my cottage so I could get a longer walk in before I turned in for the night.

"So," I said as we headed south along Amsterdam Avenue, "you and Cooper."

Dizzy glanced at me out of the corner of her eye before taking a long sip of her drink. "There is no me and Cooper."

"I'm pretty sure he'd like there to be."

Dizzy squished her lips to one side before taking another drink of her bubble tea.

"What's wrong?" I asked. "You don't want to meet up with him?"

"I'll meet up with him. I think it'll be fun. But it'll just be two new friends chatting about a shared interest."

"So, not a date?"

"Not a date," she confirmed. "Cooper lives in California and you know I don't want to leave Larch Haven."

"I know. And I'm glad you don't want to move," I confessed. "I couldn't blame you if you did, of course, since I went off for several years, but I didn't like having all those miles between us."

Dizzy smiled. "Same. I'm really happy you had so much success in Hollywood, but I'm also happy to have you back."

I tucked my arm through hers. "A non-date is perfectly fine. Cooper's a good friend and I'm glad you have a chance to get to know him. And if he's easy on the eyes, that's just a bonus, right?"

Dizzy laughed. "A very nice bonus."

We left the conversation at that and chatted about other subjects for the remainder of our journey to Dizzy's apartment. After saying good night to her, I retraced my steps to the corner of Amsterdam Avenue and Venice Avenue, and then struck a path over a bridge and toward my cottage.

Although everything that I'd heard and witnessed over the past several hours whirled around in my head, I managed to fall asleep not long after arriving home. In the morning, I discovered I'd received text messages from Sawyer after I fell asleep. He wanted to see the physical copies of the notes I'd found. I dug through my laundry hamper until I found the first note tucked away in the pocket of a pair of jeans.

I assured Sawyer that he could have the notes, even though I didn't think they were worth keeping. Then I let him know that I had something else to share with him and asked if we could get together sometime before the day's end. He responded within minutes, saying that he was scheduled to get off work at seven o'clock that evening. After more texting back and forth, we decided I'd meet him at his place shortly after he finished work.

"I'll probably get a lecture," I said to Truffles as I held her in my arms, "but I can't *not* tell him what I overheard."

Truffles purred and rubbed her furry cheek against my chin.

Binx meowed at me from the windowsill.

"Yes, I am talking about Sawyer," I said as I set Truffles down on the floor.

Binx meowed again, louder this time.

"No, he's not coming over here. Not for this visit, anyway."

Binx let out a small mew of disappointment. At least that's what it sounded like to me.

I ran a hand over his sleek, black fur. "Sorry, buddy. I'll make sure he comes to see you soon."

With that promise made, I decided it was time to get on with my day.

As I approached the hair and makeup trailer a short while later, my steps faltered. Like Cooper, I hated the thought of Alex being guilty of murder. I hadn't known him long, but I liked him, and he'd struck me as a good person. Yet, I couldn't ignore what I'd heard, and I had a terrible feeling that his sense of guilt was connected to Tony's murder.

Knowing I had a schedule to keep to, I forced myself to enter the trailer and pretend that nothing was bothering me. I expected Alex to exhibit signs of the guilt tormenting him and to sport dark rings under his eyes like he had each day since Tony's death. Instead, he greeted me with a smile and a cheery hello, looking well rested and at ease.

I hid my surprise and chatted with him about mundane topics as he styled my hair into a fishtail braid. Michaela and Diego joined us in the trailer minutes later and I found myself smiling with them as we talked about past productions we'd worked on and friends and acquaintances we had in common.

Later that morning, I filmed a scene with Felicia and chatted with her between takes. I asked her about Tony's family and she said that he was an only child. After that, she changed the subject. Although I scrutinized her expression when she wasn't looking my way, I couldn't spot any signs of the anxiety she'd displayed during her conversation with Alex the day before. I didn't know if that was because she, like Alex, had apparently banished those worries, or if she was simply putting her acting skills to use both on and off camera.

I had only two scenes to film that day and didn't have to stay on set past noon. After a quick trip home for a bite to eat and to wash off my makeup, I paid a visit to True Confections.

A bright smile appeared on my face when I opened the door of the shop and spotted Angela and Pops inside. Angie was ringing up purchases for a customer and my grandfather was straightening boxes of chocolates on the shelves.

I greeted him with a kiss on the cheek. "Hi, Pops. No bowling today?"

My grandfather and several of his friends typically met up at the bowling alley in Snowflake Canyon two or three times a week. I suspected they did as much laughing and reminiscing about the old days as they did bowling.

"I'll be back to knocking pins down tomorrow," he said, kissing the top of my head. "Today is all about family."

"Speaking of which," I said, edging toward the kitchen. "Is Lolly in the back?"

"Doing her magic," Pops confirmed.

I poked my head into the kitchen and found Lolly filling boxes with truffles and caramels.

"Let me help you with that." I grabbed a clean apron from a hook on the wall.

"Not filming today?" my grandmother asked as I kissed her cheek on my way to the sink so I could wash my hands.

"Just this morning," I replied.

"I saw Daniela Roumeliotis yesterday," Lolly said as she continued to fill boxes.

"I ran into her a few days ago." I joined my grandmother at the spacious counter and grabbed an empty box. "She doesn't seem to have changed, unfortunately."

"That's too bad." Lolly placed a lid on the box in front of her. "She wasn't exactly the kindest child."

"That's putting it mildly." I placed a salted caramel in the last vacant spot in the box I was working on. "Do you think she's here to stay?"

"I asked her that when I spoke to her, but she was vague about her plans. She told me she's exploring her options."

"Who are we talking about?" Angela asked as she breezed into the kitchen.

"Daniela Roumeliotis," I replied.

"You need to watch out for that one," Angie cautioned. "She's been helping the Gossip Grannies spread those rumors about you and Cooper."

I rolled my eyes. "Next thing you know, she'll be sharing those rumors online."

"I wouldn't put it past her," Angie agreed. "But there's something I wanted to tell you, Becca, and it has nothing to do with Daniela."

"I'm all ears," I said as I started filling another box.

Angie's face lit up with a bright smile. "You haven't seen the last of me on sct!"

"You got booked for more days?" I asked with excitement.

My cousin did a happy dance. "At least two more! Aunt Kathleen will cover for me here at the shop again."

"I'm glad you're both having such fun with this movie," Lolly said as she placed a lid on another box.

I put an arm around her and gave her a gentle squeeze. "And I appreciate you taking over for me here so I can dip my toe back into acting."

"My pleasure, sweetheart," Lolly said with a smile. "I miss this place when I'm away from it too long."

"I know the feeling."

Angela returned to the front of the shop and I helped my grandmother fill boxes until we had enough to keep the shelves well stocked for a couple of days.

With that task taken care of, I selected some of the misfits—the chocolates not perfect enough to be sold at regular price—and placed them in a small paper bag. I made sure to include several peanut butter pretzel truffles since those were Sawyer's favorite chocolates.

I left True Confections with the intention of running a few errands before the afternoon was over, but I didn't make it past more than a few storefronts. A small crowd had gathered near the empty bakery that the production had used for the flower shop. As I drew closer to the group of people, I recognized Michaela, Maggie, and a few other crew members.

"What's going on?" I asked Michaela when I reached her side.

She pointed at some bright daffodils blooming in a half barrel outside the bakery. "Maggie just found these here. We both recognized them right away, so I called the cops. We're waiting for them to arrive."

I took a step closer to the half barrel so I could see what held everyone's attention.

My eyes widened when I got a good look.

There, lying among the daffodils, were two gold chains and a watch.

Like Michaela, I recognized them immediately.

They were the items of jewelry that had been missing from Tony's body.

Chapter Nineteen

I HOPED SAWYER WOULD respond to the call Michaela had placed to the police, but Officers McNally and Nyberg arrived on the scene instead. They placed the chains and watch into evidence bags and questioned Maggie. I listened in, but Maggie's answers didn't provide any insight into how the jewelry had ended up among the flowers.

If not for the fact that Maggie had an alibi for Tony's murder, I would have wondered if she'd committed the crime and stolen the jewelry, and then simply pretended to find it, either in an attempt to deflect suspicion or because she was afraid of getting caught with it in her possession. Thanks to what I'd learned at The Oar and Anchor, however, I knew Maggie wasn't the killer.

After the small crowd dispersed, I completed my errands with my mind in a daze. Considering my level of distraction, I was lucky I ended up leaving the grocery store with the items I actually wanted and not with random products. I made a quick stop at the pet supply store and then I returned home to spend some time with my cats before heading over to Sawyer's place.

Shortly after seven o'clock, I hopped in my whisper boat and traveled along the canals, shivering as the cool evening breeze brushed over my bare arms. I hadn't realized how much the temperature had dropped since the afternoon, so I'd left home without anything warmer than my jeans and short sleeve T-shirt. I decided against turning back, though, since it would take me mere minutes to reach my destination.

Sawyer owned a townhouse in a row of timber frame units that backed right up to the canal. Each townhouse had a back door that led out onto wide concrete steps that disappeared into the water. Many of the homeowners, including Sawyer, had a boat moored behind their unit. Sawyer spent most of his time getting around town on foot or by bicycle, but he enjoyed taking his boat out on Shadow Lake during favorable weather. I was looking forward to doing the same once my schedule calmed down and summer approached.

As I drew closer to the back of the row of townhouses, I spotted Sawyer up on his second-floor balcony, lounging in a chair with his feet up.

He waved as I drew closer and called out, "The door's unlocked!"

I waved in acknowledgment and cut the engine. My whisper boat glided toward the concrete steps and I hopped out, tying up my craft next to Sawyer's boat. I let myself into the townhouse and walked through the kitchen and living room to reach the foyer and the staircase that led up to the second floor. Upstairs, I passed through the master bedroom to reach the sliding door that opened out onto the balcony.

Sawyer had left the door open about a foot, so I squeezed through the gap and joined him outside. He had his laptop set up on a small table and was streaming a baseball game.

The balcony wasn't very spacious, so I edged behind Sawyer's chair and dropped into the one next to him.

He raised his bottle of beer in greeting. "Is the acting life still going well?"

"I'm having fun with it," I replied as I got comfortable in the chair. "And I'm staying in Larch Haven. Just in case you had any lingering doubts."

Sawyer took a sip of his beer. "No doubts, but I'm glad to hear it, nonetheless."

I met his dark gaze and nervous butterflies threatened to take flight in my chest, but then I remembered that Sawyer was *Sawyer*, my lifelong friend and someone I trusted completely. That reminder sent the butterflies back to sleep.

"Did you bring the notes?" he asked.

I fished the crumpled papers out of my pocket and handed them over. He set his bottle of beer on the arm of his chair and frowned as he read the messages.

"I'd like to file a report about these," he said.

"I really don't think that's necessary," I protested. "It's just Daniela being her typical mean self."

"Maybe, and maybe not."

"I'd be willing to bet money on it," I said. "If I officially report the notes to the police and she gets wind of it, she might get nastier."

"Or she'll get scared and stop," Sawyer countered.

"I guess that's possible," I conceded.

"Please let me do this, Becca."

I relented, mostly because of the worry in Sawyer's eyes, and quickly gave him the details of how and where I'd found each note.

Then I turned my attention to the baseball game. "Who's playing?"

"The Red Sox, of course," Sawyer replied as he tucked the notes in his pocket and picked up his bottle of beer.

"Otherwise, you wouldn't be watching."

"Exactly. They're trailing behind the Texas Rangers at the moment, but it's still early."

I nudged his sneakers with the toe of my shoe so he'd make room for my feet alongside his on the padded wicker ottoman. "I guess I'll cheer for the Rangers."

He narrowed his eyes at me. "Why would you do that?"

I gave him a sweet smile. "To annoy you."

"I can show you the door," Sawyer threatened.

I patted his arm, still smiling. "I can see it from here." I leaned back and then turned my head to look at him. "Do you want me to leave?" I asked, knowing that he was just pretending to be mad.

"No," he grumbled. "Just don't cheer for the Rangers and don't ask me about the murder investigation."

"I wasn't planning on asking about it," I assured him.

He raised an eyebrow and glanced away from the game long enough to let me see the skepticism in his eyes.

"Why is that so hard to believe?" I asked.

He laughed.

"Okay, forget I asked that question," I said. "But, really, I didn't come here to interrogate you. I came to tell you what I've learned."

"By poking your nose where it doesn't belong?" he guessed, his gaze back on the baseball game.

"I prefer to think of it as helping out a friend."

"You mean Cooper Graystone," he said. It wasn't a question.

"Sawyer, he didn't kill Tony."

"If I say I believe you, will you give up your amateur sleuthing?" he asked, not sounding very hopeful.

"*Do* you believe me?"

He sighed. "For your sake, I want to."

"That's not the same thing," I said with a mixture of disappointment and worry.

Sawyer sobered and turned his full attention on me. "Becks, I know you care about the guy, but he has a motive and I'm sure you haven't forgotten that he had a physical altercation with the victim."

"I definitely haven't forgotten, but that was way out of character for Cooper."

"So he's capable of doing things that are out of character for the version of Cooper you know."

I frowned. "Murder would be so far out of character that it would be in an entirely different universe. Besides, there are way stronger suspects. Like Chanel and Heller Yearwood, just to name two. Did you hear about Chanel sneaking around in Tony's hotel room?"

"I heard about it."

"She was probably searching for incriminating evidence to destroy."

Sawyer was shaking his head before I'd finished speaking. "We'd already searched the hotel room from top to bottom."

"Maybe she thinks you might have missed something."

"She was hoping Tony's belongings were still in the room and that we would have left behind what she was looking for after deciding it wasn't relevant to the investigation."

I perked up at that. "She told you that? Did she say what she was looking for?"

"She told Detective Ishimoto this afternoon."

"Afternoon?" I echoed. "I thought maybe she was at the police station this morning when she was supposed to be on set."

"We tried to get her to come in this morning," Sawyer said, "but she had an emergency dental appointment to deal with a sore tooth. Detective Ishimoto talked to her shortly after you reported the incident at the hotel."

"So what was she looking for?" I asked.

Sawyer gave me a sidelong glance and took a long drink of his beer.

When he rested the bottle on the arm of his chair, I took it out of his grasp and raised it to my own lips.

"Hey." He snatched the bottle back before I could take a drink. "You don't even like beer."

"True," I admitted, "but I'm thirsty."

Sawyer downed the last of his beer and got up from his chair. "I'll get you something else to drink."

I sat back in my chair as he disappeared into the house. I heard the doorbell ring, followed by a quiet murmur of voices. A minute or two later, Sawyer reappeared in the bedroom and came out onto the balcony, carrying a pizza box with another bottle of beer and a can of soda balanced on top.

I dropped my feet off the stool so he could set down the pizza box.

"Ginger ale okay?" Sawyer asked, handing me the soda.

"Perfect. Thanks."

He sat down and opened his bottle of beer before raising the lid of the pizza box. "Dig in."

I was surprised to see that the pizza was half pepperoni and half vegetarian.

"You ordered some for me?" I asked, surprised.

"I figured you might be hungry."

My stomach rumbled at the sight of the food. "You figured right." I grabbed a slice of vegetarian pizza and took a bite. "Delicious," I declared.

The pizza had come from Aficionadoughs, Larch Haven's one and only pizza parlor. In my opinion, we didn't need another, because the food from Aficionadoughs was out of this world.

"You didn't answer my last question," I said after enjoying a couple of bites. "Did Chanel say what she was looking for?"

Sawyer devoured half of his slice of pizza before speaking. "I thought you weren't here to interrogate me."

I groaned. "I did say that, didn't I?"

He grinned before making short work of the rest of his pizza slice.

"But I really want to know." I popped open the can of ginger ale and took a sip of the fizzy liquid. I stared at the computer screen without really seeing the game playing out before me. I wrestled with my curiosity, trying to get it to surrender and disappear, but without success.

Eventually, Sawyer took pity on me. "I can tell you that Chanel was looking for a necklace. A family heirloom."

"From her family or Tony's?"

"Hers."

"Why would Tony have her necklace?" I asked.

Sawyer reached for another slice of pizza. "Apparently, he admired it when they were on set and told her that he wanted to make a copy of it. Something about how it would make a perfect prop for the film he was going to be working on next month. Chanel liked the idea of a replica of her great-grandmother's necklace being in a movie, so she loaned the original to him."

"But he died before returning it," I guessed. If he really intended to return it. After everything I'd heard about Tony, I wouldn't have been surprised if he'd planned to keep the original and claim that Chanel had given it to him as a gift.

"That's her story," Sawyer said.

"Do you believe it?"

He washed down a bite of pizza with a swig of beer before replying. "I wasn't present when she was questioned, but Detective Ishimoto thinks she's telling the truth. Anyway, Chanel Yearwood didn't kill Tony Fleet."

"You sound so sure."

"She and her husband have solid alibis."

"Really?" I said with surprise. "Heller too?"

Sawyer nodded. "Cast-iron."

"But how is that possible? I saw Chanel at the Larch Haven Hotel that night, so she was clearly out and about. And she didn't stay at the hotel very long."

"No, but up until ten minutes before she arrived at the hotel, she was having dinner with a friend at your brother's restaurant, and she arrived home ten minutes after she left the hotel. Her neighbor saw her coming home and invited her over for cocktails. Chanel stayed there until after Tony was found."

"So you're saying she didn't have the opportunity to set up the booby trap."

"That's exactly what I'm saying. It would have taken a while to rig the thing up. And Heller was at the bowling alley in Snowflake Canyon all evening. Multiple witnesses confirmed that."

"But Heller was so eager to leave town," I said.

"He booked a Caribbean cruise to surprise his wife. He realized that his marriage was on the rocks and wants to save it. He's hoping that taking Chanel on vacation will help."

"But a piece of Chanel's scarf was at the murder scene," I reminded him.

"She says it must have snagged on the trailer when she met Tony there to give him the necklace. That was during the morning on the day he died."

My shoulders sagged. "So much for those two suspects." I felt a renewed sense of hope when I remembered why I'd arranged to meet with Sawyer in the first place. "I need to tell you what I overheard yesterday."

I proceeded to fill him in on the conversation between Felicia and Alex.

"I don't want either of them to be guilty," I said after I'd finished the story, "but there's something going on there."

I looked at Sawyer, trying to gauge his reaction. He had his gaze fixed on the ballgame, but I could tell he was thinking as he watched.

"Felicia is definitely a suspect," he said finally. "What did you say the hairstylist's last name was?"

"Skye."

Sawyer nodded. "Now I know who you're talking about. He was questioned initially, along with all the other cast and crew, but we haven't looked at him as a suspect yet. That will have to change."

I tried to tamp down the spark of guilt that lit up inside of me. I didn't like putting Alex forward as a suspect, but I had to do it. Even if Cooper didn't have a cloud of suspicion hanging over him, I would have had to tell Sawyer what I'd overheard. It was potentially too important to keep to myself.

The sky had darkened during our conversation and I shivered, the evening breeze cutting through my T-shirt and leaving goosebumps along my arms.

"Hold on," Sawyer said as he jumped up from his chair and headed indoors.

I wasn't sure what had prompted his departure until he came back outside seconds later with a black, zip-up hoodie in hand. He offered it to me.

"I don't want you freezing," he said.

I accepted the hoodie gratefully. "Thank you."

As I slid my arms into the sleeves, Sawyer leaned over the balcony's railing and looked down at the water below.

"Evening, Caden," he called out.

Still in my seat, I leaned closer to the railing so I could see the gondola gliding along the canal. Caden Barnes, one of Larch Haven's professional gondoliers, stood at the stern of the otherwise empty gondola, rowing at a casual pace.

Caden raised a hand in greeting. "Watching the game?"

"You bet," Sawyer replied. "We're behind three-one."

"Ouch. Maybe I'll make it home in time to watch the final innings." Caden waved again as he continued along the canal, soon passing beneath a bridge and around a bend.

"Will you be competing in the gondola races this year?" Sawyer asked me as he settled back in his seat.

I didn't miss the teasing glint in his eyes. "Not quite."

"Don't tell me that lesson I gave you went to waste," he said.

"I wouldn't say that," I hedged. "But," I added with a flutter of nerves, "I wouldn't mind another lesson."

Sawyer's gaze met mine and I sensed he was searching my eyes for the true meaning behind my words. I hoped he found it.

"That can definitely be arranged," he said.

His gaze stayed on mine and I suddenly found it hard to breathe.

The sound of a bat connecting with a ball reached our ears, followed by a cheer.

We both looked at the computer screen.

"A two-run homer!" I exclaimed as we watched a Red Sox player jog around the bases. "Now the game is tied!"

Sawyer glanced my way. "I'm glad you're cheering for the right team now."

"Since I didn't refrain from questioning you about the investigation, it's the least I can do."

"I'll say," he agreed, earning a nudge from my elbow.

Smiling, we fell quiet as we continued to watch the game. Soon, though, my thoughts strayed back to the murder, Cooper's predicament, and whatever Felicia and Alex might be hiding.

Sawyer must have sensed my sinking mood because he turned his head my way and asked, "Are you all right?"

I let out a sigh. "I just want everything to work out okay."

From the way he looked at me, I suspected he knew I was talking about more than just the murder investigation.

My suspicions were confirmed when he placed his hand over mine and gave it a gentle squeeze.

"Everything will, Becks," he assured me. "Everything will."

I intertwined my fingers with his and neither of us made any move to break the contact.

As we sat there in the deepening darkness, watching the game together, I hoped with all my heart that he was right.

Chapter Twenty

I HAD IT FAIRLY easy the next day. I was done filming by noon and when I stopped by True Confections, Lolly assured me that she and my aunt Kathleen had taken care of all the kitchen work for the day. After a short visit with my aunt, grandmother, and cousin in the shop, I arranged to meet up with Dizzy at my place, since she had the day off from her work at the library. We were thinking of going kayaking while chatting about the status of our unofficial investigation.

On the way to my cottage, I decided to stop for a drink at Juice It Up, a shop that sold juices, smoothies, and mocktails. I almost changed my mind when I spotted Daniela and her mother sitting at an outdoor table at the café next to the juice shop. As much as I liked the drinks at Juice It Up, I was willing to bypass the place to avoid a confrontation with Daniela.

I didn't get a chance to change my path because three women and one man, all in their early twenties, approached me, smiling but also a little hesitant.

"Becca Ransom?" one of the women said. "We're huge fans of *Twilight Hills* and we can't wait to see the movie you're filming now."

"Thank you," I said with a smile that I hoped would put them at ease. "That's so nice to hear."

"Could we get your autograph?" one of the other women asked. She was already rifling through her tote bag to find something I could write on.

I happily agreed to the request and we chatted while I provided autographs and then posed for selfies with the four of them. I always found it so cool that people still wanted to talk about *Twilight Hills*, even though the final season had ended a couple of years ago.

The encounter left me with a smile on my face, but that expression quickly faded away when I saw Daniela striding toward me with a mean glint in her eyes.

"Becca, Becca, can I have your autograph?" she asked in a taunting voice.

"Knock it off, Daniela." I didn't have the patience for her attempt to ridicule me.

"You're such an attention seeker."

I struggled to keep my temper from flaring. "Jealousy doesn't look good on you, Daniela," I said, impressed by my level voice.

"Jealousy?" she scoffed. "Why would I be jealous of *you?*"

"You tell me." I shook my head. "On second thought, don't bother." I walked away, heading for Juice It Up. I decided I wasn't going to let Daniela change my plans.

"Break a leg, Becca," Daniela called after me. "For real."

I kept walking without looking back, but her parting jab didn't slip past me unnoticed. If I hadn't already been sure that she was the author of the notes I'd found, I would have been now. Those final words were so similar to the first note and I didn't think for a second that it was a coincidence.

It wasn't easy, but I did my best to shake off the encounter with Daniela as I entered the juice shop. I didn't want her ruining the remainder of my day.

Inside the shop, I had to wait in line behind one person, but the place was otherwise empty. Once the summer tourist season arrived, the place would be packed, like all the other eateries around town.

During my brief wait, I texted Dizzy to ask if she wanted me to bring her a drink. She replied right away, declining the offer, since she'd just finished an iced latte.

When my turn came, I ordered a paloma mocktail, made with grapefruit juice, lime, maple syrup, and sparkling water. After I paid for the drink, I asked if the shop's owner, Denise, was around. She was a good friend of my mom's.

"She's in the back," Jaida, Denise's employee, said. "You can go and see her, if you like. I'm sure she won't mind."

I thanked Jaida and made my way around the counter to the door that led to the back hallway. The door to the office stood open and I peeked inside.

Denise sat at the desk, typing away at her laptop, but she looked up when I arrived in the doorway.

"Becca, this is a nice surprise," she said as she removed her reading glasses.

"I came in to get a drink and just wanted to say hi, but I didn't mean to interrupt you. You looked like you were hard at work."

Denise gave me a sheepish smile. "Not for anything related to the business. Things are slow today so I thought with Jaida here I'd spend some time working on my novel."

"I didn't know you were a writer," I said with interest.

"I'm just starting out. It's my first attempt at writing a book, but I'm having so much fun with it."

"That's so cool," I said. "And impressive. I'm not sure I'd have it in me to write an entire book."

"That's what I thought about myself for so many years, but now that I'm giving it a try, I can't seem to stop."

"That's great," I said with a smile. "Have you heard about the literary festival that's happening this summer?"

"I saw a poster at the library," Denise replied. "I'm looking forward to it."

"Dizzy will be glad to hear that."

I stepped aside when Jaida joined me in the office doorway.

"Denise, there aren't any customers at the moment." Jaida glanced at me. "Aside from Becca. Is it okay if I take my break now?"

"Of course." Denise hit a couple of keys on her laptop—probably to save her document—and got up from the desk. "I'll take over out front.

"Thanks." Jaida smiled at me. "I can't wait to see the movie, Becca."

I thanked her and she disappeared into the break room across the hall from the office.

Denise stood up, but then sat back down and opened a desk drawer. "I know we need more of our stamp cards out front. I've got another stack of them here somewhere." She rummaged around and then pulled a stack of cards out of the drawer. "Success! Do you have one of these, Becca? It's a new thing we're trying. You get a stamp every time you buy a drink. Every ten stamps, you get a free drink."

"I don't have one, but I'd love one."

"So far, our customers seem to like the idea." She stamped one of the cards and handed it to me.

I tucked it in my pocket. "Most people like a chance for something free, especially when it's something delicious."

"Very true."

I followed her out to the front of the shop, briefly wondering if we should try something similar at True Confections. That was a thought for another time, though.

My paloma mocktail was sitting on the counter, so I grabbed it and a paper straw on my way out the door. To my relief, Daniela and her mother were no longer seated on the neighbouring café's patio. I glanced around, but I couldn't see them anywhere else either.

After my chat with Denise, I was running a little late, so I set a brisk pace as I crossed a stone bridge, heading away from Venice Avenue. I took a long sip of my drink as I walked, grimacing as I got my first taste of the grapefruit concoction. I'd tried several other drinks at Juice It Up and they'd always been delicious. This one, however, wasn't quite so good.

I took several more sips as I walked, trying to figure out what exactly it was about the drink that I didn't like. I couldn't put my finger on it. I was thirsty, though, so I kept drinking even though the quality wasn't as good as I was used to from Denise's products.

Dizzy was sitting on my front step when I reached my cottage, so I hurried to pull out my keys and let us in through the front door.

"I'm not so sure about going out on the lake now," Dizzy said as we entered my cottage. "Those clouds look a bit ominous."

Although the day had started out with a clear sky, thick gray clouds now blotted out the sun.

"According to my weather app, they're supposed to blow over," I said, "but I don't mind staying on dry land today. The wind is picking up, so it's probably a bit chilly out on the lake."

I set my drink on the foyer table after I shut the door. My cats had come to greet us and I picked up Binx while Dizzy scooped Truffles up into her arms. After we'd showered them with cuddles and kisses, we set them down and let the cats lead the way to the family room and kitchen at the back of my cottage. I took my paloma mocktail with me and drew another sip up through the straw. I made a face and decided I'd rather have a glass of water than finish the mocktail.

"What's wrong?" Dizzy asked as I set the drink aside. She must have noticed my expression.

"I ordered the paloma mocktail from Juice It Up and it's not as good as the other flavors I've tried."

"Really?" Dizzy said with surprise. "I've had that one a few times. I always thought it tasted great."

"You can have the rest, if you like."

Dizzy tried a sip of the drink and made a face. "You're right." She set it on the kitchen counter. "That doesn't taste great. Which is weird, because every other time I've had that mocktail it's been delicious."

"Strange. Maybe Jaida messed up my order somehow?" That's the only explanation I could think of.

"Something's not right, that's for sure," Dizzy said.

Forgetting about the drink, I peeked out the kitchen window at the gray sky. "Should we sit outside, or is it too chilly?"

"Let's give it a try," Dizzy suggested. "We can always move back inside if we get cold."

I opened the small door in the laundry room that led to the cat's outdoor enclosure so Binx and Truffles could choose if they wanted to be inside the cottage or out. Then Dizzy and I moved onto my back patio, where we had a view of the nearest canal.

"Guess who I ran into on my way to Juice It Up?" I said as I shut the door behind us.

Dizzy dropped down into one of the chairs on the patio. "Daniela?"

"Got it in one." I sat down beside her, but then bounced back to my feet, restless energy buzzing through me. I paced back and forth as I recounted my conversation with Daniela.

"She's awful," Dizzy said once I'd finished.

"I actually feel kind of sorry for her," I admitted.

"That's probably a waste of energy."

I shrugged. "Maybe. But anyone who's that unpleasant can't be very happy inside."

"True," Dizzy agreed.

"But let's forget about Daniela and talk about our suspects instead," I said in a rush. "We can strike two people off our list, thanks to information I got from Sawyer last night."

I quickly shared everything Sawyer had told me about Chanel and Heller Yearwood.

Maybe too quickly, because Dizzy waved at me to stop when I was partway through relaying the information.

"Slow down, Becca. I can hardly understand you."

I wasn't sure if I could slow down. Thoughts were racing through my mind at lightning speed and I felt like I needed to get them all out of my head.

"Hey, there's Sawyer," Dizzy said before I had a chance to speak again.

She waved and I followed her line of sight. Sawyer was walking along the path on the far side of the canal, dressed in his police uniform.

"Please don't tell me that the two of you are scheming up ways to get in trouble," he called out to us.

"Okay, we'll keep our lips sealed," Dizzy called back with a grin on her face.

I continued my pacing, feeling hot and jittery. Even the cool breeze couldn't seem to soothe my flushed skin.

Dizzy grabbed my hand as I passed her, forcing me to stop my pacing.

"Becca, what's the matter with you?" she asked, looking up at me with concern.

"Actually," I said with a gasp. "I'm not feeling too great."

My chest tightened and I suddenly felt lightheaded. My heart was galloping like a runaway stallion.

"And I'm having trouble...breathing." I gasped again, trying to pull air into my lungs.

"Becca, sit down." Dizzy jumped up and pushed me into the nearest chair. "Sawyer!" she yelled.

She sounded scared, but not as scared as I felt.

Why can't I breathe?

My heart's going too fast.

Those thoughts and a dozen others spun around in my head so fast that they whirled and blurred together.

I popped up out of the chair, unable to sit still.

Running footsteps announced Sawyer's arrival before he rounded the corner of the cottage.

"I think Becca might be having a panic attack," Dizzy said to him.

"No, no, no." I resumed pacing again, struggling to breathe. I kept babbling, but I didn't even know what I was saying anymore.

Sawyer gently pushed me down into a chair and took my hands.

"Becca," he said. "Look at me."

I tried but it was like my eyeballs couldn't stay in one place.

"Squeeze my hands," he instructed.

Again, I tried to do as he requested, but it was as if my entire body had gone haywire, and my mind too.

"I can't...breathe...my heart." I stopped trying to talk. I couldn't get enough oxygen into my lungs.

"I'm not so sure this is a panic attack," I heard Sawyer say.

It sounded like his voice was coming from far away, even though he was right there in front of me.

I jumped up from the chair as my heart tried to beat its way out of my chest.

"I can't...." I started to say again.

Then darkness overtook me.

Chapter Twenty-One

EVERYTHING THAT FOLLOWED THE wave of darkness was muddled, fuzzy, and punctuated by further bouts of oblivion. Sawyer lowered me gently to the ground. Dizzy called my name, sounding scared and tearful. Hands lifted me onto a stretcher. Water lapped against the sides of a boat.

All I could think was that I didn't want to die and I didn't want Sawyer to let go of my hand.

I was vaguely aware of being transported from the boat to a waiting ambulance, but then I knew nothing more until I was in the emergency department of the hospital. Even then, the world faded in and out. Doctors peppered me with questions, wanting to know if I'd taken any drugs. I answered with an adamant no. At least, I thought I did.

Needles pricked my skin and a flurry of other activity took place around me. In my most lucid moments, fear over the crazy pace of my heartbeat crept into my mind. I asked for Dizzy and Sawyer, but I couldn't process what the nurse told me in response.

One of the doctors had me drink a strange concoction that tasted worse than my paloma mocktail. She might have said something about activated charcoal, but I couldn't make sense of anything.

Eventually, my heartrate slowed and I could breathe more easily. Relief settled over me, along with the heavy weight of exhaustion.

At first, I tried to fight it, but soon I gave in and let sleep overtake me.

· · • • · • • • · ·

I WOKE BRIEFLY A couple of times, but couldn't remember much from those moments. When I finally surfaced from the fog of sleep long enough to take in my surroundings, I realized I was in a private hospital room, no longer in the emergency department. I blinked a few times, trying to get my brain to work.

"Welcome back to the land of the living." My brother stood at my bedside. He smiled down at me, but his hazel eyes held a hint of worry.

"Gareth?" I tried to sit up, but then thought better of it. My body felt as though it had been drained of energy. "What happened?"

"That's what I was about to ask you. Do you want me to raise the head of the bed?"

"Please."

He pushed a button and soon I was a little more upright.

"I got a call from Sawyer a few hours ago, telling me you were going to the hospital in an ambulance," my brother said. "He couldn't tell me what was wrong, aside from the fact that your heart was racing and you passed out."

I thought back, trying to sort through my muddled and broken memories. "It wasn't a panic attack. That's all I know."

I'd had a few panic attacks while living in Los Angeles. Although my episode at my cottage had some similarities, it had felt different somehow.

Gareth sat down in a chair next to my bed. "The doctor said you overdosed on caffeine."

"What?" I said, shocked. "No way. That can't be."

"I told her you don't drink coffee, only tea, but apparently there was a crazy amount of caffeine in your bloodstream. Dizzy thinks it might have been from a drink you got at Juice It Up."

"That's weird." I was so confused.

Dizzy rushed into the room then. "Is she awake?" She didn't wait for an answer, seeing for herself as she hurried to my bedside. "Oh my gosh, Becca! I was so scared!"

She threw her arms around me and then pulled back just as quickly.

"Sorry!" she apologized. "Can I hug you? Are you okay?"

I laughed, but only briefly. "You can hug me. And I'm fine. I think."

I glanced at my brother as Dizzy hugged me hard.

"You're fine," he confirmed. "You just need rest."

I returned Dizzy's hug before she released me.

"I called mom and dad," Gareth said.

"Oh no." I sank back against my pillow. "Please tell me they aren't jumping on a plane to get here."

"They're not," Gareth said. "Only because I knew you were going to be fine by the time I called. They send their love and mom has a thousand questions about what happened. I couldn't answer all of them."

My mom was a doctor, currently working at a hospital in Florida.

"Maybe I can get the doctor who treated me to talk to mom directly," I said.

She'd worked at this hospital in Snowflake Canyon before taking the job in Florida, so there was a good chance she knew the doctor who'd treated me in the emergency department. Or doctors. I couldn't remember how many doctors and nurses had attended to me.

"But I'll call her myself too." I glanced around, realizing I didn't have my phone.

Dizzy produced it from one of her pockets. "I grabbed this before following you to the hospital."

"Thanks, Diz." A thought struck me. "Truffles and Binx!"

"I shut them in the cottage and made sure they had plenty of water," Dizzy assured me.

"And I'll stop by to feed them this evening," Gareth promised.

I relaxed. "Thank you."

Gareth got to his feet. "Lolly and Pops are in the cafeteria. I'll go let them know you're awake." He took my hand and gave it a squeeze. "Don't scare me like that again, okay?"

"I'll try not to," I assured him. "Thanks for being here, Gareth."

"I wouldn't be anywhere else."

I let out a heavy sigh as he left the room. Exhaustion was creeping up on me again, but I didn't want to let it win yet. "I don't understand what happened."

Dizzy took over Gareth's vacated chair and inched it closer to the bed. "Sawyer stayed at the hospital until he knew you were going to be okay. Now he's trying to figure out what happened. He's worried that you were...." She bit her bottom lip.

It took a second, but my sluggish mind finally realized what she was hesitating to say. "He thinks I was poisoned? The killer might have done this to me?" I shook my head. "Surely it must have been an accident."

"You had a lot of caffeine in your system, Becca," Dizzy said. "More than you'd find in a coffee or cappuccino or an energy drink."

"Why would Tony's killer come after me?"

"You've been investigating," she reminded me.

"But I'm nowhere close to figuring out the murderer's identity."

"They might not know that."

I glanced toward the open door, half expecting the killer to come stalking through at any moment.

Dizzy caught on to my worries. "Relax, Becca. You'll have someone here with you at all times. Gareth, Sawyer, and I already talked about that and everything's arranged."

That brought me a sense of relief, although it didn't entirely wipe out my anxiety. "You need to be careful too," I warned. "The killer might know that you've been helping me with my investigation." I sat up straighter. "And Cooper."

"We're all being careful," Dizzy assured me.

I sank back against the pillow as Lolly and Pops came into the room, rushing over to hug and kiss me. I made a short phone call to my parents, assuring them that I was fine and telling my mom that I would ask the doctor to call her. Then I responded to concerned text messages from Phil, Jasmine, and Cooper. Dizzy had told Coooper about my emergency trip to the hospital and he'd passed on the news to Phil and Jasmine. I wasn't sure when I'd be back on my feet, but I hoped it would be soon. I didn't want to mess up the filming schedule.

After sending the text messages, I couldn't keep my eyes open any longer. Under the watchful eyes of Lolly, Pops, and Dizzy, I drifted off to sleep. I woke up briefly in the evening to find Gareth at my bedside again. When I opened my eyes a few hours later, Blake had taken over.

Early the next morning, I woke up slowly, momentarily confused about where I was and why. When I cracked my eyes open, I remembered what had happened. Despite the unpleasant memories, I smiled, because Sawyer was sitting in the chair next to my bed. He was unshaven and wearing jeans and a black Henley with the sleeves pushed up. He looked good, as he always did, but he had dark circles under his eyes that weren't usually there.

"Hey, sleepyhead," he greeted.

I rubbed a hand over my eyes, trying to banish my drowsiness. "How long have you been here?"

"A little over three hours."

I grabbed my phone from the table next to my bed and checked the time. It was barely past six in the morning. "Didn't you sleep?"

"I thought Blake should get home for some rest since he and Gareth have to open the restaurant this afternoon."

"So that's a no."

"I wouldn't have been able to sleep, even if I'd tried," he said. "I was too keyed up. And I wanted to be here. I'm sorry I wasn't when you first woke up."

"Don't be sorry. I'm grateful you're here now, and for looking after me until the paramedics arrived."

His eyes darkened. "I'm just glad I was close by."

I turned my hand so my palm faced up and he closed his own around it.

"Dizzy said the whole caffeine thing might have been Tony's killer taking aim at me," I said as my fingers entwined with his.

"I was worried about that, but it's been ruled out."

"Really?" My curiosity woke up. It never seemed to stay out of commission for long. "Then how did I get that much caffeine in me?"

"You were intentionally poisoned, just not by the person who killed Tony," Sawyer said.

"Why would anyone else try to poison me?" I scrubbed my free hand down my face. "I'm so confused."

"Liquid caffeine was added to your drink when you were in the back of Juice It Up," he explained.

"But Jaida wouldn't have done that." Memories surfaced in my mind. "Daniela! Does she seriously hate me that much? She followed me into the juice shop and poisoned my drink? That's low, even for her."

"It wasn't Daniela."

"Are you sure?" I couldn't think of anyone else who would do such a thing.

"Thanks to the surveillance video from inside Juice It Up, I'm sure."

"Then who was it?"

"Mrs. Roumeliotis."

My jaw nearly dropped. "Daniela's *mother* poisoned me?"

"She didn't realize there was a camera in the shop."

"But why would she do that to me? Have you talked to her?"

"Detective Ishimoto had a good long chat with her. She seems to think that Daniela would be the next Angelina Jolie if someone would only give her a chance. She was hoping that if you were too sick to finish the movie, the production company would be desperate to find a replacement as soon as possible."

"And Daniela would be conveniently waiting to step into my role? I doubt they would have picked some random woman off the street."

"Probably not," Sawyer said, "but that's what Mrs. Roumeliotis was hoping for."

"That's crazy."

"I'd have to agree."

"Did she actually want to kill me?" I asked, suppressing a shiver at the thought.

"She claims she just meant to make you too sick to work. But if that's the case, she didn't really know what she was doing. We tested the remains of your drink. She put enough caffeine in it to kill you, especially since you don't have a high tolerance for it."

That sent a chill through me. "Do you think Daniela knew what her mom was up to?"

Sawyer shook his head. "We talked with her too. She seemed genuinely shocked. When Detective Ishimoto pressed her, she admitted to leaving the notes for you, but she swears that's all she did. She seemed surprised when we brought up the fact that there were two notes."

"Why was she surprised if she wrote them?"

"I wondered about that too, so I asked her about it. She says she actually left three notes for you."

"One went astray? No loss there." I thought for a moment. "And you're absolutely sure that Mrs. Roumeliotis didn't kill Tony? I have no idea why she would, but if she's bonkers enough to try to kill me then who knows what else she might do."

"She doesn't seem to have any connection to Tony and she has an alibi for the murder. She spent the entire evening with her next-door neighbors."

"So, the two incidents are completely unrelated and I'm safe now?"

"You're safe now," Sawyer confirmed.

"I thought you were here on guard duty."

"I'm here because I needed to see with my own eyes that you're okay."

I squeezed his hand. "I am. Thanks to you and Dizzy. I'm so glad the two of you were there. If I'd been alone...."

This time he squeezed my hand. "Let's not even think about that."

"I was so scared," I admitted. "I really thought I was dying."

A shadow seemed to pass across his face. "I was scared too."

"I don't remember a lot, but I do remember that you sounded so calm."

"I'm trained to stay calm during emergencies. But afterward...." His dark gaze grew more intense. "There was no way I was going to be able to sleep without seeing you first."

I averted my eyes from his, staring instead at our entwined hands as emotions threatened to overwhelm me. "Sawyer...."

A nurse appeared in the doorway and offered a cheery greeting as she came in to check on me, putting an end to my private conversation with Sawyer. She shared the welcome news that I'd likely be discharged from the hospital that day, after a visit from the doctor. By the time the nurse left, Lolly had arrived. She sent

Sawyer home with orders to get some rest and I decided to take a nap myself. With my grandmother by my side, I drifted off into a deep and peaceful sleep.

Chapter Twenty-Two

I COUNTED MY LUCKY stars that the poisoning incident didn't wreak too much havoc on the production's schedule. Two short scenes had to be postponed because I didn't get out of the hospital until noon and I was too tired to work that day anyway. Otherwise, however, everything was able to go ahead as planned. The missed scenes were squished into the next day's schedule. That meant I had an extra early call time, but I didn't mind. I was happy to be well enough to be back to work.

My body hadn't completely shaken the effects of the caffeine poisoning. I still felt like I'd been run over by a truck, but I thought I'd be fine as long as I rested in my trailer whenever I wasn't needed on set. I skipped my morning exercise routine, instead getting extra cuddles from Binx and Truffles. Those cuddles were like medicine for my soul and helped me get the day off to a good start, even though it was so early that I left my cottage while it was still completely dark out.

If my poisoner hadn't already been identified and arrested, I would have been nervous about traveling alone in the dark. Thankfully, I didn't have to worry about that now. Although, if my poisoner had remained at large, I had no doubt that Sawyer or one of my family members would have been on guard duty.

I really was fortunate. My life was full of people—and cats—who cared about me, I'd survived the caffeine overdose, and I was working both as an actress and as a chocolatier. I couldn't ask for much more, except, perhaps, for Tony's killer to be behind bars.

With a travel mug full of chai tea in hand, I hopped in my whisper boat and navigated my way along the canals until I reached the dock closest to the town parking lot. I tied up my boat and climbed the stairs from the dock to the cobblestone walkway. As I reached the top of the steps, Sonja came into view, walking toward the trailers. She was backlit by the glow of a lamppost located a short distance behind her.

When Sonja saw me cresting the top of the stairs, she jolted to a stop and let out a scream.

"Sonja! It's okay!" I hurried to reassure her. "It's me, Becca."

She pressed a hand to her chest. "Oh my gosh, Becca!"

"Sorry," I said. "I didn't mean to scare you."

She waved off my apology. "It's okay. I just didn't see you until there was suddenly a shadow moving in the darkness."

Cooper came jogging over our way. "Everything okay here?"

"Yes, fine," Sonja said quickly. "I got startled, that's all. Sorry for the fuss."

With that apology, she hurried off.

"For a second I was worried there'd been another murder," Cooper said as we watched Sonja disappear into a trailer.

"I took her by surprise when I came up from the dock in the dark," I explained.

Cooper turned back to me and gave me a hug. "I'm so glad you're okay, Becca. I can't believe someone tried to poison you."

"Thanks, Coop. It's good to be back on my feet. Now that the police know who put the caffeine in my drink, hopefully that's the end of it." As long as Daniela didn't decide to seek revenge on me. It wasn't my fault that the police had arrested her mom, but Daniela might not see it that way.

"Sonja is sure on edge lately," Cooper remarked as we walked toward the hair and makeup trailer.

"I guess I can't blame her, considering that there's a murderer on the loose."

"That's got everyone nervous," Cooper agreed. "I have to say, though, Sonja is the last person I expected to be so jumpy."

"Why do you say that?" I asked.

"I didn't think she was scared of anything. She skydives, bungee jumps, and swims with sharks. All those crazy things."

"I guess having a killer in our midst isn't such an adrenaline rush."

Cooper opened the trailer door for me. "You can say that again."

After we had our hair and makeup done and we'd donned our outfits for the morning's scenes, Cooper and I had a few minutes to kill. The sun was rising above the mountain peaks to the east, but the air still held a definite chill, so we decided to hang out in my trailer.

Once Cooper and I got settled in the trailer, I filled him in on what Sawyer had told me about Chanel and Heller Yearwood, including the fact that they both had alibis.

"I know it wouldn't be nice for you or your fellow townsfolk for the murderer to be a local, but I was kind of hoping that one of the Yearwoods was guilty," Cooper confessed. "Otherwise, the killer is probably someone we've been working with day after day."

"I know," I said. "I wish I could believe that the murderer was a total stranger to all of us, but I doubt that's the case."

A hard rap on the door of my trailer put an end to our conversation. I jumped up and opened the door to find Geneva standing out in the early morning light, looking stressed.

"Becca, have you seen Cooper?" she asked.

Before I had a chance to answer, Cooper came up behind me and Geneva caught sight of him.

"Cooper!" she exclaimed. "I just saw your lawyer heading for his rental car. He said he's going back to California!"

Cooper rubbed the back of his neck. "He's got to be in court with another client tomorrow."

"You should be his priority!" Geneva fumed.

Cooper moved past me and exited the trailer to speak with Geneva outside. I lingered in the open doorway.

"Geneva, relax," he said in a calm voice. "Everything will be fine."

"How can you say that?" She looked ready to tear her hair out. "You're under suspicion for murder, in case you've forgotten."

"I definitely haven't forgotten," Cooper said, exasperation creeping into his voice.

"You need a lawyer to get you off the hook for the crime." Geneva pulled out her phone and started scrolling through her contacts.

"Omar will be back in a few days." Cooper gently took the phone from her hand. "If I need a lawyer sooner than that, one of his colleagues will come and help me out."

Geneva let out a noise of frustration and snatched her phone back.

"Seriously, Geneva," Cooper said, his exasperation building. "You need to chill."

She glared at him through her black-framed glasses. "I'm just trying to look out for you."

"And I appreciate that." He'd managed to get his voice sounding calm again.

"How can we resolve this mess if we don't have someone to prove your innocence?" Geneva asked, her voice rising in pitch.

"I've got Becca helping me with that."

Geneva shot me a look that I couldn't quite read, but I thought it was laced with distrust.

"She's not a cop," she pointed out. "Or a lawyer."

"The police are going to figure out who the real killer is," I said, hoping that was the truth. "Then everyone will know that Cooper is innocent."

I thought I caught a glimpse of tears in Geneva's eyes before she turned her head away.

"I've got phone calls to make," she mumbled. Then she hurried off, leaving me and Cooper alone.

"Seriously," Cooper said, watching her go. "She stresses me out, and I don't need any help with that these days."

I stepped out of the trailer and rested a hand on his shoulder. "How's your anxiety today?"

"It wasn't too bad until Geneva's outburst." He drew in a deep breath and let it out slowly. "It's easing a bit now that she's gone." He sighed. "I really miss Wes."

"How much longer until he's back on his feet?" I asked.

"Hopefully just a couple of weeks."

A production assistant waved to us and pointed at a waiting golf cart, so we headed over that way and climbed into the vehicle. After the driver had dropped us off by the front lawn of the Larch Haven Hotel—the morning's filming location—we had another moment alone to chat.

"Cooper, a few days back you said maybe you needed a change of scenery. Are you thinking of leaving California?" I asked.

"Not completely," he replied. "But after seeing this town, I'm thinking it might be nice to split my time between LA and somewhere quieter. I still want to do some acting, but I've discovered that I also love writing."

"Really?" I said with interest. "I didn't know that."

"I didn't want to tell anyone when I started working on my first screenplay, just in case it turned out to be garbage."

"I'm sure it's not garbage," I said without any doubts. "I bet it's great."

He smiled. "Thanks for the vote of confidence, Becca. And I'm actually kind of proud of what I've come up with. I'm on my third screenplay now."

"That's amazing, Cooper. Have you shared them with anyone?"

"Not yet. But I'd love for you to read one."

"I was hoping you'd say that."

"If you like it, I'm thinking of sharing it with Phil. We've talked a bit about doing more projects together. I'd like to see if he's interested in working with me as a writer as well as an actor."

I gave his arm a squeeze. "That sounds like a great idea."

We didn't have a chance to talk about the subject any further because we were needed on set, but I was happy about how enthusiastic he sounded about branching out into writing.

To start our work day, Cooper and I filmed a scene with Felicia and Diego. After that, I had a break, during which I had to change into a new outfit and get my hair styled differently. Then I was back to the front of the hotel to film a scene with Diego.

In the scene, Jorge invited Addison to an upcoming banquet. We stood on the front steps of the hotel for that exchange. Addison accepted the invitation shyly before hurrying down the steps while Jorge watched her go.

At the bottom of the stairs, Addison stopped short before turning around and rushing back up to kiss Jorge. While Jorge stood there in a happy daze, Addison hurried down the steps again to end the scene.

After the third take, Alex rushed over to tame a few of my flyaway hairs. I stood patiently while he worked, my gaze drifting toward the canal. My cheeks flushed when I spotted Sawyer, wearing his police uniform, standing near the town's main dock and watching the production.

Had he seen me kissing Diego?

I already found kissing scenes awkward to film because there were always numerous crew members looking on, but the thought of Sawyer watching suddenly made me even more self-conscious.

After a brief hesitation, I raised a hand to wave at him. He acknowledged the greeting with a raised hand of his own. Then, to my relief, he set off along the avenue. That allowed me to relax. At least he wouldn't be watching the next take.

That afternoon, we filmed a couple of scenes in the hotel's lobby, and then I was done for the day. After returning home and taking a nap with Binx and Truffles snuggled up next to me on my bed, I decided I felt well enough to make the most of the nice spring weather by going for a walk. If not for the poisoning incident, I would have gone for a run, but I definitely wasn't up to that yet.

I took it easy and set a gentle pace, taking the time to appreciate the sight of all the blooming flowers around town. I was about to turn for home when I drew to a stop. The police station was up ahead and Geneva had just come out the front door.

She didn't see me as she hurried down the steps and set off in the opposite direction from where I stood, but I caught enough of a glimpse of her face to see that she was crying.

Chapter Twenty-Three

As soon as I got home from my walk, I texted Cooper to let him know that I'd seen Geneva leaving the police station. I asked if everything was all right with her, but Cooper responded by saying that he had no idea why Geneva had paid a visit to the police. He'd just finished filming his final scene of the day, so we made arrangements to meet up at The Gondolier for dinner. I was about to suggest that I invite Dizzy when Cooper had the same idea.

I smiled as I sent a message to my best friend. I was pretty sure that Cooper had a bit of a crush on her. Even though Dizzy wanted to stay in the friend zone, I thought it was sweet that Cooper liked her and I was pleased he recognized that she was such a great person.

Dizzy accepted the dinner invitation, so the three of us met up at The Gondolier an hour later, after I'd taken another short rest at home under the watchful eyes of Binx and Truffles. Outside the restaurant, we found Sonja near the front door, frowning at her phone.

"Hey, Sonja. Everything okay?" Cooper asked her.

She tucked her phone into the back pocket of her jeans. "I was going to meet Maggie here for dinner, but she has a migraine so she's going to bed early."

I glanced at Dizzy, asking a silent question. She gave me a small nod.

"Would you like to join us for dinner?" I asked Sonja. "The food here is great."

"And she's not just saying that because she's biased," Dizzy added.

"Becca's brother and his husband own the restaurant," Cooper explained.

Sonja cast a worried look in the direction of the setting sun. "I really wanted to eat here before leaving town, but I don't want to walk back to the hotel by myself in the dark. I know this isn't LA, but with everything that has happened lately I'm not feeling super safe."

"We're staying at the same hotel," Cooper reminded her. "I'll walk back with you."

She gave him a grateful smile. "Okay. Thanks, Cooper."

We headed into the restaurant, with Cooper holding the door open for the rest of us. Before stepping over the threshold, Sonja tossed a nervous glance over her shoulder, but she seemed to relax once we were inside.

Although the restaurant was nearly full, the hostess found a table for us in a back corner. Blake came over to say hello and soon a server arrived and took our orders. I didn't mind having Sonja join us for dinner, but I hoped I'd have a chance to speak to Cooper that evening without her listening in. Fortunately, I didn't have to wait long for that opportunity to arise. After we placed our orders, Sonja excused herself and disappeared into the restroom.

Quickly, I filled Dizzy in on the fact that I'd seen Geneva in tears as she exited the police station that afternoon.

"What did she say when you mentioned Becca had seen her there?" Dizzy asked Cooper.

"She claimed she stopped in at the station to see if the police still consider me a suspect," Cooper replied.

"Claimed?" I echoed, noting the worried crease etched into his forehead.

"I'm pretty sure she was lying." He shook his head. "I don't know what's up with her. I'm tempted to have her go back to California early. Having an assistant is supposed to ease my stress, not add to it."

I took a sip of the ice water our server had brought me. "Do you think she would leave if you asked her to? She seems so overprotective. It's hard to picture her leaving you here without someone to watch over you."

"Yeah, that's what I'm worried about," Cooper said.

"Are you still a suspect?" Dizzy asked him.

"Geneva wouldn't give me a straight answer about that. All she would tell me was that the police have far stronger suspects." He shrugged. "I sure hope that's true."

Sonja rejoined us then, so we switched to talking about other subjects. Sonja wanted to know about the history of the town, so Dizzy and I told her how the town's founder, Reginald Sutton-Maxwell, had come to Vermont from England with his Venetian bride and set out to design a new home that would remind them of their places of origin.

"What's now the Larch Haven Hotel was the Sutton-Maxwell home," I said.

"And some say it's haunted," Dizzy added.

"Haunted?" Sonja shuddered and took a long drink of the margarita she'd ordered. "That's all I need."

"I thought you were into visiting haunted castles and all that stuff," Cooper said.

Sonja nodded. "Sure, but can you imagine if Tony's ghost started haunting us? What a nightmare." She downed the rest of her margarita.

"Tony didn't die in the hotel, so he's not likely to haunt it," Dizzy said. "The only ghost said to haunt the halls of the hotel is Lucia, Reginald's wife."

"Why wouldn't her spirit leave when she died?" Cooper asked.

"Legend has it that the once-passionate love she and her husband shared had faded over the years," I said.

Dizzy picked up the tale. "The story goes that Reginald had a young mistress and Lucia's heart broke when she found out."

"Supposedly she threw herself from the top of one of the turrets," I finished.

Dizzy nodded. "It's hard to know how much is fact and how much is fiction, but I'm pretty sure the haunting part is true."

"There have been a lot of reports of strange happenings at the hotel over the years," I said.

"And every so often, somebody sees the ghostly figure of a woman at the top of the turret," Dizzy added. "Usually when the moon is full."

"I'll have to keep my eyes peeled," Cooper said.

The server brought our food then, and Sonja ordered another margarita. The rest of us stuck with water or soda.

Sonja had heard about my brief stint in the hospital, so I filled her in on what had happened. After that, we chatted about our families and our various hobbies while we ate. Halfway through the meal, Sonja finished her second drink and ordered another. When it arrived, she changed the course of our conversation.

"What are the cops like in this town?" she asked.

I dug my fork into my seafood linguine. "What do you mean, exactly?"

"Are they competent? Helpful? Or do they dismiss women as being hysterical and having fanciful imaginations?"

"Definitely competent," Dizzy said.

I nodded my agreement. "And helpful. Dizzy and I have known Officer Maguire our whole lives."

"He's a really good guy." Dizzy reached for her glass of soda. "If there's something you want to talk to an officer about, we can put you in touch with him."

"Oh no." Sonja took a gulp of her third margarita. "I don't need to talk to the police." She laughed, a little too shrilly. "I don't have anything to tell them. I mean, except for what I told them when they questioned me. Just like they questioned everyone else. It's not like they think I'm the killer." She hiccoughed and turned her attention back to her food.

I shared a worried glance with Cooper and Dizzy. Sonja had started slurring her words and didn't seem like herself. I hoped she wouldn't try to order another drink.

Dizzy and I shared more history about the town as we ate. For the most part, Sonja stayed quiet. I'd nearly finished my dinner when I glanced across the dining room and noticed Daniela sitting at a table with two other women we'd gone to school with. The other women were laughing and chatting, but Daniela was looking my way. I was used to getting glares from her, so it surprised me to see worry and perhaps even guilt on her face. When she realized that I'd spotted her, she quickly turned back to her friends, her face flushed.

A short time later, I made a trip to the ladies' room. On my way back, I found Daniela waiting for me. My shoulders tensed, despite the fact that her body language screamed that she was feeling nervous and uncertain. Nothing good had ever come from an encounter with her in the past.

"Daniela," I said, stopping in the narrow hallway that led to the washrooms. I didn't let my voice betray my unease at facing her.

"Becca, I know we're not exactly friends," she said to start.

That's an understatement, I felt like saying, but I kept quiet.

She played with the strap of the purse hanging over her shoulder. "But I swear I had no idea that my mom was going to try to hurt you. If I'd known her plan, I would have stopped her."

"I'm glad you weren't part of the drink tampering, but you did leave me those nasty notes," I reminded her. "I don't understand why you hate me so much. What did I ever do to you?"

"You were always one-upping me in high school," she said, a hint of petulance creeping into her voice.

It took effort, but I kept my exasperation in check. "I was never competing with you, Daniela. I was just living my own life, chasing my own dreams."

She kept playing with the strap of her purse. "I really wanted to be a movie star. It seemed to come so easily for you. I went to three auditions in New York and didn't land a single job."

"It might have looked easy from the outside, but I worked hard for everything. And it took me seven auditions to land my first commercial. Many more before I got my first speaking role on a tv show. If you really want to be an actress, you should keep trying."

"I'm probably too old to make it big in the movies now," she said, dejected. Then she brightened. "But there's a reality TV show I want to try out for."

"I hope it works out for you." I meant those words sincerely, even though I hoped our paths wouldn't cross again. A futile wish, perhaps, if she stayed in Larch Haven. The town was too small to avoid anyone for long.

Daniela seemed to have run out of words, so I excused myself and returned to my friends.

Although our brief conversation had drained me, it also left me feeling lighter. I didn't think Daniela would be bothering me again in the future, even if she did stay in Larch Haven.

I pushed thoughts of her aside and focused on enjoying time with my friends. Fortunately, Sonja called it quits at three margaritas and we finished up our meals without incident. After we paid our bills, the four of us left the restaurant together.

I worried about Sonja's ability to walk back to the hotel and, apparently, Cooper did too. After Sonja had taken a few faltering steps, he offered her his arm. From there on, she seemed steady enough.

Dizzy and I walked with them to the Larch Haven Hotel and we lingered near the town's main dock while Cooper and Sonja disappeared inside so they could head for their respective rooms.

I told Dizzy about my latest encounter with Daniela and my feeling that she wouldn't be bothering me in the future.

"I hope you're right about that," Dizzy said. "But if you're wrong, I'll happily have a chat with her."

I laughed. "You could scare off the most menacing of enemies, Dizzy."

She grinned. "I'm small but fierce."

I hugged her. "That's for sure."

Dizzy headed home and I returned to my cottage. Before going to bed, I spent some time practicing my lines for the next day, with Truffles and Binx as my audience. Truffles purred her encouragement, but Binx was more of a tough critic. I thought I won him over eventually, and that's when I decided to call it quits.

After climbing into bed, I exchanged a few text messages with Sawyer and then set my phone aside and switched off the lamp. I had a smile on my face as I snuggled beneath the covers.

I was ready for my next gondola lesson.

Chapter Twenty-Four

I GOT UP BEFORE sunrise the next morning and struck out along the canal path as the first hint of pink touched the sky. The stately Larch Haven Hotel appeared more majestic than usual that morning with its gray stonework tinged with a rosy hue thanks to the sunrise. A single tourist stood on the front lawn, capturing the fleeting sight with his camera. I paused to take a quick photo with my phone, but the result wasn't as stunning as the real view.

Tucking my phone away, I continued on and found Sawyer waiting for me on the dock, wearing jeans and a T-shirt. I called out a greeting as I approached.

"It's a perfect morning for training for the gondola races," he called back.

"Not happening," I said as I descended the steps to the dock. When I stood in front of him, I rested my hands on my hips. "You should be impressed that I'm willing to have another lesson."

"I'm impressed," he assured me. "How are you feeling?"

"Much better."

"That's good to hear." Sawyer gently brushed aside a stray lock of my hair and tucked it behind my ear.

Pleasant tingles spread through my body, but that didn't surprise me. Lately, that seemed to be my reaction to standing in close proximity to Sawyer. What I didn't expect was the sudden rush of jumbled emotions that hit me like a crashing wave. I couldn't even identify the individual emotions, but they made my heart ache with both longing and happiness.

"Ready?" Sawyer asked, never taking his eyes off mine.

I wondered if he had any idea that I had a whirlwind of feelings twisting around inside me in that moment.

I swallowed hard and gathered myself together. "Ready."

Sawyer had already rented a gondola for us to use that morning. He gave me his hand to hold as I stepped from the dock to the boat. Once standing at the stern, I released Sawyer's hand and clutched the oar as the craft rocked beneath me.

"All good?" Sawyer checked.

As the gondola steadied, I stood with more confidence. "All good."

He made a move to climb into the middle of the gondola.

"You're sitting down there?" I asked with disappointment.

Sawyer stopped and stayed on the dock. "You want me there with you?"

I tightened my grip on the oar. Why did it sound like there were hidden layers to that question?

"Definitely." When I spoke that word, it felt like I was throwing caution to the wind.

Sawyer held my gaze for a split second longer before stepping off the dock to join me on the gondola. He positioned himself behind me and gently corrected my grip on the oar.

"Remember to keep your hands a little farther apart," he instructed.

"In line with my shoulders," I said, remembering my first lesson.

"Now, show me what you've got."

I didn't get off to the smoothest start. I nearly lost my balance a couple of times and we came close to hitting the bank before I found my rhythm with the oar. After a few bumps at the beginning, however, I had the gondola gliding along the canal.

Sawyer removed his hands from the oar, resting one on my shoulder and the other at my waist, letting me have complete control of the gondola. "You're slaying it, Becca. Just like I knew you would."

His praise brought a smile to my face.

"Maybe I'll be entering the gondola races after all," I said.

"I'll be sure to get a front row seat."

"Don't get your hopes up too much," I cautioned. "I didn't say I'd be entering the races *this* year."

Sawyer laughed. "We have plenty of time for more lessons then."

I smiled again, enjoying the way the heat from his body seeped through my T-shirt to warm my back.

I navigated the gondola beneath a stone bridge and then out into the light of the rising sun. "Do you know why Cooper's personal assistant was at the police station yesterday?" I asked. "I saw her leaving in tears."

"I think you'd better ask her about that. Better yet," Sawyer said, changing his mind, "don't ask. Focus on things other than the murder."

"Not exactly easy to do, especially when a friend of mine is under suspicion."

"What if I told you he's no longer a suspect?"

I turned to look at Sawyer and immediately regretted the move. The gondola rocked beneath my feet and I nearly toppled off and into the water.

Sawyer snaked his arm around my waist and held onto me until the gondola stopped bobbing and tipping.

"How about keeping your eyes on the canal?" he suggested as he released me.

"How about you explain how Cooper got off the hook?" I countered.

"Row," Sawyer instructed.

With a sigh, I got the gondola moving forward again. "Cooper's really off the suspect list?"

"Turns out he's got an alibi," Sawyer said. "Maybe not an iron-clad one, but good enough that we're focusing our investigative energies elsewhere."

"That's good to hear," I said with relief. "But how did he get an alibi when he didn't have one before?"

"I don't think I should get into specifics. Can't you just be glad that Cooper's not a top suspect anymore?"

"Yes. Maybe." I tried to clarify my answer. "I mean, I'm definitely glad, but I'm also curious about how that happened."

"Your curiosity does seem to be incurable."

"It really is," I admitted. "But I'll try to focus on other things. Like work."

"Good idea." He paused for a moment before saying, "I caught a few minutes of filming the other day."

"Right," I said, suddenly finding it a little harder to breathe. "My scene with Diego. Probably the only one I wasn't eager to film. Just so you know, I always find kissing scenes awkward."

"Just so I know?"

"Yes." I hoped he couldn't see my cheeks flush. "Just so you know."

We'd traveled in a rough circle through the network of canals and now coasted back to the main dock.

"You hop off first," Sawyer said as we got closer to the dock.

I managed to step off with a modicum of grace and Sawyer followed me with ease. He tied up the gondola and then turned to face me.

"Why do you want me to know?" Sawyer asked.

"Why do I want you to know what?" I asked, pretending I'd forgotten what we were talking about.

He kept his gaze leveled at me. "That it was awkward to kiss Diego."

I looked off to the side, staring at the ripples in the water, internally panicking as I tried to find a way out of the conversation. Then I realized I'd had enough of being scared. I'd had enough of dancing around and leaving things unsaid. My recent brush with death had reminded me that life was too short to let fear rule my actions.

I raised my gaze to meet Sawyer's. "Because I don't want you thinking that I want to be kissing other guys."

"Other than...." He let the question trail off, but his eyes never left mine.

I drew in a deep breath, gathering my courage.

"Morning, Becca! Morning, Sawyer!"

We both turned toward the water. Consuelo Díaz had called out the greeting. She was cruising along in her whisper boat, heading toward Venice Avenue and the café she owned.

We waved at her, but disappointment weighed down my smile.

When I turned back to Sawyer, I saw my disappointment mirrored in his eyes.

Even so, he offered me a hint of a wry grin. "Burning cookies again." He held my gaze for another second before tipping his head toward the stairs that led up from the dock. "I guess we should get going."

He turned to go, and I let him.

I glanced around at the beautiful morning.

Birds sang, the sun shone down, and Consuelo's boat disappeared, leaving the water completely still, like a mirror.

The moment was close to being perfect, except for one thing.

I grabbed Sawyer's hand as he started up the steps.

He turned back to me, but I kept hold of his hand.

Suddenly, I wasn't scared anymore.

"No more burning cookies," I said.

Then I kissed him.

Chapter Twenty-Five

As soon as my lips met Sawyer's, the rest of the world blurred and slipped away. He tugged me closer to him and my skin heated as he deepened the kiss and trailed one hand down my back and the other over my hair. I didn't know how long the kiss lasted. It was as if time ceased to exist in our little bubble of a universe. There was just the two of us, and a whole lot of feelings that had been bottled up for too long.

When the kiss ended, Sawyer had his hands on my hips and I had my arms wrapped around him. He rested his forehead against mine, both of us breathless.

I felt disoriented, lost, and yet completely found at the same time.

Something in my universe shifted, like a long-lost puzzle piece finally clicked into place.

"Becca," Sawyer whispered, "I've wanted to do that for a very long time."

I smiled, but only for a moment. "I'm sorry it took me so long to get here."

Sawyer wrapped his arms around me. "Becks, for you, I would have waited forever."

Tears prickled in my eyes even as I thought I might float away like a helium balloon. I leaned in against his chest and he held me close. I drew in a slow, deep lungful of air, breathing in his scent and soaking up the moment. I wanted to stay that way forever, but then three kids ran along the bank of the canal, laughing loudly.

I pulled back from Sawyer. The private bubble around us had popped, though the spell we'd cast over ourselves remained unbroken.

Sawyer let out a low growl of frustration before kissing me, all too briefly.

"What's wrong?" I asked.

"I have to get to work."

His obvious disappointment brought a smile to my face. "Me too."

He ran a hand down my hair. "Will you be on set today?"

I shook my head. "At the shop."

"I'll stop by if I can," he promised. "I want to see you again as soon as possible."

My smile brightened. "Same."

He gazed into my eyes like he couldn't look away. Tiny bubbles of pure happiness popped and fizzed in my chest.

He held my hands in his and took a small step back. "Okay. I should get going."

He didn't make another move to leave.

"You probably should," I agreed.

I gave his hands a squeeze and then brushed my lips against his. "Thanks for the lesson."

He still had his eyes on mine. "Nothing about that kiss suggested that you need lessons, Becca."

I poked him in the ribs. "The gondola lesson. You know that's what I meant."

He grinned. "I'm not sure you need lessons for that anymore either, but I'll give them whenever you want."

I smiled. "I have a feeling I'm going to want a whole lot more."

"That's good to know."

I took a step back because the temptation to move into his arms again was growing too strong. I couldn't bring myself to let go of his hand, though. Not yet.

"We'd better get going," I said.

"Unfortunately."

We climbed the steps to the walkway as a jogger ran past. Two women pushing babies in strollers passed by next. As the last bit of our privacy vanished, I settled more heavily back into reality.

Giving Sawyer's hand a squeeze, I backed away from him, letting my hand slide slowly out of his. "See you later."

He started walking backward, a hint of a grin on his face. "In the meantime, stay out of trouble."

I laughed. "No promises."

With a shared smile, we turned and went our separate ways, even as the paths of our lives finally merged.

· · · • • · • • • · ·

THE FIRST THING I did after leaving Sawyer was text Dizzy to tell her we needed to meet on an emergency basis. I assured her that all was well, but I didn't share any other details via text. She met me at True Confections twenty minutes later. Angela hadn't yet arrived at the shop, so we had the place to ourselves.

"What's going on, Becca?" Dizzy asked as she hurried in the front door. She took one look at my face and her eyes widened. "Oh my gosh! Finally!"

She threw her arms around me and squeezed me tight.

"Can't. Breathe," I gasped, but I was laughing at the same time.

Dizzy released me and I filled her in on everything. She left half an hour later, with a bag of misfit chocolates in her hands, but only after giving me another fierce hug and telling me for the umpteenth time how happy she was for Sawyer and me.

After she'd set off for the library, I got to work in the kitchen, a big smile on my face. I still felt like I could float away at any moment, carried off into the sky by pure happiness.

When Angela arrived an hour later, she popped into the kitchen to say hello. "You look happy this morning," she remarked after we'd exchanged greetings.

"It's a beautiful day," I said, leaving it at that.

From the way my cousin looked at me, I figured she suspected there was something more to my cheeriness, but she didn't press the matter. I was glad of that. I wanted more time with Sawyer before I told anyone other than Dizzy how things had changed between us.

After I'd put in a few hours of work, I decided I needed to get out in the fresh air and stretch my legs. As I strolled along Amsterdam Avenue, I spotted Cooper jogging down the front steps of the Larch Haven Hotel. He waved when he saw me and I stopped to wait for him to join me on the path that ran along the canal.

"Have you seen Geneva this morning?" Cooper asked.

"No," I replied. "Is something wrong?"

"She's been making herself scarce since yesterday and I need her to explain something."

I spotted the woman in question over his shoulder. "Here she comes now."

He turned around just as Geneva noticed us. She was walking along the canal path, heading in our direction. Her steps faltered, but then she continued toward us.

"Morning," she greeted, but there was a slight tremor to her voice. Her gaze darted to Cooper and away again, like she didn't want to meet his eyes.

"You haven't been answering my texts," Cooper said with a hint of annoyance.

"Sorry," Geneva mumbled. "I decided to go for a walk and forgot to check my phone."

She was a terrible liar. She hadn't forgotten anything and Cooper knew that as much as I did.

"You mean you've been avoiding me," he said. When she started to deny it, Cooper held up a hand to stop her. "Maybe you can explain something for me. I just got a call from my lawyer, letting me know that I'm no longer a suspect in the murder investigation because somebody provided me with an alibi."

Cooper and I stared at Geneva, waiting for her to say something.

She licked her lips as she continued to avoid meeting his gaze. "That's great news, right?"

"Did you lie to the police, Geneva?" Cooper asked.

Her eyes widened behind her glasses. "Of course not!"

"But you're the one who provided me with the alibi."

Geneva didn't confirm or deny that.

"I saw you leaving the police station yesterday," I said. "You were crying."

"Come on, Geneva," Cooper said, his patience wearing thinner by the second. "Tell us the truth."

She blinked away tears. "Okay, yes, I'm the one who provided you with an alibi."

"But how is that possible?" Cooper asked. "I went out for a walk on my own that night."

A thought struck me. "Were you following Cooper?"

"Not exactly," Geneva replied.

"What does that mean?" Cooper pressed.

She heaved out a breath and seemed to know that he wasn't going to settle for anything less than a full explanation. "Okay, so I followed you for part of the way. I lost sight of you when a bunch of teenagers got between us, but I was still able to tell the police where you went."

"How?" I asked, beating Cooper to the question.

She hesitated before speaking in a rush. "I've been tracking you through your phone."

Cooper stared at her. "Seriously, Geneva? What the hell?"

"I need to know where you are so I can make sure you're safe!"

Cooper ran a hand through his hair. "Looking out for my safety isn't in your job description. And neither is tracking me without my knowledge or permission."

"But thanks to the tracking app, I was able to show the police exactly where you were at any given time that evening. It proved that you did nothing more than walk by the props trailer."

"Even so, you've really overstepped," Cooper said. "I want you to go back to California."

Geneva's eyes widened again. "But you need me here!"

"No, what I need is someone to keep my life organized without stressing me out and invading my privacy."

Geneva burst into tears. "I just wanted to be the best personal assistant you've ever had so you'd want to keep me on!"

She turned and ran for the hotel.

We watched her go, Cooper looking both exasperated and dumbfounded.

I rested a hand on his shoulder. "I'm sorry you're having to deal with this," I said. "But I'm glad you've got an alibi, even if Geneva did overstep."

He huffed out a breath and rubbed the back of his neck. "Same. I guess I should go talk to her."

"Are you going to let her keep working for you until Wes is back?"

"Heck no," he said. "I'll do without a personal assistant in the meantime. I can't trust Geneva anymore."

"I don't blame you."

Cooper drew in a deep breath and let it out slowly. "All right. I'd better go take care of this."

"Good luck," I said.

He gave me a wry grin. "Thanks, Becca. See you later."

I turned back toward Venice Avenue, deciding I'd been away from True Confections for long enough. As I walked, I mulled over everything Geneva had said. As wrong as it was for her to track Cooper without his permission, she'd provided him with a good alibi. I recalled that Sawyer had mentioned that it wasn't an iron-clad alibi, but still a pretty good one. I figured that was because, in theory, Cooper could have planted his phone on someone else to cover up the fact that he'd spent an extended amount of time at the props trailer, setting up the booby trap. But even if he'd known that Geneva was tracking him, or if he'd worried that the police would be able to access the location history of his phone at a later date, it would have been easier to simply turn his phone off for a while. Thankfully, the police must have thought the same.

The fact that I no longer had to worry about clearing Cooper's name meant I could forget about the murder and focus on my own life.

Okay, so forgetting about the murder wouldn't really be possible, especially with a killer still roaming free, but I could leave the investigation to the police.

As I returned to True Confections, I resolved to do just that.

Chapter Twenty-Six

IN THE MIDDLE OF the afternoon, I wrapped up my work in the kitchen and cleaned until the place was spotless. After tossing my apron in the laundry hamper, I ventured out into the front of the shop. Right away, I regretted the move. Delphi and Luella stood in the middle of the store, speaking to a rapt audience of three other local women.

"If the police knew what they were doing, they'd realize that there never actually was a murder," Delphi said.

Agnes Lawrence, a local senior citizen, widened her eyes. "But there was a body, wasn't there?"

Luella jumped in to explain their theory about the body being nothing more than a clever prop.

I was about to interrupt and attempt to set them straight, but then I spotted Sawyer, dressed in his uniform, through the front window. I skirted around the gossiping women and motioned at Sawyer to go around to the back of the shop. I didn't want him walking right into the clutches of the Gossip Grannies.

His gaze shifted to the women gathered in the middle of the store and he nodded in understanding. He continued walking along Venice Avenue and disappeared from sight.

The women were still deep in conversation, and Angela was attending to another customer over by the display case, so I slipped into the back without saying a word.

It was probably for the best that I didn't try to refute the Gossip Grannies' ridiculous theory, anyway. They'd believe whatever they wanted, no matter what the evidence to the contrary.

All thoughts of gossipy senior citizens flew from my mind as I unlocked the back door. I opened it to find Sawyer waiting outside and my heart gave a funny flutter at the sight of him. I put a finger to my lips and then took his hand, quickly leading him along the hall to the office. We made it inside without being noticed by anyone in the front of the shop. I shut the office door and leaned my back against it.

"Thanks for saving me," Sawyer said. "Again."

"I think we all need saving from the Gossip Grannies." I pushed away from the door. "But let's forget about them." I wrapped my arms around Sawyer and hugged him as a surge of emotion nearly overwhelmed me.

He put one hand to my back and ran the other down my hair. "Are we okay, Becca?"

I nodded against his chest but didn't release him. I frowned against his vest. "Argh."

"What's wrong?" he asked with concern, and maybe a bit of apprehension as well.

I stepped back so I could see his face. "I can't hug you properly when you're in uniform."

His vest and all the equipment on his duty belt weren't conducive to snuggling up nice and close.

Sawyer's face relaxed with relief. "And here I thought you were about to say you regretted what happened earlier."

I stepped into him again and kissed him. He put one hand to my face and deepened the kiss, leaving me weak at the knees.

"Never," I said, looking him right in the eye once the kiss ended. "And I do love the vest, because it helps to keep you safe. I'm just looking forward to hugging you the way I really want to once you're off duty."

"You're not the only one," he assured me as he brushed his thumb across my cheek. He took my hands in his and regarded me closely. "I just wanted to make sure you were okay, because I know the thought of changing things between us made you anxious."

"You knew that?" I shook my head. "I shouldn't be surprised." I squeezed his hands. "I'm not frightened anymore." That was the truth. In that moment on the dock, when I decided to kiss him, the fear had left me. "We've got a lifetime of friendship between us. That's not going to change."

"You're right about that," he agreed. "We can build on it, but the foundation is unshakable."

I smiled, wishing I could spend the entire day with him, but I knew I had to let him leave.

"Let me get you some chocolates before you go. I wouldn't want you leaving empty-handed in case that makes you less likely to come back."

"Becca." He didn't continue until I looked him in the eye. "The chocolate here is fantastic, but it's never been the draw."

I slid one hand from his so I could press it to my chest. "You'd better stop saying things like that. My heart can only take so much in one day."

He tugged me closer and rested his forehead against mine. "Becca," he said, completely serious, "I want you to know that if you ever get scared again, about us or anything else, you can tell me."

I put all my joking aside. "Thank you. I don't mean to get scared, but sometimes it just happens."

"And that's okay." He kissed my forehead. "Now, I'd better get out of here or I might never leave."

With a smile, I let go of his hands so I could open the office door and peek out into the hall. I heard voices coming from the front of the shop, but I couldn't see anyone from my vantage point and the voices didn't sound like Delphi's and Luella's. I motioned to

Sawyer to follow me across the hall to the kitchen, where I packed up a small bag of misfit chocolates for him.

I told him about my latest conversation with Daniela as I added salted caramels and peanut butter pretzel truffles to the bag. "I don't think she'll be a problem anymore."

"I don't think so either," Sawyer said. "I had a stern chat with her the day her mom was arrested. Between that and the fact that her mom nearly killed you, I think she's been scared into changing her ways."

"I wish I could have been a fly on the wall during that chat." I handed him the bag of chocolates. "Did you use the full force of your cop face?"

"My cop face?"

"You know," I said, "when you do that thing with your face. And your eyes. Like this." I tried to give him my most intimidating, stony-faced stare.

"I don't know what that is, but it definitely isn't a cop face," Sawyer said. "More like a ticked off puppy."

I shoved him in the chest, sending him a step backward, with him grinning the whole time.

"You know what face I mean. It's very intimidating. For other people, anyway. It doesn't work on me."

"No?" He leveled a hard stare at me.

I smiled. "Not even a little."

"If only it *would* work on you," Sawyer grumbled, "maybe you'd listen to me and not get into so much trouble."

"What would be the fun in that?" I asked, still smiling.

Sawyer shook his head with exasperation that was only partly feigned. Whatever percentage of it was real faded away when I gave him a quick kiss. It was too quick for my liking, but anything more than an ever-so-brief one would run the risk of turning into a much longer one and I knew I should let him get going.

"I'm working late tonight," Sawyer said on his way out the door. "Otherwise, I'd ask to see you later."

"Sometime tomorrow then?" I asked, hopeful.

He flashed me a grin that nearly made my heart burst. "You can count on it."

· · · ● · ● · · · ·

DIZZY CAME OVER TO my place that evening and helped me practice my lines for the next day, though not until after we had a good long chat about Sawyer. Once I felt certain that I had my lines memorized, I heated up some vegetable lasagna. While I was in the hospital, Gareth had stocked up my fridge and freezer with homemade meals so I wouldn't have to cook anytime soon. Having a talented chef for a brother definitely had its perks.

"How are things going with the plans for the literary festival?" I asked Dizzy as I slid the lasagna into the microwave.

The library would be hosting the festival in the summer and Dizzy was in charge of organizing the event.

"Great!" she said with a smile as she got two plates out of the cupboard. "I booked another two authors to speak and do book signings."

While we ate, she told me about the authors and some of the activities she had planned for the festival. It was nice to chat about something completely unrelated to murder, poison, or any other dark and troubling subject.

"I met Cooper at the coffee shop this morning," Dizzy said when we'd finished our meal. "We had a fun chat about all things paranormal. He says he wants to stay in touch."

"He likes you, Dizzy," I said with a smile as I rinsed our dishes.

A hint of pink showed in her cheeks. "And it's flattering that a Hollywood star would have any interest in me." She took the plates from me and stacked them in the dishwasher.

I dried my hands with a towel. "It's totally understandable that he would. I know you don't want to go beyond friendship with him, but I'm happy he sees how amazing you are."

Her cheeks still pink, Dizzy smiled and shut the dishwasher. "Thanks, Becca. But I really do want to draw the line at friendship. I don't think a small-town girl like me would keep his interest for long, and I'm not cut out for that kind of life anyway."

I gave her a hug. "A smart, beautiful, funny, kind, caring, and awesome girl like you could easily hold his attention forever, but I absolutely won't push you to be more than friends with him."

Dizzy rested her head on my shoulder. "I don't want to cry, so you'd better stop saying such nice things about me."

I held her at arms' length. "It's easy to say good things about you, Diz."

"Stop!" she demanded with a smile on her face and with tears shining in her eyes.

I returned her smile and gave her shoulders a squeeze before releasing her. "I'm really glad you two are friends now. And I get what you mean about not wanting that life."

Dizzy busied herself with opening the bakery box she'd brought over from Love at First Bite. "While we were chatting this morning, we got interrupted three times by fans wanting to talk to Cooper and take selfies with him. I'm happy he's so popular, but that's just the tip of the iceberg attention-wise. These days, I bet anyone who dates Cooper would end up in the tabloids right along with him."

The remnants of my smile disappeared. "Unfortunately, that's true, and it makes me sad for Cooper."

Dizzy set two cupcakes out on clean plates. "Hopefully, the negative attention will die off."

"Now that Tony's no longer feeding photos and videos to the tabloids, I think there's a good chance of that." I sat down at the kitchen table. "It's just too bad that Tony had to die for things to get better for Cooper."

Dizzy sat down across from me and pushed one of the cupcakes my way. "Good thing he's not a top suspect anymore."

"I'll say."

I'd texted Dizzy with that piece of good news after Geneva had revealed how she'd been able to provide Cooper with an alibi.

"Speaking of Tony," Dizzy said after we'd started in on our delicious and beautifully iced cupcakes. "Have you made any progress with identifying the killer?"

"I haven't given it much thought since Geneva came forward with Cooper's alibi," I admitted. "I figure I can leave it to the police now that he's pretty much in the clear."

"Or maybe you've just been preoccupied with thoughts of a certain police officer," Dizzy said with a mischievous grin.

"That too," I admitted with a smile. "But I'm hoping the police will catch Tony's killer soon so we can all relax. And now that Daniela's campaign against me seems to be over, maybe life can be smooth and drama-free from now on. At least for a while."

Chapter Twenty-Seven

WHEN I STEPPED OUT onto my back patio the next morning, a clear sky greeted me. I didn't have to be on set for a few hours and I'd already gone through my usual yoga and Pilates routine, so I enjoyed a leisurely breakfast out on the patio while Binx and Truffles hung out in their enclosure, intently watching the birds hopping about on the ground and in the maple tree on the bank of the canal.

A little later, I set out along the canal path with the local coffee shop as my intended destination. I'd barely made it a stone's throw away from my cottage when I saw Sawyer crossing a bridge, heading my way.

I stopped on the path and waited for him to reach me. We stood there, facing each other, both of us with smiles on our faces, but neither of us closing the last bit of distance between us.

"I really want to kiss you," Sawyer said at last, making my smile grow brighter. "Can I do that in public?"

I appreciated that he'd asked. "As much as I want you to, I'd like to talk to my family first."

Sawyer nodded with understanding. "I figured as much. They don't need to be hearing about us through the grapevine."

"And especially not from the Gossip Grannies." I gave a dramatic shudder at the thought. "I don't even want to guess what crazy story they're going to come up with about us."

"I still wish I could toss them in lockup. At least for a while."

"As much as I understand the temptation," I said, "I'm pretty sure Detective Ishimoto would frown upon that."

"She might not if she were locked in a room with the Gossip Grannies for five minutes first."

I laughed. "True." I tucked my hands behind my back because they itched to reach for Sawyer.

His dark eyes held mine and the heat from his gaze was almost palpable. "Can you do me a favor, Becca?"

"Name it," I said without hesitation.

"Talk to your family as soon as possible?"

My smile widened. "I'll go see Lolly and Pops right now. Walk with me?"

We fell into step together and Sawyer tucked his hands in the pockets of his jeans.

My fingers twitched at my sides. "I really want to hold your hand," I confessed.

He grinned. "Why do you think I've got my hands in my pockets?"

"What about your mom?" I asked a moment later. "Do you plan to tell her about us?"

"Of course. Next time I talk to her. She'll be thrilled."

"Really?" I said, pleased.

"Becca," Sawyer said, gazing at me with so much affection that my heart gave a painful squeeze, "she adores you."

I smiled for what felt like the hundredth time that morning. "The feeling is mutual."

I couldn't help myself. I tucked my arm through Sawyer's as we continued to walk. That was something I would have done even before our relationship shifted, so I figured it didn't matter who saw us.

When we reached the path leading to Lolly and Pops' front door, we drew to a stop.

"I'll leave you here," Sawyer said.

"You're not coming in with me?" I asked with surprise.

"It's probably best that I don't. What if your grandparents aren't keen on the idea of us as a couple?"

"Sawyer, Lolly and Pops love you. They'll be as thrilled as your mom's going to be." I had no doubts about that.

"And your brother?"

I thought about that one for a second. "Gareth knows you're a good guy. It might take him a moment to get used to the idea, since you and I have been friends forever, but he won't disapprove. Even if he did, he'd have to learn to get over it."

"I still think I should let you talk to your family on your own," Sawyer said. "Besides, I need to get to work."

"That's okay," I assured him. "But at least walk me into the back garden."

I figured we were close enough to breaking the news to Lolly and Pops that I could take Sawyer by the hand. I led him past the front door and through the side gate. Instead of following the path around the cottage to the back door, I tugged Sawyer off to the side of the gate, where a large rhododendron bush hid us from view of anyone who might be walking along the canal out front.

"I like the way you think," Sawyer said with a grin before kissing me.

When the kiss finally ended, he held me close and inhaled deeply, like he was breathing me in. Tears flooded my eyes as a wave of emotion washed over me.

Sawyer stepped back, just far enough so he could see my face, his hands resting on my shoulders.

Concern darkened his eyes. "Why are you crying?"

I smiled, my vision shimmering. "Because I'm so happy."

That wiped away his concern. He brushed one of my tears away with his thumb and then rested his hand against my face. "I know this is all new and I don't want to rush anything, but after almost losing you, I don't want to hold back. I love you, Becca, and I want you to know that. I don't want to leave it unsaid. And, just to be clear, I've loved you my whole life, but I mean I'm *in* love with you. I have been for a while."

Another tear slipped out of my eye, a sign of the happiness that was brimming out of me. "I'm in love with you too, Sawyer. So deep I don't think I can see the surface anymore."

His slow grin lit a warm glow in my chest and made my head buzz in a pleasant way.

He leaned in close so he could whisper in my ear. "That's okay. There are no lake monsters down here."

My joyous smile was cut short by another kiss, one so luxurious and sweet that it felt like a dream.

Eventually, Sawyer rested his forehead against mine. "I guess I should go," he said with obvious reluctance. "Before your grandparents catch us making out in their garden."

I laughed against his chest. "That would be one way of breaking the news to them."

He kissed the top of my head and finally stepped back. "But not the way you want to go about it. Text me to let me know how it goes?"

"I will," I promised.

"And you can tell me the truth, no matter what it is," he said.

I slowly walked backward along the path, away from him. "It'll be good news."

"Then we can celebrate."

"And you can kiss me for the whole world to see," I added.

"I'll hold you to that, Becks."

"Please do."

With a wave, I rounded the corner of the cottage.

And found myself face-to-face with my scowling brother.

"Were you spying on me?" I asked with suspicion.

Gareth stood with his arms crossed over his broad chest. "It's not spying when I just happened to see you out the window. You and Sawyer."

My cheeks flushed. "Why are you glaring at me?"

"When were you going to tell us?"

"That's exactly what I came here to do," I said. "Well, I came to tell Lolly and Pops. I was going to tell you and Blake next."

He continued to scowl at me.

I put my hands on my hips, doing my best to hide my flutter of nerves. I wanted my family to be happy for me, not disapproving. "Seriously, what's your problem? Sawyer's a good guy. You know that."

"Sure, but is he good enough for my baby sister?"

"I'm not exactly a baby anymore, in case you haven't noticed," I said.

The back door opened and Lolly poked her head out. "What are you two doing out there? Aren't you coming in, Rebecca?"

I was about to answer when I saw one corner of Gareth's mouth twitch.

My jaw dropped. "I don't believe it!" I said to him. "You've been pulling my leg!"

Gareth uncrossed his arms and laughed. "Of course I've been pulling your leg. Did you really think I wouldn't approve of Sawyer?"

I narrowed my eyes at him. "You're evil."

He laughed again. "Not evil, remember? Just a big brother."

"Argh." I tried to storm past him, but he grabbed my arm and pulled me into a hug.

"Seriously, Becca. I'm happy for you. And I'm so glad you're okay."

My annoyance melted away. "Thank you." I returned his hug before releasing him.

Lolly stood waiting in the doorway. "Are you going to tell me what's going on here?"

"Absolutely." I jogged up the porch steps and put my arm around my grandmother as we entered the kitchen. A delicious aroma greeted me. "Lolly, have you been making your famous cinnamon rolls?" I spotted the pan of fresh, gooey rolls on the counter. "I knew it!" My mouth watered.

Blake and Pops were seated at the kitchen table, mugs of coffee in front of them.

"I'm about to dish them out," Lolly said. "There's hot water in the kettle. Get yourself a cup of tea and sit down. Then you can tell us everything."

"Everything about what?" Blake asked.

"Becca's in love," Gareth said, drawing out the last word.

I tried to give him a light punch in the arm, but he dodged it.

Blake regarded me over the rim of his coffee mug. "With Cooper?"

"Those Gossip Grannies," I said with a heavy sigh. "No, not with Cooper. Let me get my cup of tea and then I'll fill you in."

· · • • · • • · ·

THANKFULLY, NO ONE ELSE tried to play a joke on me by pretending they didn't like the idea of me getting romantically involved with Sawyer. Lolly's eyes lit up and she gave me a hug and a kiss. I thought I saw tears of happiness in her eyes, but she blinked them away before I could be certain. Pops seemed pleased too, and relieved that I wasn't about to run off to Hollywood with Cooper.

I stayed and chatted with my family as we enjoyed the scrumptious cinnamon rolls, and then Gareth, Blake, and I hugged our grandparents and left the cottage. We walked a short distance together and then went our separate ways, with me heading for the hair and makeup trailer.

We were filming scenes for *Love on the Canal* at the cute café owned and operated by Consuelo Díaz. Two wrought iron tables had been set up outside the café and that's where Felicia and I filmed our first scene of the day. After a few takes, Jasmine was satisfied and ready to move on to the next scene.

Felicia and I got up from our seats at one of the two outdoor tables, ready to head back to our trailers. We both had a break ahead of us while Cooper filmed a scene with the woman playing the part of the town's mayor.

We'd taken only a few steps away from the outdoor table when Detective Ishimoto appeared on set, flanked by Sawyer and Jared Tuffin, another uniformed officer. Felicia's steps faltered when she saw the police and fear flashed in her eyes before she smoothed out her expression.

Jasmine Singh, the director, stepped forward to meet Ishimoto. "How can we help you, Detective?"

"We're here to see Ms. Blessing," Detective Ishimoto said, her gaze on Felicia as she spoke. She produced a set of handcuffs from the pocket of her blazer and stepped forward. "Felicia Blessing, I'm arresting you for the murder of Tony Fleet."

Felicia's eyes filled with wild fear. "No!"

She shoved aside a chair and made a run for it. Sawyer tried to grab her arm, but she tripped and stumbled into him, knocking him off balance.

He fell to the cobblestones, right into the path of an oncoming golf cart.

Chapter Twenty-Eight

SOMEBODY SCREAMED AND I thought it might have been me until I realized that I had my hand pressed over my mouth.

I dropped it as the golf cart lurched to a stop. Cooper, riding in the back, nearly got thrown from the small vehicle.

"Sawyer!" I ran around the small group of people that stood between me and the place where he'd fallen.

He was on his back, in the midst of trying to get up.

"Are you okay?" I asked, fear squeezing my chest so painfully that I could hardly draw in a breath.

"I'm good," he assured me. "No damage done."

Cooper appeared next to me. I grabbed one of Sawyer's hands and Cooper took the other. Together, we pulled him to his feet.

I wanted to hug him, but refrained since he was on duty and in the company of his colleagues. He gave my hand a squeeze before releasing it and I appreciated that extra bit of reassurance. Even so, I looked him over carefully. It was only once I was certain he was fine that my heart slowed to a normal rate.

When I finally allowed my focus to stray from Sawyer, I saw that Officer Tuffin had Felicia in handcuffs. Tears ran down her cheeks as she sobbed quietly. The other members of the cast and crew stood around, watching in shocked silence.

Detective Ishimoto came over to check on Sawyer. Once he assured her that he was fine, she nodded at Officer Tuffin, who then led Felicia through the stunned crowd to one of two police cruisers that had quietly pulled up to the scene.

Fortunately, it didn't appear as though anyone other than the cast and crew had witnessed Felicia's arrest. Nevertheless, it likely wouldn't take long for the news to spread around town and across the Internet. I didn't know if I should feel sorry for Felicia or not. If she really had killed Tony, she didn't deserve my sympathy. Yet, even though I'd suspected her, I still had trouble believing that she was a murderer.

Jasmine Singh ran after the detective and tried to speak with her as she was climbing into one of the cruisers. Detective Ishimoto said something I couldn't hear and then shut the door. Within seconds, Jasmine had her phone pressed to her ear.

"This is crazy," Cooper said from where he stood next to me. "Do you really think Felicia did it?"

"The police must have reason to think she did." I shook my head, still shocked by everything that had transpired in the last couple of minutes. "I can't seem to believe it, but maybe that's just because I don't want to."

There was a delay in moving on to the next scene, but eventually Jasmine declared that Cooper and the actress playing the mayor would keep working. Everyone appeared dazed, but focusing on work seemed to help. As for me, with nothing to do in that moment, I wandered off toward my trailer, feeling numb.

I'd almost reached the town parking lot when Leanne, the actress who played Felicia's mother, came hurrying over to me.

"Becca, I heard what happened. Surely it can't be true! Felicia couldn't hurt anyone."

"I have trouble believing it too," I assured her.

"But the police really arrested her?"

"I'm afraid so."

Leanne blinked away tears. "Poor Felicia. And maybe it's terrible for me to be thinking about this, but what will happen with the film? Will it get finished or are we all out of jobs?"

"I really don't know," I said. "Hopefully Jasmine or Phil will let us know soon, but I guess it all depends on what happens with Felicia."

"Even if she gets out on bail, will she be allowed to keep her part?"

"I'm sorry, Leanne," I said, at a loss. "I wish I had some answers for you."

She patted my arm. "And I'm sorry for bombarding you with questions. I'm just so stunned."

"Me too."

Leanne rushed off, heading in the direction of the day's set. I'd almost reached my trailer when Alex came running toward me with tears on his cheeks.

"Becca, have you heard?" he asked, anguish on his face.

"About Felicia's arrest? I was there when it happened."

"It's terrible," he choked out over a sob. "Becca, you've got to help me."

"Help you how, Alex?" I asked. "What does Felicia's arrest have to do with you?"

Tears ran down his face. "That's what I have to tell the police. I can't let Felicia take the blame. She didn't kill Tony." He grasped my arm. "Please, Becca. I don't even know where the police station is in this town."

I patted the hand that had a tight grip on my arm. "I can show you."

He choked back a sob. "Thank you, Becca."

To my relief, he loosened his hold on my arm, though he didn't let go. As I walked with him in the direction of the police station, I was glad to see that there were plenty of people out and about.

If Alex was Tony's killer, I didn't want to be alone with him, even if he did seem ready to confess to the crime rather than kill again.

Alex cried silently the whole way to the station. When we stopped at the base of the steps leading to the double front doors, he kept hold of my arm.

"I know it's asking a lot, Becca," he said, desperation in his eyes, "but will you come inside? I'm terrified to go in alone."

"All right," I agreed.

Since I'd already come that far with him, I didn't see any harm in accompanying him into the building, especially since there would be multiple police officers inside.

I led him up the steps, wondering if the murder case was about to be solved with his confession.

When we entered the lobby, Sawyer was in the midst of crossing it. He stopped short when he saw Alex and me.

"Becca?" he asked with concern, his gaze going from me to Alex's tear-stained face and back to me again. "What's wrong?"

"Alex needs to talk to Detective Ishimoto," I said.

Beside me, Alex nodded but said nothing.

"It's about Tony's murder," I added.

"All right," Sawyer said. "Alex, you can come with me."

Alex's grip on my arm tightened again. "Can Becca come too? Please? I don't think I can do this alone."

Sawyer hesitated, looking between us again, but then he nodded. "Come this way."

He led us through a door and down a hall to an interview room.

Alex finally released my arm and collapsed into a chair, pulling up the hem of his T-shirt to wipe his tears away.

"Becca, can I talk to you in the hall for a minute?" Sawyer requested.

Alex didn't protest, so I slipped out of the room with Sawyer, pulling the door shut behind me.

"What's going on?" he asked in a low voice.

"I'm not entirely sure," I admitted quietly. "He says there's something he has to tell the police because he can't let Felicia take the blame."

"For the murder? Is he about to confess?"

I shrugged. "Maybe."

"Then I don't want you in there alone with him," Sawyer said. "Leave the door open and wait right here, okay?"

"I will." I touched his wrist to keep him from turning away. "You're really okay after your fall? I thought the golf cart was going to hit you."

"You and me both." He put a hand to my face, ever so briefly. "But I'm fine. I promise." He waited until I nodded and then he opened the door to the interview room and poked his head inside. "I'll be back with Detective Ishimoto as soon as possible," he said to Alex.

I lingered in the hall as Sawyer strode off around a corner. I rubbed my arms and glanced through the door at Alex. His face looked unhealthy and pale in the room's artificial light, but he wasn't crying at the moment. As I watched, he folded his arms on the table and rested his head on them.

He seemed like such a sweet guy. Could he really be a murderer?

Thankfully, I didn't have to wait with my unsettling thoughts for long. Sawyer reappeared within a minute, Detective Naomi Ishimoto on his heels.

I preceded them into the interview room and sat down next to Alex. He raised his head and took my hand, holding it firmly but not so tightly that it hurt. His eyes were wide and full of fear.

Detective Ishimoto informed him that she'd be recording the conversation and Alex acknowledged the statement. Sawyer stood by the closed door, his expression serious.

"I understand you want to talk to us about the murder of Tony Fleet," Detective Ishimoto said once she was seated around the corner of the table from Alex.

He nodded. "Felicia Blessing didn't kill Tony."

"How do you know that?" Ishimoto asked.

Letting go of my hand, Alex drew in a shaky breath and let it out before replying. "I know," he said in a clear voice, "because I was with Felicia when she found Tony's body."

Chapter Twenty-Nine

"YOU AND FELICIA FOUND Tony's body?" I said to Alex with surprise. "I thought a police officer found him."

When I saw a hint of disapproval on Detective Ishimoto's face, I warned myself to keep quiet. I didn't want to get kicked out of the room and miss out on whatever else Alex had to say.

"We didn't tell anyone that we found him," Alex said, staring down at his hands as he twisted them in his lap.

"Why is that?" the detective asked.

Fresh tears rolled down Alex's cheeks. "We both took something from Tony," he admitted. "The first time I worked with him, he acted all friendly, like we were good buddies. After we'd known each other for a few weeks, he asked me to loan him some money. I gave him five thousand bucks. Big mistake."

"He didn't pay it back," Detective Ishimoto surmised.

Alex shook his head. "And his personality changed. Now I know that he was just showing his true colors, that he never really saw me as a friend. My boyfriend and I are trying to buy a condo in LA. I really needed my money back, but Tony said I'd given it to him as a gift. He knew that wasn't true, but he told me I'd never see a cent of it again."

I remembered the argument I'd witnessed between Alex and Tony. It must have been about the money.

"When Felicia and I found him lying there, dead, I saw an opportunity. He had that expensive watch and those gold chains.

I thought if I sold them, I'd have at least some of my money back." Alex swiped at fresh tears with the back of his hand. "But I never did sell them. I felt too guilty. Even though he owed me money, what I did felt wrong."

"So you dumped the jewelry in the barrel of flowers," I said before remembering that I'd meant to stay quiet.

Alex nodded. "I hoped someone from the cast or crew would see the watch and chains and recognize them as Tony's. That way they'd get returned to his estate without anyone knowing what I'd done."

"How does Ms. Blessing fit into all of this?" Detective Ishimoto asked.

"We were walking together when we found Tony's body," Alex said. "She knew about the money he owed me and she wanted his phone because...." He trailed off.

"Because he had intimate photos of Felicia stored on the device," the detective finished for him.

Alex nodded again. "From back when they were married. Tony had been threatening to post them online or sell them to the tabloids. His phone was just lying on the ground next to him and Felicia was mortified by the thought of anyone seeing the photos."

"Even without the phone, we were able to access Mr. Fleet's photos through his service provider," Detective Ishimoto said.

"I was worried that might be possible," Alex said. "But I didn't have the heart to tell Felicia."

"Is that why you arrested Felicia?" I asked, once again ignoring my own warning to keep my mouth shut. "Because you saw the photos?"

I was surprised when Detective Ishimoto actually acknowledged my question. She kept her eyes on Alex as she did so. "And we found Mr. Fleet's phone hidden in Ms. Blessing's hotel room. Frankly, Mr. Skye, Ms. Blessing still could have killed Mr. Fleet. Maybe to get his phone, maybe because she no longer wanted to pay alimony. Either way, she had motive, and the fact that you came upon the body together doesn't mean she couldn't have set up the booby trap."

Alex clasped his hands together so tightly that his knuckles turned white. "She has an alibi."

"How long were you two together before you found Mr. Fleet's body?" Detective Ishimoto asked.

"Not long," Alex replied. "Maybe fifteen minutes."

The detective consulted her notebook. "Then there was still a significant gap between the time she left set and the time she met up with you."

"But she wasn't alone during that gap," Alex insisted.

"That's not what she told us," Detective Ishimoto said.

"That's because she's trying to keep a secret, but she can't do that anymore. There's too much at stake."

I desperately wanted to ask about Felicia's alibi, but I managed to stay quiet. Fortunately, Detective Ishimoto asked the question that was trying to bubble out of me.

"Who was she with?"

Alex let out a deep breath. "Jasmine Singh, the film's director. They recently started a romantic relationship. They've been trying to keep it under wraps, at least until this film is done. Felicia got Jasmine to swear that she wouldn't tell anyone, including you. Felicia didn't think she'd be a suspect for long—because she's innocent—and she was worried that people might say she got the lead role in *Love on the Canal* solely because of her relationship with Jasmine. That's not true, of course. She got the job before they became involved, but people can be cruel, especially online."

Detective Ishimoto wrote something in her notebook. I couldn't tell from her expression what she thought about every-thing Alex had told her. I glanced at Sawyer, but his face was just as inscrutable.

"Is there anything else you'd like to tell us?" the detective asked Alex.

"I think that's everything." He seemed far calmer now, as if telling the truth had relieved him of a great burden.

Detective Ishimoto closed her notebook and got to her feet. "I'd like you to remain here for the time being. I might have further questions for you."

Alex nodded and stared at the tabletop.

"Ms. Ransom," the detective said to me. "I don't think your presence is required any longer."

I stood up, knowing I'd been dismissed. I rested a hand on Alex's shoulder. "You'll be okay?"

He reached up to squeeze my hand. "I'll be all right. Thanks, Becca. It means a lot that you were here with me."

I gave him a quick hug and then left the interview room, with Detective Ishimoto and Sawyer following behind me.

"Let's get Jasmine Singh in here," the detective said to Sawyer. "We need to speak with her."

"I'm on it," he assured her.

Detective Ishimoto walked off down the hall and disappeared through another door.

"Does this mean Felicia will be released?" I asked, hopeful.

"It's too soon to say," Sawyer replied. "We have to wait and see what Jasmine has to say. Even if she confirms what Alex said, it's possible that Jasmine would lie for Felicia."

"But then why not do that from the start?"

"Maybe they were hoping it wouldn't come to that."

"What about Alex? Do you think he killed Tony so he could get the watch and gold chains?" I didn't think that was the case, but I wanted to know what the police thought.

Sawyer put a hand to my lower back and guided me along the hall, toward the lobby. "Alex has an alibi."

"Really? I didn't know that."

Sawyer's mouth twitched. "That's because you're not a police officer and therefore not privy to the information we've collected."

"But you said earlier that he might be coming here to confess to the murder, and you didn't know he was with Felicia or that they found Tony's body."

"The time he spent with Felicia was the only gap in his alibi and now it's been filled, as long as Felicia confirms what he said. For the rest of the window of time when the booby trap could have been set up, he was either with other cast and crew members or in the midst of a video call with his boyfriend."

"That's a relief," I said. "I like Alex and I really didn't want him to be the killer. I feel the same way about Felicia."

Sawyer opened the door at the end of the hall and held it for me. "Hopefully she wasn't involved in the murder either."

"Then you'll be back at square one," I said as I preceded him into the lobby.

"Not quite."

Maybe that was true, since the pool of potential suspects had dwindled since the start of the investigation.

"If Jasmine confirms Felicia's alibi, I won't have many people left on my suspect list," I said, thinking out loud.

"I'm guessing it would be a waste of time to remind you that you shouldn't even have a suspect list."

"You know me so well," I said with a smile.

As we drew to a stop in the lobby, near the front door, Sawyer's face grew more serious. "You know why I don't want you investigating."

"Because you don't want me ending up in any danger." I remembered the terror I'd felt when he'd fallen in the path of the golf cart earlier. "I get that."

He brushed a lock of hair off my shoulder. "Good. Please don't forget it."

"I promise to keep it in mind."

He regarded me with suspicion but changed the subject. "I'm glad things went well with your family this morning."

I'd sent him a text message to give him that news.

"They think we make a good match," I said.

He looked at me with an intensity that left my knees week. "I happen to agree with them."

I had to remind myself to breathe. "Me too."

Sawyer put a hand to my back and guided me a few steps away from the door as a middle-aged couple entered the building and headed for the reception desk.

"Since we don't yet know if we've got the killer in custody," he said once we had some privacy again, "please don't ask questions that could put a target on your back."

"I plan to focus only on acting and making chocolates," I said.

"That'll be the day."

"No, really," I assured him. After the morning's drama, I didn't want to think about the murder. Not for a while, at least.

"Uh huh." He was entirely unconvinced. "I'll call you later."

"Please do."

With a wave, I pushed open the door and left the police station.

· · • • • • • • · ·

UNSURPRISINGLY, FELICIA'S ARREST WREAKED havoc with the filming schedule. It also didn't help that Jasmine had to attend the police station and didn't know when she'd be back on set. She had assistant directors working with her, but we still needed Felicia for most scenes. In the afternoon, I filmed a short scene with Diego, but everything on the schedule after that had to be postponed.

After spending some time at home with my cats and then dropping in at True Confections, I decided to join some of the cast and crew for dinner at the local pub. When I arrived at The Oar and Anchor, I found Sonja, Diego, Cooper, and Maggie already there. Soon after, a few other crew members joined us. We had two tables pushed together and I ended up sitting between Cooper and Sonja. When we all had drinks in front of us and had placed our food orders, the conversation turned to Felicia's predicament, but I decided not to say anything about her alibi until the police had a chance to double check it.

Sonja rubbed her arms as if she were cold. "I can't believe they arrested Felicia."

Everyone else chimed in with their agreement, but I kept my eyes on Sonja. Her face was pale and she had dark rings beneath her eyes.

"Are you okay?" I asked her quietly as everyone else talked about Felicia.

She forced a smile and wrapped a hand around her cocktail glass. "I'm good." She took a sip and then glanced my way. "Don't worry. I'm not planning on getting drunk again."

"That's not what I was worried about," I said. "I thought maybe you were upset about Felicia."

"I am," she admitted. "I can't wrap my mind around the fact that she's a killer. You don't think the police will let her out on bail, do you?"

The question took me aback. Everyone else seemed to be hoping that Felicia would get released soon, preferably because the police realized she wasn't the murderer.

"I'm not sure," I said in response.

Despite her assurances, Sonja ordered a second cocktail after she finished up the first, and she followed the second with a third. By the time we all left the pub, she was more than a little tipsy. I stationed myself on one side of her, with an arm around her back, and Cooper held her other arm as we made our way along Amsterdam Avenue, heading for the Larch Haven Hotel.

"I'm so sorry," Sonja slurred as we walked. "You must think I'm so unprof...unprofessional."

"It's been a difficult time," I said.

A tear rolled down her right cheek. "I can't believe Felicia would want to kill me," she whispered.

"Kill you?" I asked, exchanging a startled glance with Cooper.

He shrugged at me.

Sonja's head jerked up and she suddenly seemed more alert. "Not *me*. Tony. I can't believe it."

"None of us can," Cooper said.

Sonja fell silent. When we reached the hotel, Maggie and Diego took over and got Sonja inside so Cooper could walk me home. I was grateful for his company on the short journey, but we were both too tired for any further socializing, so we said good night as soon as we reached my cottage.

When Sawyer called me later, I was already in bed, reading a book while my cats snoozed away, Truffles by my feet and Binx snuggled up in the crook of my arm.

"What happened with Felicia and Jasmine?" I asked after we'd exchanged greetings. "Or is that confidential police information?"

"I can tell you since it'll be obvious in the morning that we released Felicia at the end of the day."

Relief helped me to relax into my pillows. "Jasmine must have confirmed her alibi then."

"She did," Sawyer said, "and we found some video evidence to back it up too."

"How come you didn't have that video before?" I asked.

"We had it. We just didn't know what we were looking at."

"Please tell me you can explain that." If he couldn't, my curiosity might keep me awake all night.

Sawyer laughed and the sound sent warmth spreading through my chest.

"The video is from the Larch Haven Hotel's surveillance camera by the front door," he explained. "We checked the footage at the start of the investigation to see if we could track the movements of anyone who knew Tony. Felicia previously claimed that she was alone in her hotel room during the window of opportunity for setting up the booby trap. There were some people who came and went from the hotel that we weren't able to identify. It turns out that one of those people was Felicia. She and Jasmine were caught on camera entering the hotel a few minutes after seven. The camera didn't get a good angle on them and Felicia was wearing a coat with the hood up. Once Felicia showed us a distinctive purse that she was carrying at that time and Jasmine showed us her pink leather jacket, we were able to confirm from the footage that they entered the hotel at the time they said they did."

"And they didn't leave again that evening?" I checked.

"Not through the front or back doors. Both are covered by security cameras. Plus, it turns out they ordered room service. The hotel employee who delivered their food saw the two of them in the room. Since they wanted to keep their relationship under wraps, they paid the employee not to say anything once we started asking questions."

"If they'd kept their money, they would have saved Felicia a whole lot of trouble," I said.

"I think they see that now."

"So, Tony's killer is still out there somewhere." I didn't like that thought.

"I'm afraid so."

"Do you know what the Gossip Grannies have been saying about the murder?" I asked.

Sawyer groaned. "I probably don't want to know."

"Probably not," I agreed, but I told him anyway. "They're saying that Tony's body was just a prop and he's actually still alive."

I could almost hear Sawyer's eyes rolling.

"Those ladies are nuttier than your hazelnut truffles," he said.

"Nuttier than the hazelnut truffles and the peanut butter truffles combined," I amended with a smile.

"Now you've got me craving your chocolates."

That made me smile even more. "Do you have any left from the last batch I gave you?"

"They never last long," he said.

I snuggled deeper beneath the covers. "I guess you'll have to visit me at the shop to get some more."

"I can't wait."

"To see me or to get more chocolates?" I asked.

"Both. But mostly you, Becca. You know that, right?"

I practically glowed with happiness. "I do."

Chapter Thirty

THE NEXT MORNING TURNED out to be a hectic one. It started with an emergency meeting for the cast and crew of *Love on the Canal*. At least it was a happier gathering this time, with everyone cheering and clapping when Phil delivered the news that Felicia had been cleared of suspicion. The only person in the room who didn't appear to be rejoicing about the announcement was Sonja. The shadows under her eyes had grown darker since the night before and she gripped her mug of coffee like it was a lifeline. Maybe her exhaustion stemmed solely from drinking too much while in Larch Haven, but I suspected otherwise.

When the meeting broke up, I had the rest of the morning free. On my way out of the conference room, I saw Sonja climbing the stairs to the second floor. I'd planned to head straight for True Confections, but I changed my mind and followed Sonja up the staircase. As I passed by the suit of armor, memories of Tony came flooding back. Maybe the antique would always remind me of the murdered props master.

I reached the second floor in time to see Sonja disappear into her room, so I knew exactly where to find her. When I rapped on the door, she opened it within seconds.

Surprise registered on Sonja's face when she saw me. "Hey, Becca. What's up?"

"I just wanted to check in with you to make sure that you're doing okay."

She winced. "Do I look that terrible?"

"No, of course not," I said quickly. "Just...a little tired, maybe."

"And hungover?" She gave me a hint of a smile as she stepped back so I could enter her room. "I know I'm not making a good impression."

"I wouldn't say that. The circumstances haven't exactly been normal." I stayed close to the open door, not wanting to be shut up in a room with one of my suspects.

Sonja grabbed a hairbrush that was sitting on top of the room's dresser. "Seriously." She ran the brush through her hair and then tugged a hair elastic off her left wrist. "And the police still haven't caught the killer."

I didn't miss the worry in her eyes as she faced the mirror above the dresser and tied her hair back in a ponytail.

"But it's a relief that Felicia's not a murderer," I said, watching her reflection.

"It didn't seem right that it was her. I'm so glad it wasn't." She stared at her reflection for a second, fear and anxiety etched in a line across her forehead. Then she turned my way and forced a smile. "Thanks for checking on me, Becca. I promise I'm not usually so fragile."

"I believe you," I said. "I'll let you finish getting ready for the day."

As I turned to leave, a small piece of paper on the room's desk caught my eye. I froze when I read the note.

It's time for you to exit stage left. Permanently.

It looked and sounded like the notes Daniela had left for me.

"Where did you get this?" I asked, pointing at the note.

"Oh, that." Sonja swept it off the desk and crumpled it in one hand. "I found it on the floor in the hallway." She tossed the ball of paper into the wastepaper basket. Then she grabbed a messenger bag off the desk chair. "Sorry to run out on you, but I need to get going."

"Of course." I took the hint and left the room, all the while thinking about the note.

Sonja came out behind me and shut the door. "Thanks again, Becca. I appreciate your kindness."

She waved over her shoulder as she hurried off down the hall.

I followed at a slower pace, my thoughts churning.

I got the sense that Sonja's breeziness when throwing the note away had been forced and her story about finding the note in the hallway didn't ring true.

But why else would Sonja have one of Daniela's notes? And why would she lie about it?

I shook my head, trying to clear it, and picked up my pace. Nothing about this case made sense to me. Maybe if I spent a few hours focused on making chocolates, my thoughts would clear on their own.

Doubtful, but it was worth a shot.

· · • •• • • · · ·

I RELAXED AS SOON as I stepped in the front door of True Confections and breathed in the delectable aroma of chocolate. Despite the emergency production meeting and my detour to talk to Sonja, I was still the first to arrive at the shop. I made a beeline for the kitchen and got right to work. I spent the next few hours making batches of London fog truffles, peanut butter pretzel truffles, chocolate-coated salted caramels, and raspberry creams.

I stayed so focused on my work that I was surprised to find it was nearly noon when I finally emerged from my chocolate-making trance and looked at the clock on the kitchen wall. After stretching my arms over my head, I started cleaning up. I'd planned to work only half a day at the shop since I had to be on set later for scenes that would be filmed inside the Larch Haven Hotel.

When I ventured into the front of the shop after cleaning the kitchen, I realized it was a good thing we'd be filming indoors that day. Thick, steely gray clouds had rolled in and strong gusts of wind whipped along the avenue, rippling the water in the canal and setting the hanging baskets swinging.

"Looks like there's rain on its way," my aunt Kathleen remarked.

She was looking after the shop that day so Angela could work as a background performer again, much to my cousin's delight.

"I hope it holds off until I get to the hotel," I said as I shrugged into a light jacket.

A group of three customers hurried into the shop, eager to escape the wind. I waved to my aunt and pushed out the door.

A damp gust of wind hit me as soon as I stepped outside. My hair danced around my head and whipped at my face. I tried to tame it with my hands, but I was no match for the wind. In the end, I gave up and stuffed my hands in my pockets to keep them warm.

Huddled in my jacket, I walked briskly to the hotel. Fortunately, Alex and Michaela had set up inside the former mansion. Even if I'd ridden in a golf cart from the trailers to the hotel, my hairstyle would have been ruined during the short trip, no matter how much product Alex used to hold it in place.

When I arrived at the conference room temporarily in use as a hair and makeup studio, Alex greeted me with a fierce hug.

"How are you doing?" I asked as I rubbed his back.

"I feel so much better now that I've got everything off my chest and Felicia is free." He released me and patted his chair. "I can't thank you enough for going to the police station with me."

"Yes, thank you," Felicia chimed in from Michaela's chair. "You, Alex, and Jasmine really saved me."

"I don't think I did very much," I said as I settled into the chair, "but I'm glad things have turned out all right for the two of you."

Alex got to work on my hair. "We might end up facing minor charges for tampering with the crime scene."

"But I'm going to make sure we both have good lawyers," Felicia said. "I've already talked things over with mine. Since Alex and I both have previously clean records, there's a good chance we won't do any jail time."

Alex lifted his gaze up toward the ceiling. "Thank heavens!"

After I had my hair and makeup done, I moved to another conference room that was being used by the wardrobe department. Then, when I was finally needed on set, I made my way to the lobby. Diego and I would start the next scene there, with Angie and several other extras dressed as party guests and mingling in the background. Then Cooper would stand in awe as Felicia descended the grand staircase to join the party.

Once we'd finished that scene, the crew began the process of moving all the equipment into the dining room, the next filming location within the hotel. Craft services had set up in yet another conference room, so the other actors and I stopped in there for a bite to eat. After a snack and a cup of tea, I wandered back toward the lobby, with Felicia accompanying me.

All the equipment had been moved out of the lobby, but a production assistant informed us that there would be a short delay in starting the next scene. Felicia decided to wait in her room, so she set off up the stairs. I settled on the couch in the seating area and Diego and Cooper soon joined me. Any time someone opened the front door of the hotel, the wind rushed in, cold and fierce. Rain splattered the windows, making me all the more grateful that we were indoors.

After a few minutes, I noticed Sonja hurrying up the staircase with a clipboard in hand. More time passed and Diego got up to stretch his legs. I was considering whether I should do the same when a powerful wind gust whistled around the building and rattled the front doors.

The lights blinked out, shrouding us in darkness.
Then came an almighty crash, followed by a scream.

Chapter Thirty-One

I JUMPED TO MY feet, my heart pounding.

Had the killer struck again?

A series of thuds and clangs followed the loud crash. I heard a cry of pain amid all the other noises, coming from the direction of the staircase.

I took a step forward and banged my shin against the coffee table. Wincing from the pain, I edged my way around the table in the dark as startled murmurs and exclamations rang out from all around. Once away from the seating area, I picked up my pace, only to trip over something on the floor.

I fell forward. Before I could hit the ground, someone grabbed me from behind.

I gasped and tried to jerk my arm free.

"Becca!" Cooper's voice sounded right by my ear. "It's just me."

Although the hotel's lights remained off, the production's lights were powered by generators. They were stationed in the dining room now, but the double doors to the restaurant stood open, allowing a glow to spill out into the lobby. Together with the faint gray light seeping in through the window, I could make out the shapes of furniture and people once my eyes adjusted.

The crash and scream had come from the direction of the staircase, so I looked that way. It took me a second to realize what I was seeing. Then I ran forward.

Sonja lay sprawled at the bottom of the staircase, with pieces of metal around her. When I got closer, I realized that the metal was actually the suit of armor. Somehow it had fallen down the stairs as well. It had come to pieces, with various parts scattered over the stairs and on the lobby floor.

I picked my way around the bits of armor so I could reach Sonja's side. Cooper followed right behind me.

"Sonja!" I said as I knelt down beside her. "Are you all right?"

To my relief, she opened her eyes, staring up toward the ceiling. She winced and let out a groan. "My arm."

A couple of crew members moved one of the production's lights into the lobby, illuminating the area. That allowed me to see that Sonja's upper left arm was bleeding. The blood came from a gash about three inches in length. I didn't have any first-aid training, but the cut looked nasty and I was pretty sure it would need several stitches.

Sonja raised her head and got a look at the freely flowing blood. She groaned again and set her head back down.

"Stay still," Cooper cautioned her.

He and I got up and moved out of the way as the set medic hurried over to attend to Sonja. Jasmine and the first assistant director rushed over as well.

"Sonja, what happened?" Jasmine asked.

Sonja groaned. "I'm so sorry for the drama." She put a hand over her eyes. "When the lights went out, I thought they were going to kill me."

"Who did you think was going to kill you?" I asked.

"Whoever killed Tony." She left the "of course" unsaid, but I still heard it in her voice. She glanced at the medic, who was trying to staunch the flow of blood. Then, with another moan, she stared up at the ceiling.

"But why did you think the murderer might come after you?" I pressed, hoping she would explain.

"We've all been on edge lately," Jasmine said.

That was true, but Sonja had been more jittery than most of us.

"Sonja?" I prodded. When she didn't respond, I made a guess. "Was it because of that note you found?"

Tears pooled in her eyes. "I'm a terrible liar, aren't I? But it wasn't just the note."

Two paramedics came into the hotel, rolling a stretcher. A gust of wind and a spattering of rain followed them.

Reluctantly, I backed away from Sonja again. I desperately wanted to know what else she might have to say, but she needed medical attention more than I needed answers.

The emergency lights were now on in the lobby, providing the paramedics with more illumination to work by. Cast and crew members stood around in groups, chatting, while Ellen Smart and another hotel employee worked at collecting the pieces of the suit of armor.

I picked up the helmet, which sat near my feet. "I hope it can be put back together."

"It might take a bit of work, but I think it can be," Ellen said.

Something rattled within the helmet. I turned it so I could look inside.

"What the heck?" I pulled out a cell phone.

"What's that?" Ellen asked, coming over my way.

"There was a cell phone inside the helmet."

"That's strange." Ellen looked puzzled. "Maybe it belongs to the woman who took the tumble. It could have fallen down the stairs with her and landed in the helmet."

I nodded and Ellen got back to picking up the pieces of armor.

While that was a possible explanation, I wasn't so sure it was the right one. I'd seen Sonja's phone before and knew it had a bright blue cover. This one was in a plain black case.

If someone had put the phone inside the antique, it easily could have ended up in the helmet as the suit toppled over and bounced down the stairs.

There was one way to find out for sure, though.

Sonja was sitting on a stretcher now while one of the paramedics bandaged her arm and the other shone a light in her eyes, asking her questions.

I waited for a lull in the examination and then stepped closer.

"Is this your phone, Sonja?" I asked, holding up the black device. "I found it near where you fell."

She patted her pocket. "Nope. Mine's in a blue case and I've got it right here."

"Was anyone else on the stairs when you fell?" I checked.

"No." She looked sheepish. "I freaked out for nothing."

The paramedic started talking to her again, so I moved a discreet distance away. The phone hadn't landed in the helmet after bouncing down the stairs. So how *did* it end up in there?

I recalled how Tony had lingered by the suit of armor before his death. Had he slipped the phone inside?

Probably not, I decided. After all, why would he do such a thing?

Maybe a child staying at the hotel had hidden a parent's or sibling's phone as a prank. If I couldn't figure out the identity of the owner in the next few minutes, I'd ask Ellen if any of the guests had reported their phone missing.

I tried turning on the device, wondering if it had a charge. It booted up and didn't even have any security features preventing me from accessing the phone's contents.

Ellen and her colleague had finished cleaning up the scattered bits of armor, so I wandered over to the seating area while the paramedics continued to tend to Sonja in the middle of the lobby.

Cooper dropped down on the couch next to me. "What have you got there?"

I explained about finding the phone in the helmet.

"Weird," Cooper said.

I agreed with his assessment of the situation.

"Is there any way to tell whose it is?" he asked.

"That's what I'm checking for." I navigated my way around the phone. "No photos." I left the empty gallery and opened the contacts. "Talk about strange."

Cooper leaned in for a look. "What?"

"There's only one number listed as a contact and there's no name attached to it." I opened the call history. "And there aren't any phone calls listed in the log."

"What about texts?" Cooper asked. "Some people hardly ever make actual phone calls."

I opened the texting app. "There's just two sent messages, none received. And both texts were sent to that number in the contacts, one right after the other." I froze, my pulse thudding in my ears. "Cooper." I held the phone closer to him. "Read the messages."

He did so, out loud. "'I need you to meet me at the props trailer.' And then, 'ASAP. It's important.'" Some of the color drained from Cooper's face. "Those messages were sent the night Tony died."

I nodded as a chill settled over me. "Cooper, I think this phone belongs to the killer."

Chapter Thirty-Two

"So that's Tony's phone number?" Cooper asked after taking a moment to digest what I'd said.

"Maybe," I said. "And this is how the killer lured him to the props trailer that evening."

The hotel's front door opened and Sawyer entered the lobby with Officer Jared Tuffin, both of them in uniform, their jackets and hair wet.

I jumped up from the couch, but had to hold myself back while Sawyer and Jared spoke with the paramedics, Sonja, and Jasmine.

Soon, however, Sawyer's eyes found mine from across the room. I held up the phone and gave it a wiggle.

After exchanging a few more words with Jasmine, Sawyer broke away and headed in my direction. I met him halfway, holding the phone with my thumb and one finger, belatedly wishing I hadn't left my prints all over it.

"Did someone call the police?" I asked him.

"We received a report of screaming after the lights went out, but it appears it wasn't anything too serious." He looked at the phone. "Whose is that?"

Cooper appeared at my side. "The killer's," he said in a low voice.

Sawyer's gaze sharpened as he looked to me for an explanation.

"I think Cooper's right," I said. "It was in the suit of armor." When Sawyer's gaze flicked toward the landing, where the relic no longer stood, I added, "It got knocked down the stairs when Sonja fell."

Sawyer removed a pair of gloves from his pocket and pulled them on. "Why do you think the phone belongs to the killer?"

I handed the device to him. "There's only two sent text messages on it and both went to the same number. Read them and the date and time they were sent. Then you'll understand."

He did so. His expression, already serious, became even more so. "Did anyone else touch this?"

I shook my head. "I'm sorry about getting my fingerprints all over it. I didn't realize it was connected to the murder until I saw those messages."

"Hold on a moment." Sawyer strode off to join Jared.

As I watched him show the messages to his colleague, I hoped Sawyer wasn't angry with me. I hadn't intended to tamper with evidence by touching the phone, but I might have accidentally smudged any fingerprints that could have helped to identify the owner of the phone and therefore the killer. That possibility made my stomach sink.

Cooper stayed at my side as we watched the officers. They moved over to the reception desk and spoke with Ellen, who passed Sawyer a stylus.

"Hey," Cooper said quietly as Sawyer used the stylus on the phone's screen. "I think they're going to call the number that received those messages."

"But wasn't Tony the recipient? And don't they have his phone at the police station?" I asked. "They seized it when they searched Felicia's room."

"Right," Cooper agreed. "So what's he doing then?"

I had no answer to that question.

We edged closer to the officers, apprehension mixing in with my bubbling curiosity.

Sawyer tapped the device's screen with the stylus and then looked up, his gaze sweeping over the lobby and everyone in it.

A second later, a phone rang nearby.

Chapter Thirty-Three

OVER ON THE STRETCHER, Sonja tugged her ringing phone from the pocket of her jeans with her right hand. She took one look at the screen and gasped. The phone fell to her lap as her face turned alarmingly pale. That got the attention of the paramedics, who zeroed in on her again as she tapped the screen of her phone.

The ringing stopped. Sawyer and Officer Tuffin approached Sonja. Cooper and I followed in their footsteps.

Sonja now had a tube feeding oxygen to her nose. The paramedics started wheeling the stretcher toward the door, but Sawyer asked them to wait a moment and addressed Sonja.

"Who sent you those text messages on the night Tony was killed?" he asked.

"I don't know!" Sonja cried, distraught. "Whoever the killer is." She burst into tears.

I hurried around the officers and took her hand. "The killer tried to lure you to the props trailer?"

She gripped my fingers. "I've been feeling so guilty, Becca. The killer wanted *me* dead. Not Tony. And I'm so scared they're going to finish the job."

"Why didn't you say anything earlier?" Officer Tuffin asked.

"I was so scared you'd think it was some elaborate ruse I'd set up to make myself look innocent. Everybody knows Tony and I didn't get along. And I was a suspect, just like I worried I would be. I didn't want to make things worse for myself."

"When you told me it wasn't just the note that had you worried, you meant the text messages as well," I said.

Sonja nodded as a tear trickled down her cheek. She released my hand and wiped at the tear.

"We need to get her to the hospital," one of the paramedics said.

She and her partner wheeled the stretcher out the door to the waiting ambulance.

Sawyer and his colleague accompanied them out of the hotel. After a brief hesitation, I trailed after the group and Jasmine fell into step with me.

"Do you know what's going on?" the director asked me.

I quickly filled her in as we descended the front steps. I had to raise my voice as the wind swirled around us and the rain lashed our faces.

As the paramedics loaded the stretcher into the back of the ambulance, Sonja looked out at us with panic in her eyes. "What if the murderer tries to kill me at the hospital?"

"You're going to be fine," Jasmine said in a reassuring voice.

The panic didn't leave Sonja's eyes.

"We'll be right behind the ambulance," Sawyer said.

The paramedics shut the ambulance door.

Sawyer turned my way and held up the phone, now in a plastic evidence bag. "Thanks for this, Becca."

The ambulance pulled away, moving slowly along the wide paved path leading from the hotel to the avenue. A police cruiser was parked close by. Sawyer and Officer Tuffin jogged over to it and climbed inside.

I wrapped my arms around myself as I shivered in the rain and wind, watching the cruiser follow after the ambulance.

Jasmine touched my shoulder. "We should get inside, Becca."

As the vehicles drove off, I followed Jasmine into the hotel.

Fortunately, Sonja had an assistant who stepped into her role, allowing us to finish filming the day's scenes. When evening arrived, the storm was still raging and darkness had fallen over the town. One of the production assistants kindly offered to drive me home in a covered golf cart. I accepted with relief. If I'd walked, I would have ended up drenched and I would have worried about Tony's killer sneaking up on me in the dark and noisy storm.

Once safely in my cottage, I took a quick shower and changed into cozy clothes. I heated up one of the dinners Gareth had left in my freezer before practicing my lines for the next day, with my cats offering silent encouragement (Truffles) and criticism (Binx). When I felt fully prepared, I set the script aside and picked up a book. Rain continued to lash at the dark windows and the lights flickered overhead. That sent a shiver of unease running through me, so I got out my battery-operated candles and set them around the room, just in case.

I read one chapter of my book before someone knocked on the front door. Binx leapt up from the couch and ran for the foyer. I followed in time to see him skitter to a stop near the door. He paused for half a second and then shot up the stairs to the second floor, his green eyes comically wide.

I shook my head, laughing. "You're crazy, Binx."

I hesitated with my hand on the doorknob, suddenly uneasy about who might be standing on the other side of the door.

"Becca, it's me." Sawyer's voice sounded muffled, but it was still easy to identify.

Relieved, I opened the door with a smile.

Wind and rain rushed over the threshold.

"Quick," I said, opening the door wider.

As soon as Sawyer stepped inside, I shut the door behind him.

"It's not letting up out there," he said as he unzipped his rain jacket.

"It's a good night to be tucked up inside."

Binx ran back down the stairs and came to greet Sawyer, winding figure eights around his legs.

"Can you stay a while?" I asked.

"If you're not busy," he said. "I probably should have texted before coming by."

"You can drop by unannounced any time, Sawyer," I assured him.

He shrugged out of his coat and I took it from him, careful not to let it drip water on my dry clothes as I hung it up. He kicked off his shoes and took my hand, tugging me close for a kiss that warmed me right down to my toes.

With his hand still in mine, I led the way down the hall to the family room. Binx galloped past us and then pounced on the catnip banana he'd left on the kitchen floor.

"I figured your curiosity would be running at full throttle," Sawyer said, "I thought I'd come and share what I can."

"You're right about my curiosity, but you can keep me in suspense a while longer while I get us something to drink."

He agreed to that and picked up Binx for a cuddle while I brewed us some decaf tea.

"Do you know how Sonja's doing?" I asked as I filled two mugs with tea.

Sawyer set Binx on the floor and sat on the couch. Truffles immediately hopped onto his lap, purring.

"She's back at the hotel now," Sawyer said as he stroked my tabby's fur. "She needed a few stitches but otherwise she's fine."

I set our mugs on the coffee table and settled on the couch next to Sawyer. "I'm glad to hear it."

"You'll also be glad to hear that the case is solved."

"What? Really?" I shifted to face Sawyer and tucked one leg beneath me. "Did the phone help?"

Sawyer continued to run his hand over Truffles' fur. "I should probably say no so I don't encourage your amateur detective tendencies."

"Dizzy will always encourage me, so you're fighting a losing battle if you want to deter me."

Sawyer raised his eyes heavenward. "Don't I know it."

"Besides, I didn't find the phone because I was sleuthing. It was just there in the helmet when I picked it up."

"I guess I have to concede that one," he said grudgingly.

"You definitely do." I poked him in the arm. "I take it the phone did help then."

"It pretty much cracked the case wide open," Sawyer said.

I smiled with triumph, but then my expression grew somber. "Okay, so who's the killer?"

"What do you think, Truffles?" he asked the purring cat. "Should we tell her?"

"You should definitely tell me," I said over Truffles' purrs.

"Hmm."

"Sawyer!" I gripped his arm. "Don't keep me in suspense any longer. I'm worried it's someone I like."

"I don't think you need to worry about that," he said, puzzling me. "Are you ready for it?"

"Long past ready."

"All right. Prepare yourself to be shocked," he cautioned, "because there is no killer."

Chapter Thirty-Four

"I DON'T UNDERSTAND," I said. My eyes widened as a thought struck me. "Don't tell me the Gossip Grannies were right. I mean, how could the medical examiner confuse a prop for Tony's body?"

"No prop," Sawyer said. "Tony wasn't murdered, but that's about all the Grannies got right."

I gave his arm a shake. "Sawyer, explain, please."

He relented with a grin. "Tony's fingerprints were all over the phone. The only other prints likely belong to you."

I winced. "Not my proudest moment."

"Don't worry about it," Sawyer assured me. "We'll need your prints for elimination purposes, but that can wait until tomorrow. We were able to trace the purchase of the phone to a store in Los Angeles. Although the phone was bought with cash, the store's surveillance footage from the time of the purchase confirmed that Tony was the buyer."

"But you found his phone in Felicia's room," I pointed out. "He had more than one?"

Sawyer nodded. "We think he treated the one you found as a burner phone."

"Wait." My thoughts clicked together. "Tony's the one who sent the text messages to Sonja, trying to get her to go to the props trailer." My eyes widened.

"I think you've got it now," Sawyer said, watching me.

"Sonja was right. She was the intended victim." When Sawyer nodded, I continued voicing my thoughts out loud. "And...Tony was the one planning to kill her?"

"He used the burner phone to research booby traps on the Internet."

I sank deeper into the couch. "Tony set up the booby trap to kill Sonja but ended up dying himself."

"We think he accidentally triggered the booby trap when he was trying to leave the trailer," Sawyer said.

"Right after he set it up?"

"We believe so. He was probably backing out the door when he triggered the trap."

"But how did he expect to get away with killing Sonja?" I asked. "Everyone knew about his grudge against her and he had access to the props trailer."

"We don't have a definite answer to that question, but we do have theories."

"Please tell me you can share them," I said, hoping he wouldn't leave me to perish from curiosity.

"Tony reported his key to the trailer missing the day before his death. He was provided with a copy to use from that point on."

I considered that information. "So maybe he was trying to make it look like the original key could have been stolen?"

"That's what we're thinking," Sawyer agreed. "And it's possible he was hoping to get back to the scene of Sonja's death before anyone found her. If he disassembled the booby trap and locked up the trailer, it's possible no one would have known that she wasn't stabbed outdoors by a person. In that case, the stolen key could have been a backup."

"Covering all his bases," I mused with a nod. "And since it would have been a hands-off murder, Tony could have established an alibi for the time when Sonja died. As long as no one figured out that there was a booby trap involved, he would have been in the clear."

"Exactly."

"Still, it was risky," I said.

"I get the impression that Tony thought a lot of himself and his abilities."

"Same. I guess he believed he could pull it off." Something still didn't make sense to me. "But if Tony wanted an alibi, why did he send the text messages to Sonja while he was still at the trailer? Wouldn't he have wanted to lure her there after he was long gone from the area? And how did the burner phone end up in the suit of armor after Tony died?"

I hoped I wasn't asking too many questions at once, but I couldn't help myself.

"He had a text scheduling app on the phone," Sawyer explained. "He wrote the messages ahead of time and set them to go out later that evening. He must have hidden the phone in the suit of armor before he even set up the trap."

That made sense, but the amount of premeditation and maliciousness involved sent a chill down my spine, and the thought of Sonja walking into Tony's trap triggered a wave of queasiness in my stomach.

Sawyer continued to fill in some blanks. "When Sonja first received the texts, she thought her ex-boyfriend had followed her to Vermont and was trying to get her to meet him using a new phone number. She was worried he'd track her down at the hotel, so she went out for a walk."

That explained why she wasn't in her hotel room like she'd later claimed.

"After phoning her ex's sister, Sonja found out that he was still in Los Angeles," Sawyer said. "She went back to the hotel and fell asleep. It wasn't until she heard about Tony's death the next day that she realized someone had wanted to harm her."

"Why did Tony want to kill Sonja?" I asked. "Because of the screenplay he accused her of stealing?"

"Apparently. The thing is, he started telling people about his idea just over a year ago. Sonja has files on her computer proving that she started her screenplay long before that."

I shook my head. "I can't believe Tony took it so far."

"It backfired on him."

I took a moment to digest everything. "I'm glad there's no killer on the loose, but what an unnecessary tragedy."

Truffles climbed onto my lap and meowed at me.

I ran a hand over her fur. "You're right, Truffles. We should focus on happier things."

I scooted closer to Sawyer and he put his arm around me. Truffles hopped up onto the back of the couch and curled up for a snooze.

"There is something I wanted to ask you," Sawyer said.

I leaned into him, relishing the fact that I could now do things like that without any worry or hesitation. "Something unrelated to murder?"

"Completely unrelated," he assured me. "Do I now have high enough security clearance to read those notes you and Dizzy wrote to each other in middle school?"

I laughed, recalling my embarrassment when he found those notes in my attic last December. Then I pretended to carefully consider what he'd asked. "I'd say you're getting pretty darn close."

He ran his hand down my arm, leaving a trail of pleasant tingles. "One more question."

"No, I won't be entering the gondola races this year," I said.

"Wrong question. This one's way more important."

I snuggled in closer to him. "Okay, what's your important question?"

"Will you go on a date with me, Becca?"

I tipped my head back and smiled up at him. "That's a definite yes."

Chapter Thirty-Five

THE FULL MOON HUNG in the star-studded sky, reflected in the rippling water of Shadow Lake. On the beach of Mad Hatter Island, I sat by a campfire with Sawyer, Dizzy, Cooper, Alex, and Michaela. Logs served as benches around the fire pit, where flames danced and crackled. The six of us had gathered there so the non-locals could have one last taste of Larch Haven on their final night in town. In the morning, the cast and crew of *Love on the Canal* would be leaving Vermont for Los Angeles.

"I haven't toasted marshmallows since I was in Girl Scouts," Michaela said as she jabbed a large marshmallow with a pointed stick. "And don't ask me how long ago that was."

"It doesn't matter how many times Becca has toasted marshmallows over the years," Sawyer said. "Hers will always catch on fire."

At the exact moment that he stopped speaking, the marshmallow I held close to the red-hot coals burst into flame.

Everyone else laughed as I blew on the marshmallow to extinguish the mini fire.

"Wouldn't want to break with tradition," I said.

I pointed the marshmallow end of my stick at Dizzy and she pointed hers at me. She tugged the blackened, gooey confection off my stick while I slid the perfectly toasted one off of hers. We stuffed the marshmallows into our mouths, smiling at each other. We'd been trading marshmallows ever since we were kids. Dizzy had a knack for toasting them perfectly, just the way I liked them, but she preferred eating charred ones. As Sawyer had mentioned, mine always caught on fire and turned black. Trading was the perfect arrangement.

"It's amazing out here," Cooper said as he toasted his own marshmallow. He sat on a log next to Dizzy. I'd already caught him looking at her a couple of times while she was chatting with the rest of us. His crush was still alive and kicking.

I tipped my head back so I could look up at the night sky. "It's a great place to watch for shooting stars."

"And UFOs," Dizzy added.

"Have you ever seen one here?" Cooper asked with interest.

"When we were sixteen," Dizzy said.

I shook my head. "I still can't believe I missed it."

"You weren't here?" Alex asked.

"Oh, she was here." The firelight danced on Dizzy's face, making her smile extra mischievous. "But she went for a moonlit stroll among the trees."

"Ooh, with a boy, Becca?" Alex asked, his smile just as mischievous as Dizzy's.

I slid another marshmallow onto the end of my stick. "I was dating Jackson Webb. That's when we had our first kiss."

"Was the kiss worth missing the UFO for?" Michaela asked.

"No way," Sawyer said.

I nudged him with my elbow. "How would you know?"

"It was Jackson Webb," he replied, as if that explained everything.

I laughed. "Good point. I don't know what I was thinking back then."

"Your taste in guys has definitely improved." Sawyer took the bag of marshmallows from me so he could have one for himself.

"Exponentially," I agreed with a smile.

"I need to hear about this UFO," Cooper said.

I settled in to listen as Dizzy told the tale with her usual flair. A chilly breeze blew across the lake, ruffling my hair and making me shiver. I didn't mind, though, because that gave me an excuse to snuggle closer to Sawyer. He wrapped an arm around me while he continued toasting marshmallows. I rested my head on his shoulder, utterly content.

Even if we did see a shooting star that night, I didn't need to wish for anything.

I already had everything I needed.

London Fog Truffles

Ingredients:

- 9 oz white chocolate

- 3 oz heavy cream

- 1 tbsp loose leaf Earl Grey tea

Instructions:

Finely grate 1 oz of the white chocolate and set aside.

Finely chop the remaining 8 oz of white chocolate and place it in a heat proof bowl. Set aside. In the top of a double boiler, heat the cream until it's just starting to bubble. Remove the cream from the heat and add the tea (you can use one tea bag instead of loose leaf tea). Leave it to steep for approximately 10 minutes.

Heat the cream again until it's just starting to bubble. Strain out the tea as you pour the cream into the bowl of chopped white chocolate. Let it sit for approximately two minutes, then mix the cream and chocolate together until all the chocolate has melted and the ganache is smooth.

If the chocolate won't melt completely, heat the mixture in the microwave for 10 second increments. (Be careful not to heat it too much, as that could cause the ganache to split.) Leave the smooth ganache to set at room temperature. If necessary, chill the ganache in the fridge to help it set.

Use a melon scooper or roll the ganache into 1-inch balls. Roll each ball in the grated white chocolate until completely coated. Store the truffles in an airtight container in the refrigerator.

Makes approximately 15 truffles.

ACKNOWLEDGEMENTS

When I found out that the publisher of the first two True Confections Mysteries would not be continuing the series, I knew right away that I would keep it going on my own. However, venturing into self publishing for the first time was a daunting task, one that would have been all the more challenging without the help of some amazing people. Thank you to Jody Holford, Karen Stallman, and Helen Lee for lending me your eagle eyes and helping me to make this a better book. Thank you to Sarah L. Blair for answering all of my questions and for supporting me on this journey into the indie publishing realm. Thanks also to Francesca D'Ottavi for creating such a beautiful illustration for the cover. Last but definitely not least, my heartfelt thanks go out to all of my readers and to everyone who wanted more of Becca's sleuthing adventures.

Sarah Fox is the author of several cozy mystery series, including the *USA Today* bestselling Pancake House Mysteries. She was born and raised in Vancouver, British Columbia, where she developed a love for mysteries at a young age. When not plotting (fictional) murders or doling out sardines to her mini panther (black cat), she is often reading her way through a stack of books or spending time outdoors with her English springer spaniel. You can visit her online at:

www.authorsarahfox.com
www.facebook.com/authorsarahfox
www.instagram.com/the_write_fox

Printed in Great Britain
by Amazon

49555251R00148